THE CHRISTMAS PIC

Rena Sapon-White

Ella Schaefer

For Eddie Ginsberg and Matthew Nordquist

SPOILER-Y CONTENT WARNING!

You've got a fun read ahead of you. However, it is still an adult story with adult themes, language, and spice. We'd estimate it's a four chili pepper read (out of five) and includes discussions of death and grief, as well alcohol use.

If you're still down, stick a rainbow candy cane in your drink of choice and settle in for a romantic tale about the gayest season of all: Christmas!

THEY CALL ME THE GRINCH. Am I green and hairy with a general distaste for society? Perhaps the latter and, admittedly, hairy when I don't feel like doing the dreaded full-body shave. But I'm definitely not green, either in the sense of color or inexperience. I am at the top of my game in the world of tech, and being a woman in this industry is no sleigh ride. As CEO of Gramsta, the biggest social platform on Earth–yes, *Earth*–I'm considered "unrelatable" to the general public. All the men at my level get to indulge in the world's most elitist hobbies, like polo or yachting with Russian oligarchs, yet if I charter one little private jet to the Maldives so I can actually enjoy my holidays for once, I'm smeared across the press as a Christmas-hating eco-destroyer.

Eco-destroyer? I think not. Gramsta is supported by one hundred percent renewable energy. Christmas-hating... They might have one on me there.

Christmas and I, we have a history. My haters didn't realize how apt a villain they chose to denigrate me with when they picked the Grinch. Believe it or not, I'm not the only person in this world who isn't a fan of the holidays. We did a user poll and over thirty percent of those who voted would rather stay home than load up their cars for a week of hellacious travel to be surrounded by people they hardly know and hardly like.

Which is exactly why I created Gramsta's AI Christmas Card Generator. All you do is upload pics of the people you want in your photo, then wham, bam, thank you person of unspecified gender–you've got yourself a hassle-free Christmas card. The AI might still be a little finicky, but it's the best image generator on the market that absolutely no one is giving me due credit for. Yet.

Which is why I'm getting my nose powdered by a makeup artist on the set of a commercial my marketing crew has arranged for me. My team consists of pedants with an extravagant flare, and I'm usually here for it, but this set is far from my personal brand–typically professional, elegant. Today, we're on a studio lot somewhere way too deep in the Valley for this Westside girl and the cramped honey wagon they're making me up in is a long way from my perfectly curated executive office in Venice with killer views of the Pacific. Not to mention there's no treadmill in sight–an absolute must-have for the moments when I need to get out of my head and on the move.

But for now, I'm stuck in this chair with Charlene, the makeup artist, gabbing away about the first assistant camera, who she clearly has a crush on, as she adds an ungodly amount of rouge to my cheeks.

That's the thing with crushes: they distract you from doing your job at the top level required to run a Fortune 5 company (no, I did not stutter or miss two zeroes, thanks). Why would I take time out of my insanely busy schedule running a company I love to talk to strange men from the internet who want to mansplain my expertise back to me? Matchmakers don't appeal either–I've fired enough headhunters to have a healthy disdain for people who think they can suss out a better match than me. All of my contradictory opinions on modern dating might give off red flags that I'm "too much" or "difficult," and to that I say… No shit.

I gaze at my garishly rosy cheeks in the mirror.

"Can't say I've ever looked this… cheery."

"That's what we're going for!" Charlene chirps.

I'm trying to be kind, really, I am. But it's difficult to see yourself staring back like one of those haunted Christmas composition dolls. Luckily, I keep my mouth shut long enough not to let that one slip. I have to work on what comes out of this yapper. I'm quick, but sometimes too quick for my own good. Most people can't keep up, but that's what it takes to be in my position. Lonely? Sometimes. But not always.

I breathe a sigh of relief as my assistant, Max, knocks on the door.

"We're ready for you on set, Ava." Max picks up their head from their tablet and recoils. "Oh dear god, what happened to your face?"

So it is as bad as I thought. The patriarchy makes even *me* doubt myself sometimes.

But Max, with their petite stature and unmatchable gusto, has been there for me for five long years. Longer than anyone else. As soon as this new product launches, we're headed to the Maldives for our annual trip to free ourselves of the absolute chokehold *All I Want For Christmas Is You* by Mariah Carey has on every public space in this Santa-forsaken country. It's the closest thing we have to a Christmas tradition.

"We can fix it in post. Let's go." Max closes the door behind us. I clear my throat and they know what to do.

Max peeks their head back in the honey wagon. "Oh, and, Charlene? You're fired."

Max escorts me across the lot. "Doing your dirty work is exhausting."

"You're only doing my *excess* dirty work, I'm up to my knees," I tell them as we approach the set.

"Things are off to a rough start," they say, "but remember why we're here."

I roll my eyes. "The Board is the last thing I need to hear about right now, Max."

"I understand, but let's think beyond this moment and about the future of Gramsta. You have so much innovating to do with this company, and for that we need their support."

Max is my favorite person on this Earth who, at times, totally exasperates me with their even-keeled perspective. But they're right. I have ideas galore on how to move the internet forward for the betterment of humanity, and unfortunately, that will also require involving the worst of humanity: old white men and their cash.

We approach the set and in front of us stands a cartoonish facade of a house, decked out in holly jolly maximalism.

"Talent is on set! Last looks!" the assistant director calls.

Max shoos away the wardrobe team and adjusts the collar on my cream-colored pantsuit. "You're gonna kill it."

"I know."

I take my mark and read off the teleprompter, explaining the ingenuity of my Christmas Card Generator. Some of the crew trade glances over my spiel, probably because their minds are blown by the AI revolution they're witnessing in this very room. People are busier than ever and I'm here to make their lives easy and obnoxious-family-free. *You're welcome.*

"And... cut!" The director approaches me as I slide on my Dolce sunglasses, ready to put a bow on this shoot and get back to putting the final touches on the actual product. But she has other ideas, chirping, "Now let's do another take with a heavy dose of Christmas spirit!"

I've already spent the better part of two years frosting my invention in Christmas to appease the masses and convince the Board to let me release the generator. The director might be doing her job, but she's struck a nerve that's already raw for me.

"I've doused this project in enough Christmas spirit to drown Rudolph," I inform her. "I've got places to be."

But this director chick doesn't want to back down, folding her arms at my rebuttal.

"One more take," she presses, her voice raising enough to catch the crew's attention. "We want the audience to feel like Ava Garcia-Greene is in their living room on Christmas morning, presenting the best gift imaginable to her loved ones. Think of warmth, coziness, togetherness. *Family.*"

Now that this exchange is being observed by everyone on the lot, I refuse to be publicly condescended to about what *my* audience is meant to feel about the program *I* created.

"I don't need to pander to anyone more than I already have with all of this Christmas garbage. This is the most prominent advancement in AI history under the *guise* of holiday cheer. Which I couldn't care less about. I care about my business."

Max winces in my periphery. I sense the PAs whispering amongst themselves. *Have fun gossiping about this at lunch later.*

"But if we do it right," the director insists, "this commercial could be good for your business–"

Any semblance of decorum I have left goes out the window. "I don't need you to tell me what's good for my business. I have enough people doing that already," I snap, churlish as fuck.

She's speechless, giving me and Max plenty of time to scoot to the black Caddy that pulls up to whisk me away from this North Pole hellhole.

In my mind, I'm not always a bitch. It's just sometimes I have to do what it takes to protect myself. I'm a busy woman. Places to go, people to boss around, et cetera et cetera. I don't have time to pretend I'm emotionally invested in this holiday.

Max opens the back door of my SUV. "I'll see you tomorrow for the launch! Then after that, beautiful beaches with nary an ornament..."

"Nor snowmen, nor..."

"Christmas carolers!" we exclaim together.

I slide into the backseat and am assaulted by the unmistakable sickly sweet scent of Fuji Apple Strawberry Nectarine. Materializing through a cloud of smoke is the beefy elder tech bro who runs my life.

"Jason, what the hell?" I hiss. My driving time is my sacred space, the time I can (maybe) take a breath and be alone. Of course a Board member would impede that.

"Thought I'd catch you the only way I know how," he says, taking another puff of his vape. "I'm gonna keep the main thing the main thing. The Board is on the same page: you are on some slippery ice, my friend."

I try hard not to totally dismiss his inarticulate blathering and mixed metaphors.

"We put some big bucks into this Christmas Card doohickey of yours, and if you continue to pull your typical little Ava 'I don't need to paint inside the lines' stunts, we *will* pull the plug."

"I'm not–" I start. He stares at me doubtfully.

Okay, so perhaps I *am*, but innovation should far outshine this bureaucratic bullshit.

"You can't pull the plug, it's coming out tomorrow," I argue, cringing as he takes another hit.

"It doesn't matter if it comes out tomorrow or in ten years," he says, vape clouds whooshing out of his face hole. "The truth is, Ava, you don't play the field. We need you to play the field."

A laugh escapes my lips; he definitely means play the game, but how the hell could I play any sort of game with someone who doesn't even understand basic idioms?

He stares at me like I'm proving his point. "It's like I can hear what you're thinking: 'no male CEO would have to deal with this!'" His impersonation of me is misogyny at best. "And that may be true, but that's life, kiddo. You got the raw end of the stick and you have to work with it."

The car slows.

"This is my stop!" He crawls over me and gets out.

"Thanks for the pep talk," I deadpan.

He shakes his head at me. "This generator needs to be a hit, Ava. And to make it a hit, you've got to do as you're told."

Before I can point out that the success of Gramsta is entirely owed to me not doing as I'm told, he slams the door.

All in a day's work.

I'VE TAKEN thousands of photos in my life, but the one that means the most to me isn't nicely matted and framed and hung on a wall. It's a tattered Polaroid of my dad and me, doubled over laughing in our snowsuits after my mom, wielding the camera, hurled a snowball at us right after we said *cheese*. I keep it tucked into the visor of my mobile photo studio–a hulking vintage milk truck we've nicknamed Chrissy–and peek at it when I'm going cross-eyed after a long day of back-to-school portraits and engagement sessions. That little 2x4 patch of cellulose reminds me why what I do matters. I'm capturing the soul of a moment with each shutter-click.

There's what I can see and control when I'm behind the camera in my little mobile studio: proper lighting, focus, poses. And then there's what shows up in the actual photo: its soul, that ineffable quality that separates a good photo from a bad one. When I think about what that photo of my dad means to me now that he's gone, it reaffirms for me that my purpose is to capture other people's moments of magic so that they, too, can double-dip in life's fleeting joys.

"Big yikes." Emma, sitting in the passenger seat glaring at a video on her phone, snaps me out of my reverie.

"Who's canceled now?" I ask, expecting my assistant's face to brighten as usual, ready to spill the tea. But she remains bleak, fiddling with her septum ring. She shoves her phone at me.

On the screen is the most beautiful woman I've ever seen, and I mean that in the gayest way possible. A red-lipsticked smirk that contains a hint of knowing, striking blue eyes with a gaze that is at once razor-sharp and mysteriously distant. Sometimes I see a girl so stunning that I have to come out to myself all over again in my head to digest the fraction of a possibility that I could get to be with that person. *God, I love women...*

I must let slip a contented sigh because Emma shoots me an incredulous glare. I actually tune in to what the woman in the video is saying, trying to catch up in case my Gen Z peanut gallery of one decides to quiz me.

"...won't have to sit for another time-consuming studio portrait session ever again–"

Wait. What?

"Who is that?" I ask.

Emma's eyes widen. "What rock do you live under?"

"My celebrity knowledge consists of the Real Housewives and former members of the Detroit Shock."

Emma rolls her eyes. "This is the AI revolution, Jo. They're coming for us. We're so screwed."

I turn the phone off, needing that woman's bewitching face out of sight so I can focus on the apparently imminent apocalypse.

"So it's AI Christmas cards. People don't want that. No one would pay us to composite a bunch of individual photos into a fake family card in Photoshop, they want an experience." I gesture around to the truck, decked out in holly jolly joy. "Why would they ever pay for *that*?"

Emma sighs. "They literally don't have to pay for it. It's free. Fueled by ad sales. Were you even listening?"

I yank the lever to recline the driver's seat, trying to find a comfier position to wallow over life's curveballs and the current economy. But of course, my photo truck opts for irony instead. The lever splinters off in my hand, hurling me backward, and now I'm stuck lying down in a seat that refuses to snap back up.

"That is… not good, Jo."

I'm not ready to form words yet, because they won't be pretty ones. The Photo Truck, her name so aptly coined many moons ago by my father, is a true mechanical testament to blind faith. It's a miracle she's even made it this far. But for the past year, it's been a repair every other week in a good month, which means the business' cash flow is more like a cash hemorrhage.

Emma can sense me spiraling, and she's been around long enough to know what's called for. She reaches across the console and plucks out the worn Polaroid, handing it to me.

"Go on, ask Roger."

As I've matured, I find myself combing through old memories of him, turning to them like scripture for guidance, even as the challenges of adulthood have grown increasingly complex. I've always been a visual thinker, something that serves me well in my line of work. To that end, it's easier for me than most people to roam the halls of my memory palace.

I land with myself at ten years old, crouching on the stairs while my parents exchange harsh whispers in the dining room. My dad's accounting books are spread out in front of them and my mom is wringing her hands. In an instant, he clasps both of her overactive hands in his, grounding her for a moment. Suddenly his head turns and he looks straight at me in my supposed hiding place. He winks before shifting his attention back to Mom. *Worrying is borrowing trouble from the future, Care.*

"Huh." I let my father's pragmatic wisdom sink in.

"What's today's fortune cookie?" Emma asks.

"We're not gonna borrow trouble from the future, Em. We

gotta focus on what's directly in front of us and keep our heads down."

"And that means…?"

I sit up in the driver's seat, even though it's still fully reclined.

"We get the seat fixed, we do the shoots on our schedule, and maybe we take that gig photographing Mrs. Lupinsky's Christmas bobblehead collection."

"And the artificial intelligence that's single-handedly dismantling our very niche industry in alarmingly fast, free fashion?"

"It's simply not of concern to us."

What is it they say about famous last words?

CHAPTER 3
AVA

WHEN I SAY I walk through the doors of Gramsta HQ like I own the place, it's admittedly an understatement. I saunter past poster-size magazine covers of my face, from *Forbes* 30 Under 30 to *Rolling Stone*'s 'Next Steve Jobs.' Also decorating the sleek entry is my 'Next Wicked Witch of the West' *People* cover. I put this up in the lobby alongside my biggest successes, since I firmly believe life is all about an ironically spiteful laugh in the face of your enemies. Plus, I look good in green.

You wouldn't believe that the year before *People* named me Boss Bitch of the Year. The haters over at that celeb gossip shit-show went in on me because I wouldn't bend to their will and give them the Gramsta handle they wanted. Boo-hoo, bitch. Haven't you learned that you don't always get what you want in life, Wendy? The so-called editor had her Photoshop lackeys turn my face green, sparking the Grinch nickname, and hasn't called Max for a comment since. But I digress.

Sure, I have my Board that I have to answer to, but really, I run this ship. I've never liked things being out of my control, because when they're in my hands, they'll be done the right way. I don't know what it's like to be normal, but god it feels good to always be right.

I stride into the office on my high horse–a practice not just for show, but a ritual that's almost as life-giving as the espresso waiting for me in Max's hands. Building this company from the ground up, I recognize the power of an entrance. Clad in a sharply tailored suit, red-bottoms, and hair pulled back into a slick no-nonsense bun, I embody the force I've fought to become as I stomp in–later than I should on a launch day. I've earned it, though. My employees, a mix of tech nerds and suits, still pause to watch the spectacle as I breeze past their desks at the start of each day.

But this morning is different. Usually no one looks me in the eye out of fear, but today, they're avoiding me in a much different way.

Max rounds a corner and spots me, greeting me at the foot of the gorgeous custom glass staircase with my morning venti quad shot–yes, Pedro Pascal and I have the same order, and *yes*, I did learn that from the same *People* issue I graced the cover of. I take a long sip as Max waits to let something spill. They know better than to speak before I have my first hit of the caffeine good-good, but I can tell something is off.

"Spit it out," I say after I come up for air. Their eyes go wide. I haven't seen Max act this hesitant in front of me in years, not since we had our heart-to-heart about their transition, which I accepted with open arms. I've been accused of being cunty at times, but hating people for being themselves is where I draw the line. Unless they suck, then hate away.

Max gulps and squeaks out what they can muster. "There's been, uh… some *feedback* on the new launch."

"We don't listen to the Board." I brush them off as I head up the stairs to my office overlooking all my scurrying minions.

"It's not only the Board," Max says. "It's… worse."

Up in my office, Max trembles as they hand over their phone. It's open to Gramsta's comment section on the Christmas Card Generator launch post.

"Ava Garcia-Greene is like if Scrooge and the Grinch had a baby," I read, droll. "This is what you wanted me to see? The internet being the internet?" I continue to scroll past hateful comments, including one from Wendy–something about her utter distaste for me, blah blah blah. Unfortunately when you invent the means with which hate is dispersed, it opens you up to more of it. I wouldn't say I've gotten used to it, per se, but it's been affecting me less as the years go by.

"No, this is much, *much* worse." Max pulls up backend numbers. "#GoodbyeGramsta is trending like crazy."

"They'll be back and we'll recover before the week is done. We always do."

But Max grows more anxious. "Some comments from the commercial set leaked," they blurt out.

"That director? So much for women helping women," I yawn. Contrary to popular belief, I'm not the villain here; I'm too busy busting my ass through the glass ceiling to engage in petty bullshit.

"One of the PAs…" Max pulls up a video of me on set talking to the director about Christmas being garbage. I watch myself go in on her. Sure, it's not my *best* look, but it's nothing to lose our collective minds over. I hop onto my in-office treadmill to think through our plan of action.

"Everyone thinks you hate Christmas and they're saying the generator is soulless," Max stresses.

"Well, they're right: I do hate Christmas and the generator does not have a soul. None of us do. Show me one peer-reviewed study on the existence of a *soul*."

"Ava! They're gonna burn the place down!"

"*Pfft.*"

"You think I'm kidding?" Max shouts, frantically flipping through windows on their phone. "And I quote, 'Burn the godless corporate scions profiting off of our beloved holiday!'"

"Clearly that person didn't do their research," I say. "I'm definitely not a descendant of wealth."

"That's besides the point, Ava. They're boycotting the app completely!" Max hands me their phone, open to a user summary of the generator.

"Over 500 *million* uses in twenty-four hours? Some boycott," I snort. "That's double our projections for day one."

Max points to the screen. "That is a decimal."

Five million. A measly five million. The worst performance of any launch I've ever had. I grasped that people hated AI images, but I thought that was because they were shitty–adequate at a glance, but disintegrating the moment you zoomed in on any detail. I thought the masses would be grateful for my unprecedented advancement. *I thought they would thank me.*

"The Board is calling it a crisis–PR, financial, you name it. Jason called a few minutes ago. They have some emphatic suggestions on how to fix this."

"You can call them what they are: commands," I snip, accelerating the treadmill to 4.4, entirely too fast for these Louboutins. If anyone should dictate how to guide this ship back on course, it's me. All the Board does is lounge on their piles of Daddy's money, spouting the most elementary buzzwords imaginable–from 'hashtag' to 'handle'–as if they're profound insights. I started Gramsta from my middle school computer lab, armed with nothing but sebaceous hyperplasia and a dream. I transformed what could have been a simple photo app into the multibillion-dollar corporation it is today. The idea that my all-male Board, a necessity when funding a startup in 2008, understands better than I do how to navigate a crisis is rich. And not the kind of rich I've made them.

"They say you need to prove to the public that you don't only talk the talk, but that you walk the walk."

"Shocking that Jason nailed an idiom for once," I sneer, *beep beep beep*-ing the treadmill even higher. "I would be able to fully walk my walk if they hadn't pigeonholed my literally ground-breaking AI photo generator into being a Christmas gimmick in the first place!"

Max sighs. "On the topic of Christmas... that's your cut-off. Jason's adamant about not dragging this into Q1."

"But tomorrow–"

"I know–"

I screech like a banshee. "They can't take away my Maldives!"

Buzz buzz. My SyncCircle ring warns me of my accelerated heart rate, but I ignore it, pushing the treadmill faster.

"Ava, be–"

"You've been here this whole time. You've seen what I've done! For them! For this company!"

"It's true–"

"You've walked the walk with me!"

"I have–"

"You've seen me do nothing but walk!"

Beep beep.

"The!"

Beep beep beep.

"Walk!"

"Ava, stop!"

Sometimes I should listen to Max, but that would bruise the ol' ego, probably even worse than it was contused post-treadmill rage-walk tumble. Not that I can't get another custom-tailored pair, but a snapped $6,000 heel is never a good way to start the day. Still on the ground, I elevate my leg with a nearby stack of *Tech Times* as Max rushes in with an ice pack. The patriarchy can't get me down, but a sprained ankle might.

"Ava...." Max bends down, trying to force eye contact. They're getting sentimental again, my least favorite Max trait.

While I admit I need an emotional being in my life, it still gives me the heebie-jeebies to see an over-salinated peeper peering into my personage.

"What now?" I groan.

"It's just..." they take a deep breath. "You've had some important people in your life fail you."

"Max, we don't need to go all *Psychology Today–*"

"But you're not them, Ava. You'll never fail yourself."

"Sure, but–"

Max stands, emboldened. "If there's one thing about Ava Garcia-Greene it's that, out of anyone on this planet, she's got this. She talks some dang good talk, and she will walk that flippin'–"

"MAX!"

They realize I'm still on the ground. "So sorry."

They help me up into my bespoke leather executive chair, propping my swelling ankle onto my desk. "You've gotta stop apologizing," I reply with a wince.

"Right, sorr–I mean, no, I mean..."

"*My* apology, however." I refocus. "What do they want? Me to beg for the public's forgiveness on my story? A grid post? God forbid... an extended multi-platform plea for the planet's pardon?" I hate giving the competitors any of my heat, even if it's for the good of Gramsta.

"Er... worse," Max struggles. "Jason said those things haven't worked in the past, so the Board wants you to be held publicly accountable their way or... you have to resign."

My jaw drops. "Resign?!" The Board has pushed my buttons before, but they've never threatened anything like this. They supported this app with their whole dicks. They've *never* postured their power in a way to intimidate me out of my own company. It's preposterous.

And that's how I know it's serious. I don't play their games, but sometimes to stay in power, you must bend to the whims of... *gag...* men.

I sink further down into the made-to-order leather and roll my eyes. I exhale a big *shhhhhh* through my teeth, like my mental coach taught me.

"Fine. What's their way?"

Max doesn't have to say a word because their reluctant face says it all. I realize where I'm headed.

Not again.

IT'S NOT hard for me to distract myself from impending doom, in fact I've probably gotten a little *too* good at it. When I'm on The Photo Truck, adjusting lights, switching out lenses, coaxing out genuine smiles from my clients when their faces start to freeze during a long shoot... all of it fades away. I'm in the zone, and in the zone, everything comes easily.

There are fleeting moments where the zone wavers, like when I'm bending down to rummage through my kit and my lower back twinges from driving with the broken seat all week. But I power through. *Mind over matter, baby.*

"Yoo-hoo!" George Bennington's beaming face pops into the truck. He's in his sixties, an OG fixture of Harmony Springs' drag scene when donning his Neverland alter ego, Captain Hooker (or Captain Ho Ho Hooker at Christmas). When he's not in eight-inch pleasers, he's our town's sole Uber driver.

Emma's face lights up. George and his husband Jeffrey are two of her favorites.

"Georgie! Jeffy! Come on in!" she beckons them inside. Jeffrey blows me a kiss while George struts toward me and I happily allow him to crush me in a bear hug.

"Jojo Jolly Rancher! We haven't seen you at drag brunch in a minute." He turns to Emma. "You can't let her work all the time! Even Annie Leibovitz takes vacations!"

Now it's Emma's turn to roll her eyes. "You say that like *I'm* in charge around here."

"Speaking of who's in charge"–I point to myself–"let's get you divas into first looks! What's the vision today?"

George gestures to Jeffrey. "Darling?"

George in plainclothes still has the airs of a drag queen, but Jeffrey is a little more reserved in his day-to-day life. He's a construction contractor whose uniform is a tattered flannel and Carhartt workman cargos, so I can't help the delighted grin that breaks out on my face as he lays out the kookiest, gayest Christmas sweaters I've ever seen. I'm talking rainbow reindeer, Santa in leather chaps, and a gingerbread man–nay, *queen*–in a sash and tiara.

"Brand new shipment from Mistletoe M*Porium," George grins.

Emma snaps. "You're both icons."

Jeffrey shrugs, resigned. "George won a bet, so we're doing Christmas cards his way this year. Conservative cousins in Appalachia be damned."

"We live in Harmony Springs, Jeffy," George points out, "Your extended family already knows we're *gay*-gay."

I don't bother mentioning that they've been married for as long as I've been sentient, their playful bickering the secret sauce to their lasting love. My parents weren't so different, preferring witty sparring to gushy platitudes. I wouldn't mind a bit of both. I have a tough shell but there's a timid romantic in me that hasn't come out to play in a frustratingly long time.

You'd think that living in a historically queer enclave–despite it being in the notoriously straitlaced Midwest–a lesbian would have better luck in love. But Harmony Springs is still a small town, and living here my entire life has made it even smaller. I've already dated every other local lezzy who had potential, and while many of them are still my friends (sometimes stereotypes are based in truth, okay)? I'm resigned to the fact that my soulmate has probably never set foot in, much less heard of, Harmony Springs.

Perhaps labeling my sex life over the past decade as 'dating' stretches the truth. I've been in love once before, and the devastation of that heartbreak built walls around me that I have yet to dismantle. Even in Homoville, USA, uncertain 'straight' girls will trample your heart without a second thought. Wynnie Tatum, Harmony Springs' Homecoming Queen and WASP cheerleader extraordinaire, toyed with my emotions for an entire year while secretly dating Taylor, the Homecoming King from our neighboring town. When Taylor proposed, Wynnie dumped me before anyone ever knew we were together, citing a jumble of family expectations and biological timelines. I should have known better than to let it drag on for so long when she wouldn't even kiss me in public, but embarrassingly, things truly ended when Wynnie decided it was time. I've been reeling ever since, vowing not to go on so much as a flirty farmer's market stroll without confirming my counterpart is a GLAAD-card-carrying, carabiner-clipping, out and proud member of the queer community.

I fiddle with my camera setup as Emma weighs in on sweater combos and touches up George and Jeffrey's makeup.

"You need a quote for that driver's seat, Jo?" Jeffrey asks.

"I can't afford whatever it'll cost, so why rush the disappointment?"

George elbows Jeffrey, who glares at him, exasperated. "Don't steal my thunder, George! I was about to tell her to talk with Mikey Stutz. He recently moved back and bought Hal's auto body shop. Gave me a great deal on my window tinting last week!"

"Stutz?" I recognize the surname. "Is he related to Amanda? We were in Girl Scouts together. She toasted a mean marshmallow."

Jeffrey finger-guns me. "He's Mikey now!"

"Send him my way. Thanks, J." I'm still pretty sure I can't afford the fix until after our Christmas rush is over, but I'm in no position to turn away a potentially discounted repair.

"Shall we begin? Any music requests?"

George bounces excitedly. "Mariah Christmas, please!"

Jeffrey cackles. "How do you not know the name of that album?"

"Does it matter?" George retorts. "Jo gets what I mean!"

Emma and I lock eyes in silent conversation–*let's get this show on the road.*

For the next ninety minutes, we work in tandem, shuffling around the cramped photo truck, juggling the soundtrack, costume changes, and a range of poses while George and Jeffrey banter.

At one point, George whispers something to Jeffrey, who throws his head back, laughing, as I click the shutter. Emma is seated behind me, watching the big monitor to flag the best photos as we go. She clocks the blur and nudges me.

"Delete?"

I shake my head. "It's not about the blur, it's the energy we captured. They're gonna love this one. As Roger always said, never delete a memory that precious."

"Hm." She digests this. Emma can spar as well as these clients, but when it comes to morsels of photography wisdom, she takes my guidance to heart. I appreciate her dedication to the craft and the way she listens to me. It reminds me of me and my dad back in the day, quippy but serious about the job at hand.

George gives me another bear hug as he and Jeffrey pack up their wardrobe.

"You're a talent, Jo, just like your pop. Don't forget to take breaks!" He kisses me on the cheek.

Jeffrey scribbles on the pad that's always in his front pocket, tearing off a sheet and handing it to me.

"Give Mikey a shout."

Emma and I wave them off. She shuts the door to the truck and we both take deep breaths.

"Okay. That was good. Slow start to the holiday card season, but we're back! Shall we prep for our three p.m.?" I ask her. The zone is exhilarating, and the energy of one successful shoot always snowballs into more energy for the rest of the day.

But Emma is on her phone, worrying her lip. "The Jamesons canceled their session."

"Did they give a reason?"

She shakes her head. "That's our third cancellation this week, Jo."

"Right. Fuck."

"They could always reschedule. It stayed warm later this year, maybe people aren't feeling… Christmassy yet?"

I appreciate her optimism, but reality is getting tough to deny. "Harmony Springs is almost as holiday-obsessed as it is gay, Emma. Pretty sure this has to do with a certain free Christmas Card Generator."

"We'll figure this out. We always do. You always do."

I offer a weak smile. "Totally."

And because the zone has now officially slipped from my fingertips and I am spiraling into masochistic misery, I snap some photos of the broken driver's seat and text them to Mikey for a quote. I may as well know how deep the shit I'm in actually is.

As if she can sense her daughter's wallowing, my mother's face pops up on my phone. I attempt to bottle my frustration as I pick up.

"Ma?"

"What's wrong?"

Dammit. Carol's telepathy is unmatched.

"I'll tell you later."

There's a long pause. My mom is not a big fan of being out of the loop and I swear I can hear the gears turning in her head as she strategizes.

"Jolene, come home for dinner tonight, okay? We're eating early. Lena and Matt are coming."

When she calls me Jolene, she means business. Which is exactly what I do not want to be grilled on right now. I need a buffer.

"Emma's coming with me."

Emma's expression turns dubious. I mouth *please* and *meatloaf*. She acquiesces.

"She's not a good buffer, Jolene. Her mouth will be full of meatloaf."

I can't get anything past this woman.

Standing on the front porch of my family home, I stop Emma from ringing the doorbell.

"Repeat the safe word to me once more, please, Emma."

"Fruitcake." She smirks. "Ironic."

I sigh and gesture for her to ring the bell.

The door swings open and my sister Lena stands behind it, looking a bit like a snowman version of her former self (file that under Inside Thoughts). Pregnant and glowing, she wraps me in a tight hug at the front door of our family home and whispers in my ear, "Mom is on one tonight."

Carol comes flouncing around the corner, a glass of chardonnay in one hand and a cooking mitt on the other.

"Jo, for someone who lives in my backyard, I don't see you as often as I figured I would when you moved back in."

My mother knows how to lay on the guilt. She means well, but if I don't cling to my last scrap of boundaries by cooking for myself in my backhouse most nights, I will no longer be clinging to my sanity either.

"Nice to see you too, Ma."

Emma foists a jar into my mom's arms. Carol is delighted.

"More pickling, Emma? Oh, what do we have here?" She holds the jar up to the light.

"Greek giardiniera! Great for snacking, salads, you name it."

My mom coos. "Exotic! Why don't you put that by the cutting board, Em?" She turns to Lena. "And where's that man of yours? Why isn't he downstairs for dinner?"

Lena shoots me an I-told-you-so glance as she ventures off to find her husband Matt, leaving Mom and me alone together in the foyer. She brushes a lock of hair out of my eyes contemplatively.

"Are you happy, Jolene?"

I snort–typical Carol question. "I find pockets of joy."

She clucks. "I saw Elise Stutz at Chandler's picking up the filets for tonight. That truck is a money suck, dolly."

"Mikey hasn't even sent me a quote yet but he told his mother?!"

"Mikey is a good boy. And you're a good girl."

Here we go.

"You don't need to keep your father's legacy alive in that shabby truck! You have the talent, Jo. Why won't you push yourself?"

I swallow back a hard lump in my throat as I try to formulate an adequate retort, but before I can, Matt, smelling of the greenery he recently partook in, waltzes out of the depths of the house followed by Lena. His shirt is pulled up to reveal the belly he lovingly refers to as his snack sack.

"Ladies, I think my water just broke," he quips, his expectant grin faltering as he takes in the tension.

"Hi, Matt. Congrats." I high-five him, as is our standard greeting.

His tummy rumbles and he looks at my mom expectantly. "Dinner, Ma?"

Carol sighs deeply, as if the weight of the world is on *her* shoulders, and she wasn't picking apart my livelihood for sport. Lena pats my mom's back.

"What, Mom?" she asks.

My mom lifts her arms up in exasperation. "You know how I feel about your sister and that truck."

Lena twists her mouth, giving me an apologetic smile before saying, "I mean, Jo, she's not wrong. You pour all your energy into Chrissy when you have so many more options than dad ever had."

"I thought you were on my side tonight," I tell Lena.

"I *am* on your side, Jo. I wish you saw that," she says, and before I can respond, my mom summons us into the dining room.

I slide into my seat beside Emma, muttering to her, "Fruit-cakefruitcakefruitcake."

Emma speaks below her breath. "That might be record time, Jo. Can we at least eat the meatloaf first?"

I resign myself to a delicious dinner before we can make our escape. Mom doesn't go in on me again, instead pressing Lena and Matt on their stroller options. She doesn't mean to drive us crazy. She's got such specific ideas about each of her children's ultimate happiness that she can't be entirely happy without her fingers in our business.

After ice cream sundaes, Emma loudly asks me for a ride home and we excuse ourselves before my mom can corner me about my apparent lack of ambition.

As soon as we slam Chrissy's doors shut, I lean forward on the wheel and let out a wail. I started this day so high and mighty about my ability to dissociate from impending doom, but by the hour, my certainty in that capability has faltered more and more.

Face still pressed to the wheel, I grunt out, "Music, and please no Mariah Christmas."

Emma flips on the radio, scanning through stations until we land on the euphoric chorus of *American Teenager*. Ethel Cain is the soundtrack of queer Midwestern angst.

As I'm starting to float atop her harmonies, the deep voice of the DJ cuts in over the final notes.

"Coming up next, we've got an exclusive live interview with the enigmatic CEO of Gramsta, here to discuss her controversial new app."

My heart drops into my stomach. Great, the woman currently ruining my livelihood won't even let me listen to Ethel Cain in peace.

Emma makes a move to change the station but I stop her. It's time to borrow a little trouble from the future and face at least one of my demons head-on.

I pick up my phone.

I STEP into the studio at the radio station and am overwhelmed by the saccharine coziness of the space. The locally-made vanilla candles. The fluffy faux-fur blankets. The overzealous embrace from none other than the biggest multimedia host in the world, Aspen Rune. These things are meant to put guests at ease, but they put me on edge. I'm not necessarily nervous for the interview, but I never feel more out of my element than in the cloying comfort of this team. You'd think the gay Joe Rogan would be a little too busy to be kind or caring, but down to the production assistant tasked with getting my coconut water, everyone is so… eerily nice.

"Lovely to see you again, my ice queen!" Aspen trills, not a hint of insincerity in his voice. "Have you met my new producer, Andy?"

I turn to see a tall man with floppy hair. He's cute, but, like, the kind of cute you once associated with being a "nice guy," before you realized that average-looking men are not actually obligated to be nice.

He offers his hand. "Nice to meet you."

Called it. In four words, I can read this guy. His eyes run me up and down and his monkey brain has already decided he'd have sex with me. I'd bet money he's tried to sleep with the last three female celebrity guests.

"Pleasure," I say, only slightly unpleasant.

"We're about to come back from commercial," Aspen chimes. "Make yourself at home."

I sit in the stiffest chair I can find–a literal bean bag–and practice the Board's directions in my head. *Apologize, say we care about our users, blah-de-blah-de-blah.*

Andy counts us in from outside the booth and I put my cushy headphones on. Max gives me a thumbs-up, the very minimal reassurance I don't actually need but can appreciate in times like these.

"Welcome back to Getting Real with Aspen Rune! My next guest is the uber-successful CEO of Gramsta, Ava Garcia-Greene."

"Thank you for having me," I say, convincingly enough, into my mic.

"Are we gonna get another million dollars for charity from you this time?!" He's referencing my last visit where I wanted to vacate the premises so desperately that I signed a check for a millie to support his capybara charity.

Yes: *capybara charity.* Allegedly, he saw a 'cute' video of one of the little gremlins on Gramsta and immediately went all Save the Rodents™ on us. They're not even going extinct, he just wants an excuse to cozy up with some vermin outside of Hollywood. Mogul sees mogul, and he recognized exactly how to get what he wanted out of me. Not again, though.

"Let's cut the crap, Rune, I'm here to apologize." The words spill out of my mouth. I see Max wince outside the booth so I let out a belated chuckle. Kidding, *see?* All sunshine and rainbows here.

Aspen is surprised by my candor. "And that is why we wanted to get you in the studio! For those who haven't heard,

Gramsta's new Christmas Card Generator launched this week and is causing quite the stir."

"It is, indeed. And I'm here to say I'm–" *Ugh*, this part is always the hardest. Time and again, I've faced criticism for the tone of my apologies, feeding into a growing paranoia about my demeanor in moments like this, which then quickly spirals into an ouroboros of anxiety. *Suck it up, get it out.*

"I'm... sorry. Gramsta loves the holidays as much as our users, from individuals to small businesses and beyond."

"Are you sure Gramsta loves Christmas?" he prods. "Or is this a cash grab capitalizing on customers' sentimentality?"

"Well, now that you mention it," I straighten up in this contemptible excuse for a chair. "On the way here, I got to thinking... doesn't every corporation act in the same way? Don't they all degrade the apparent sanctity of Christmas with their hyper-consumerism? We're simply using tech to make things easier for people, which has always been Gramsta's mission."

"That's an... interesting perspective. Which is why we've asked listeners to weigh in," he beams.

I can't say I didn't expect this, but including laypeople in the conversation about something the majority of them have no experience with is never helpful for the cause.

"First up, we have Rita from Topeka!"

"Hi!!!! This is Rita!" An incredibly typical listener of Aspen, Rita is giddy to the nth degree and not afraid to let you hear it. "Ava, my family used your Christmas Card Generator since we can't get together this year due to my husband's shingles flare-up." *TMI, Rita.* "It worked like a charm! Bless you, darlin'!"

I take it back. I like Rita.

"Thank you," I reply. "I'm so glad we could help your family this year. Aspen, this is exactly why we made the generator. To help people like Rita."

"Touching," he says. "Thanks, Rita. Up next, we have Jo from Harmony Springs."

"Thanks, Aspen." The low, honeyed voice on the line catches my attention. There's something to it–a mystery that has me holding on for more. "I think Ava has a point about everyone monetizing Christmas. We can't deny that."

"Thank you, Jo," I say, relaxing into the chair beans. This whole thing is going a lot smoother than I thought.

"But what Ava fails to realize is that her artificial stupidity app completely lacks heart, which is the entire purpose of a Christmas card," Jo spews. The honey in her voice becomes venom–a trick I frequently pull out of my own toolbox. Yes, I may be intense, but at least I'm self discerning. I understand exactly what it looks/sounds/smells/even *tastes* like to feel as strongly as I assume Jo is feeling in this moment (for the record, the taste is metal from biting my own tongue, but don't rule out that it's the blood of my sworn enemies). Luckily, all of this gives me the edge, something I love to have in any old-fash-ioned debate.

I goad her. "First-name basis, I see." Aspen lives for this kind of drama.

"Sounds like you have some skin in the game, Jo. What is it that you do?" Aspen soothes, playing mediator.

"I own a mobile photography studio," she says. *Ding ding ding,* we have a hater. "We had another customer cancel because they used Ms. Garcia-Greene's ridiculous app. She's not only ruining Christmas, but she's also taking down small businesses with this garbage. We might not even be open by Christmas because of her."

"That's a big accusation." Aspen turns to me.

"It is." I try not to smile, ready for battle. "Jo... I'd love to hear more about your business."

"Well, it's called The Photo Truck and we're based in Harmony Springs–"

"Got that part," I retort, clicking the imaginary pen in the imaginary boardroom of my brain. "Can you tell me about your business plan?"

"Sure, yeah, I mean, the truck has been around for a while now so we're a local staple. You can check us out on Gramsta." I can tell she impulse-called into the show, nary a game plan in her mind. "We take photos and drive around town, in Harmony Springs, all day–"

I feign a mutter. "And people accuse me of irresponsibly burning fossil fuels." She has no idea who she's dealing with, which is shocking because–ask literally anyone on Earth–I'm an infamous figure these days.

I continue. "What are some of your KPIs this quarter, Jo?" A pause. "Sorry, that stands for key performance indicators." *Zing*.

"I know what it means," she snaps. "We don't really–we're a small business so we don't operate like–"

"Like… what? Gramsta?"

"Well, yeah."

"Just because a business is small doesn't mean it shouldn't be run like a business. You wanna talk about small–Gramsta started in my middle school computer lab."

"That's great, but The Photo Truck is–"

"–Different, right. Since you're so unique, your company must be growing like crazy. What's your year-over-year?" This is almost *too* easy.

"I don't have that number right now–"

"Ad spend?"

"We don't do ads–"

"Of course you don't," I sigh. "Yet it's Gramsta's fault that your business is failing."

I turn to Aspen who's eating this up. Ratings are ratings, and I'm giving *ra-tings dah-ling*. "I'm starting to think her business has no growth potential at all. Perhaps even going in the opposite direction…"

He tries to keep his composure from my sick burn. My words are so scorching that I am almost *literally* killing it.

Jo grows even more defensive. "I'm in a small town, growing a business here is different."

"Small town girl, born and raised," I admit... if you consider a population of 100,000 a small town, which I do. "Most business owners dream of being in your scenario, having less competition and a one-of-a-kind idea."

"Thanks, I guess?" She's beyond flustered.

"I suppose you could take that as a compliment," I snort.

Aspen steps in. "Wow! This has been... fiery." As if he didn't intend for this to happen. "It sounds like The Photo Truck could use help."

"I'd be inclined to agree, Aspen," I purse my lips. I wasn't planning on totally wrecking someone in a debate today, but I'm always down for a cherry on top of a contention sundae.

"And wouldn't it be in line with Gramsta's mission to help Jo out?"

Annnnnd, there it is. Damn Aspen and his scheming ways.

"Well, I don't know about that–" I look to Max. Now would be the perfect time for them to step in and *get me the hell out of here before I lose another million.*

"I remember you saying something about your users at the top of the show," Aspen says, "how small businesses mean so much to you at Gramsta. We can find the sound bite..."

"That won't be necessary–" My eyes scream at Max. *MAYDAY, MAYDAY.*

"Yeah, that won't be necessary," Jo chimes in. Thank God–I didn't think we'd be playing for the same team here. "I don't expect a bigwig CEO to actually care about a small business like mine. If I know anything, it's that they all talk the talk, but they can't even begin to walk the–"

Trigger: hit. I hate to admit it, but she must've done at least some research to know that this is exactly how I was persuaded, nay *conned*, into donating last time. Aspen accused me of not walking the walk, something he heard from his 'source' on my Board (definitely Jason). They love to pull it out when they need something from me. It's my singular weakness; it gets my goose *every damn time*. And, unfortunately, my goose is a bitch and a half.

"With all disrespect," I spit, suddenly totally out of control. "I have been walking the walk since apps were invented. I have innovated some of the most groundbreaking tools of the twenty-first century and I will *walk my walk* all the way to Harmony Springs to prove to you that you have no idea what you're talking about."

"Oh-ho-ho!" Aspen chimes. "Is that an offer I hear?!"

I see Max and Andy, jaws dropped.

This is worse than losing a million dollars to the capybaras.

EMMA and I sit in stunned silence, the truck idling in my mother's driveway. Emma speaks first.

"What… just happened?"

"I'm not entirely sure."

That's the honest truth. How did we end up here?

"You definitely spoke your mind," Emma remarks.

My dad would be laughing at me right now. My mom always said I was his mini-me, but Dad would retort that I was merely a sleeper cell of my mom. He claimed my sharp tongue could be awakened by the proper circumstances, often when others least expected it. I can admit it gets the better of me at times (*see: recent events*).

"Let's get you home." I pull out of the driveway, purposely not looking at Emma.

"Jo, being in shock doesn't mean we shouldn't discuss the utterly insane thing that just happened between the youngest Fortune 5 CEO and you on national radio."

"I don't regret giving her a piece of my mind, but I also don't think anything is gonna change."

Emma scoffs. "You heard her, she pledged to save the truck

on the most-listened to show on the air! How could she go back on that?"

We're at a stop sign so I turn to Emma, who has a giddy grin on her face. I need to let her down easy.

"Big companies make gestures and promises all the time for PR, and when it's for PR, that means the outcome doesn't matter, so long as people are buying the story they're selling."

"Oh, so you're a marketing whizz now, huh?" she goads. "What if we can hold Ava to it? Don't you want help? A cash infusion could save us right now."

"First of all, she didn't promise a cash infusion, she promised *herself* coming to 'fix' everything that's apparently wrong with our business. I've never wanted a partner on this truck and I definitely don't want *her*."

Emma winces. "Um, ouch?"

"Oh, Em, I didn't mean it like that." Why did I bother scarfing down dinner when I've been eating my words all day?

We pull into the parking lot of Emma's apartment complex and I pointedly unlock the doors. Emma pauses before she gets out.

"We need help, Jo. On the off chance that this offer is real, we should take it, whether it's coming from a good place or not."

I love Emma and I don't want to crush her precious optimism. So I make a promise I'm sure is moot. "If there's a real offer, we will… consider it."

"Thanks Joj, get home safe. Bring some leftover meatloaf for lunch tomorrow?"

With that, she flounces off into the night.

I drive home in silence, parking down the street so I can sneak into the backhouse and avoid a run-in with my mother.

When my dad passed away five years ago, I moved out of my apartment in downtown Harmony Springs and into my childhood bedroom to be there for my mom. Lena was living in Portland, chasing her Etsy-selling dreams, and my dad had made me promise before he died that I wouldn't let my mom isolate herself. My mom and I made it about eight weeks before both of us decided we needed a bit more space. My dad had a small life insurance policy, so we used it to build the backhouse. I could live there for the foreseeable future, with the bonus of the ADU increasing the value of the property. They say not to make major life decisions when grieving, but the backhouse made so much sense at the time. We were both desperate to honor his wishes without killing each other in the process.

I don't regret moving in when I did, but I never imagined I'd stay this long. I thought I'd eventually get married and find my own place. But I haven't found my person, and my mom likes having me close. Somehow, five years slipped by in the blink of an eye, and our once-separate lives have blurred into a complicated, codependent tangle.

Locking the door behind me, I flip on the lights and take in my safe space. The ADU isn't some prefab box-in-a-box XXL shed from Home Depot. Jeffrey oversaw the construction, and dozens of townsfolk chipped in with finishes and free services to honor my father, whose legacy of communal spirit was storied amongst Harmony Springsers.

My photographs are hung on every surface, harking back to my high school years when photography was purely a passion, untainted by the need to earn a living. I loved hanging out in my dad's tiny darkroom while he taught me about every film photography technique imaginable. I was sixteen when my dad initiated me into the enchanting world of cyanotypes. I was captivated by the poetic interplay of light and chemicals, a process that I could only describe as painting with the sun. Among my cherished works in the backhouse are a series of cyanotype portraits from that time: little Emma in silhouette, her features softened into whispers of blue, and a street scene of Harmony Springs' Pride parade, where blurred, ecstatic passersby are immortalized in a moment of ethereal stillness. My days now leave little room for artistic indulgence, but I gaze at those portraits often, attempting to remind myself of the unadulterated essence of my passion in that formative period in my life.

Sharing wall space with my art are a select few framed concert posters for the musicians I have a soul connection with. Connie Converse, Alice Coltrane, Sinead O'Connor, Kate Bush, Brandi Carlile. I was lucky enough to see Sinead before she passed, may God rest her soul. I've seen Brandi multiple times because of an obsessed ex-girlfriend. She stole every last temperature-curated lightbulb from my apartment when we broke up, but I forgive her because she introduced me to the queen of lesbian Americana.

I'm a photographer through and through; that is my art form, my passion, my proficiency. But in my soul there is also music, and the music I listen to fuels my artistry as a photographer. I inherited my dad's massive record collection, and listening to his vinyls always feels like time spent with him, however fleeting. I'm lovingly thumbing through a few Magnetic Fields albums when–

Bzzzzzzt. My phone lights up with an unknown number. It's Mikey. He can do it for $1800 with salvage parts, which is more than we've made in the last six weeks.

Bzzzzzzzzzzzzzt. I wonder why Mikey is bothering to call after he just texted. Surely he's not taking some sick glee from making me tell him over the phone that we can't afford his cut-rate services.

"I appreciate you drafting up the numbers, though I'm not sure why my mother needed to be involved. But that's neither here nor there because we can't afford–"

"Am I speaking to Jolene Fisher?" An unfamiliar voice cuts me off.

"This is sh–sorry, who is this?"

"Max Navarro." There's a loud sigh on the other end. "I work with Ava Garcia-Greene."

In my defense, I had a long day. I had a glass of chardonnay at dinner. A showdown on national radio while digesting my dessert. My filter was long gone.

"Well, fuck me."

CHAPTER 7
AVA

I SIT ON MY COUCH, head in my hands, pouting. Where even is Harmony Springs, Michigan? Any town with a name like that has to be two stops away from hell. It'll just be me, alone, at Ye Olde Mitten Nook Inn.

Oh, and Max.

"Max?" I shout to my room. Max runs out, my poofy Patagonia under their arm. "What time's the flight tomorrow?"

"Four a.m." Max frowns. "And you'll have to be photo-ready."

Not only has Aspen gotten me into this mess, he's also gotten my Board involved. Aspen suggested to Jason that Max document our 'adventure'–his word, not mine–so he can get content for his Gramsta *and* the Board can keep an eye on me. At least Max knows my good side.

"And I also... rebooked the Maldives. But come Christmas Day, we'll be on the beach, don't you worry."

I've never said this before, but Christmas can't come fast enough.

Since my island paradise is on the backburner for now, I have to deal with the whole reason I'm being sent to Harmony

Springs in the first place–Jo Fisher. On my reconnaissance mission, my in-app AI chatbot tells me:

- Jo is a lifelong resident of the Springs
- Jo took over The Photo Truck from her dad
- Jo did one failed GoFundMe for the truck
- Jo loves her family
- Jo is actually a guinea pig with 1.6 million followers on Gramsta

Oh, uh... AI malfunction. We're working on that.

Guinea pig or not, Jo has delayed the one thing I anxiously await every year. My annual trip that takes me to the middle of the ocean to my favorite island, away from people and the holidays and all other things generally annoying. No, instead of sitting on the beach, soaking up the Maldivian sun rays with a Maldivian Sunrise, I am going to be stuck in Bumfuck, Michigan in the freezing cold trying to convince some You Betcha bitch that I, the number one tech CEO in the world, am better at building a business than she is. As long as I turn her shit ship around in the next couple of weeks, though, Max and I will be in the Maldives by Christmas.

Shouldn't the top CEO on Earth have more control over their schedule, you might be asking. Of course *he* would. But those early contract negotiations with financiers hit me right in the naivete. I was the youngest woman ever to seek (and receive) the millions I was asking for the development of my empire. And make no mistake, I had a *vision* for Gramsta. I didn't start it all because I was some snot-nosed Ivy brat trying to find hot chicks online.

No, I had been envisioning a universal online social space since I powered up my very first computer. I came up on the early internet, learning about friendship and connection through a screen, rather than in person–which, if I'm being honest, was much more suited to me. I was strange to my peers in school, but online, I was creative and forward-thinking and *cool*. Inspiration struck to develop a safe haven for all my little weirdos where we could be ourselves, free of judgment. Thus, Gramsta was born.

I signed the Gramsta contract at eighteen with no real guidance. I was smart, but I wasn't yet aware of the extent people (namely men) will go to maintain their power. The Board has been fairly quiet prior to the AI boom of the past couple years, but the tension with the new programs has been building. They're not letting me develop them the way they should be: for the good of humanity. They don't care about the search bot; their concern is how Gramsta looks on that infamous Nasdaq ticker.

So is my Boss Bitch attitude a facade? No. I understand what I'm capable of. I can run a company on my own... I *have*. It's what comes with the territory of playing with (read: getting duped by) others in this slimy little world of tech.

And if I can't use it to build my own business, I guess I might as well help this Jo Schmo use it to her benefit. If she'll listen.

The next morning, Max drags me out of bed and we roll into our Escalade. Luckily, I have a private jet out of Santa Monica and don't have to face the public at LAX, which would be the icing on this already stale Christmas cookie. I pull out my noise-canceling headphones, order a mimosa, let Max snap a photo of me 'doing research' on the truck, and relax into that PJ life for the few remaining hours of me-time that I have.

I'm walking down the holly-draped hallway of my childhood home. A pathetic little Christmas tree sits in the corner of the living room, its sparse needles holding on for dear life. I kneel beneath the fir to a plainly wrapped box marked 'Ava.' I open it.

Inside the box is my very first computer, an old Macintosh, in pristine condition. I tear off the box around it and run my fingers over her lovingly. The machine that started it all.

The computer purrs to life, the Apple logo shining at me on the like-new screen.

I go to move the computer to my old desk, hungry to explore the ancient device.

"Time for dinner, Ava," I hear my mom shout from the kitchen. But I can't pull my attention away from my new acquisition, as focused on its magnificence as the day I got it.

"Ava... Ava...."

I race to the kitchen, but my mom isn't there.

"Ava!"

I run to her room. Empty.

"Ava! Help!"

The backyard offers no sign of her either.

I dash back to the living room where the Macintosh sits, waiting.

"I'm right here Ava."

Her voice emanates from the glowing screen.

"Will you listen to me now?"

I startle awake to the plane *thumping* onto the runway. The pilot apologizes over the speakers—a cold front caused the bumps, of course. Add 'being cold' to my list of things I abhor.

All I have to do is get through the next couple weeks, I repeat to myself.

"All you have to do is get through the next couple weeks," Max says, eyeing me from the seat across the aisle.

"It's that obvious?" I grumble, grabbing my handbag.

"You were grinding." Max chomps their teeth together, imitating my sleeping self.

My anxiety manifests in all sorts of fun ways, one of which is teeth-grinding. I usually have my extra cushy bespoke mouth guard to keep the grinding at bay, but you wouldn't catch me dead wearing that around anyone. I'd rather grind my teeth down to pre-veneer levels than be witnessed in that state, even if the only witnesses are Max, a stewardess, and a pilot I definitely won't be hiring again.

The stewardess fights the wind to thrust open the plane door, and I am met with air so frigid that I fight not to turn around and command the pilot to fly my ass back to SoCal.

I step off the plane and into a putrid puddle of slush, which fills the toe of my left heel. My digits freeze up like little Jimmy Dean sausages.

"I need. A coffee." I try to keep it together. *In through the nose, out through the mouth,* I remind myself. Breathing is hard sometimes, also due to anxiety, but lucky for me I'm too stubborn to let it win.

"I've already got a place pulled up," says Max, holding up their phone. We approach a sedan painted with a giant rainbow flag.

"This is cute and all, but where's *our* ride?"

"Uh, this is it," Max says, hesitant. "They didn't have any other drivers in the area so we had to order... this."

The driver, a cheery old man on the verge of getting his license revoked, honks at us. It's meant to be friendly, but all I can hear is the grating sound of a Toyota Corolla.

He rolls down his window. "Pulling up right on the runway... you must be important." He winks at us.

I muster a smile. "Not that important, apparently."

I buckle myself into the cramped backseat. The floor is freshly wet from a previous passenger's boots and the overwhelming smell of Christmas Cookie air freshener pervades my senses. I try not to gag.

"I'm George. Gum?" George offers us a Christmas-ified Wrigley's tin.

"No, thank you," I say.

Max takes one and mutters, "Plane breath."

"Going to Slay Ride Rentals?" George confirms.

Max nods.

"So how'd a couple of hot shots like you wind up in Harmony Springs?"

I do *not* do small talk, and Max knows it. They give an 'I've-got-this' nod, so I put on my noise-canceling headphones to meditate.

After a few deep breaths, I feel the car moving beneath me. I'm centered, I'm calm, I'm cool. *Especially* cool. Collected, too.

I pop open an eye to see Max animatedly telling George about Gramsta, when the town outside the window grabs my attention.

Every last building, street sign, stoplight, and traffic cone is decorated for Christmas, but these aren't any old holiday decorations.

A Rudolph with a blinking rainbow nose.

Mrs. Claus with a shirt that reads 'Santa's Beard'.

A Christmas tree whose ornaments are hundreds of tiny yellow bottles labeled... *Rush?*

Where the hell am I?

George catches me gawking.

"Welcome to Harmony Springs, the gayest little town you'll ever see!"

CHAPTER 8
JO

I WAKE up from a fitful sleep at five a.m., still processing the phone call with Max the night before. Unable to lull myself back into dreamland, I throw on my running shoes and jog through the quiet misty dawn to my favorite highway exit to sit and ponder. And, well, mope a bit.

I guess it's weird, but my sanctuary is a stretch of off-ramp on the East side of town with a series of giant murals painted on it, depicting the origins of Harmony Springs, Michigan. When I was in third grade, the city council commissioned a renowned queer muralist from the West Coast to revive the drab blank wall. On the final day of painting, she invited all of the elementary school students to add their handprints to the border. I still remember dunking my hand in purple paint and applying it with purpose to the gritty cement facade. Not so different from the dopamine hit I get from taking a photograph, I suppose; that sticky silicone handprint captured a moment in time permanently. It was the first time I had truly made my mark somewhere. The very existence of this place is a sort of defiant, anachronistic miracle. When I'm in need of a bit of inspiration (okay, and some humbling), I go and sit on one of the benches by the tableaus and consider my miniscule part in that legacy of resilience.

I stare up at the founding members of Harmony Springs, trying to remind myself that people historically survived much tougher circumstances than a perturbingly hot and bitchy CEO swooping in to make over an admittedly floundering business.

In 1855, somewhere in Northern California, an orphaned teenage prospector named Silas Montgomery had sold his last earthly possession for one more chance to sift through the silt in search of gold. Legend has it that in the dwindling light of his final day, moments before the sun set on his dreams for good, Silas wandered off to relieve himself in the river and stumbled upon one of the largest gold nuggets anyone had ever seen. Excitedly digging around, he confirmed he was on an unprospected deposit. Silently, he took some gold and cleverly left the rest, telling no one. He feigned despair and told the other prospectors he was finished searching, urging them not to follow him as he was done for. He then caught a ride to San Francisco, assumed a new identity, safely deposited his gold and began the process of purchasing the land with the hidden treasure before anyone else could claim it.

Silas Montgomery became a very wealthy man. He subscribed to American ideals, like the cutthroat nature of doing business. He never looked back at his former comrades sifting silt in the riverbank, never gave them a second thought. He invested his money well, and was willing to turn a blind eye to the means by which his money grew.

He was purportedly so busy doing business that he forgot to marry until he was very old. Even so, he carried out his mission of marriage much like a business deal, finding the wealthiest bachelorette in San Francisco and promising her a child; an heir to his fortune. Matilda Montgomery went on to give birth to his only offspring when Silas was sixty-five, a son they named

Bartholomew. She did not survive the birth, leaving the aging Silas a single father.

Bartholomew was different. He was finely clothed, well-mannered, and attended the most expensive Catholic boys' school in the Bay Area, but there was something about him that the other children noticed, something he didn't yet notice about himself. It made them wary of him. He felt like an imposter, handsome and well-heeled, yet rejected for some essence that he couldn't fully grasp.

The one place where Bartholomew found respite was in choir. He sang in an angelic, lilting countertenor that fulfilled the conductor's dreams of performing choral pieces that often required women's voices. As the choir won competitions and he earned recognition from his peers, Bartholomew was allotted this one small pocket of acceptance during his schooldays. The other boys started calling him Harmony, as that was what the choir director would call out to pull his part into a rendition. The nickname stuck everywhere but at home.

In spite of Silas' refusal to acknowledge his son's talent or new moniker, Harmony Montgomery's new name imbued him with an air of confidence, a quality that intensified as he matured. In tandem with his name change, Harmony's deepest, most secretly held yearnings intensified as well. But he kept his sexuality hidden, knowing with certainty that his corrupt father would disown him if his son's identity jeopardized his business dealings with bigoted criminal associates.

When he came of age, he defied his father's wish that he focus on math and economics in order to attend USC's Thornton School of Music instead. For all the years masking his identity as a gay man, the thing Harmony Montgomery was ultimately disowned for was his choice of undergraduate degree.

Thankfully, Harmony had real talent, and he was able to attend university on a full scholarship, bartending nights at LA's first gay bar, Jimmy's Backyard. The year was 1929, and Harmony had figured out his place in the world.

Of course, that optimism was abruptly cut short as the Great Depression swept across America. In place of the roaring twenties, with its underground speakeasies and jazz explosion, was the thirties: a world where every penny went toward survival, not entertainment. Harmony made it through his schooling, but he and his classmates were overwhelmingly unemployed upon graduating.

Without his father's money to live on, Harmony took the advice of the migrant workers who passed through Jimmy's Backyard and headed to Detroit to find employment in the auto industry. He worked on an assembly line where he was paired up with different partners each shift. One day, the foreman paired Harmony with Colin Merkowski, a ginger lad from South Carolina with a relentlessly sunny disposition. Harmony worked better with Colin than anyone he had ever been paired with, and the foreman, knowing a good thing when he saw it, paired them up permanently.

For a while, Harmony couldn't tell if Colin liked him in a special way, or if he was the most charming and attentive individual on the planet. Turns out, it was a bit of both. They worked together on that line for two entire years before one night, drinking together on his fire escape, Harmony worked up the nerve to mention the place he had bartended during college. Colin, ever the active listener, wanted to hear every detail of Jimmy's Backyard, this institution whose tips had gotten his best friend through school, and whose patrons had encouraged Harmony to move to Detroit in the first place. As he tried to encapsulate the cast of characters who populated the bar, Harmony struggled to be adequately evasive. After so many years of talking around the truth, he reached a moment where he stared deep into Colin's eyes. He knew that no matter what, Colin was going to be okay with the truth.

Of course, Colin's reaction was better than okay. He flushed a deep crimson that blotted out all of his darling freckles, and declared that there was no use denying it any further, rejection be damned: he had feelings for Harmony and that was that. Harmony didn't wait another second to embrace Colin, and they shared their first kiss under the smoggy Detroit stars.

For the next year, they lived together in Harmony's apartment as 'roommates' to the outside world. To their small queer circle, their full relationship was known, but otherwise they lived in fear of being outed, losing their precious jobs, or at worst, facing fatal violence. In spite of their shroud of secrecy, they thrived as partners, with Colin encouraging Harmony to revisit his passion for singing, and Harmony editing the opinion pieces Colin published in grassroots queer publications.

On his estranged father's ninety-fifth birthday, Harmony sent Silas a photograph of himself and Colin with an update scrawled on the back. He didn't want to hide from his only living relative anymore, and there was no worse thing that could happen than his father continuing to cut him off.

For eleven months, Harmony heard nothing from Silas. But then, one blustery early December morning, a letter arrived with familiar handwriting. It was from his father, but atop the parchment was a notice: *to be delivered to my son in the event of my passing.* Silas Montgomery had died. This was a shock, to be sure, but the contents of the letter were all the more shocking.

My dear son,

It is with a heavy heart that I pen these words, words which I cannot bear to deliver face to face, and which you shall read when I have departed this earthly realm. I confess now, through this letter, the sins of a lifetime, for I have failed you as a father. I was consumed by a self-loathing so profound that, by the time of your birth, the capacity to love had long escaped me. Your innate purity, your zeal for song, your relentless curios-

ity, and your very essence were more than I could endure, having myself been ensnared by a life of avarice and ruthless ambition.

The tragic irony of seeing you now, content in the company of another man, could very well shatter one's sanity. You know so little of who I truly am. I implore you, burn this missive, lest my failings taint what little remains of my legacy.

Yet, should you come to understand me in this final confession, consider it the scant penance I can offer for the damage I have wrought. I might have lived as freely as you do now, had cowardice not held me in its grip. Heed my warning: do not barter your true self for the hollow allure of acceptance.

In the twilight of my years, I recognize that the approval I so desperately sought from those unworthy of it holds no value as I face death in solitude, unacquainted with genuine romantic affection. I leave you my estate, not as a testament to my affection, but as a burden you must bear wisely. You are undoubtedly a better man than I ever was, but beware the corrupting lure of wealth, a temptation understood only when confronted directly.

With deep regret,
   Your father,
   Silas Montgomery

At thirty-one years old, Harmony Montgomery found out his father was gay and became a multi-millionaire at the same time. In the ensuing weeks, he and Colin debated what they should do with the money. They had lived in the roughest of circumstances for so many years, and while they aimed to improve their quality of life with the influx of cash, they were also closely embedded with their fellow queer community members, the majority of whom were struggling to make ends meet.

On Christmas Eve that year, Harmony and Colin gathered

their friends in their cramped Detroit apartment. Together, they celebrated the fact that, even with nothing, they had all that they needed in the company of one another, their chosen family.

As the evening wound down, with their guests huddled around the fireplace, Harmony unveiled his visionary project: he had acquired ten thousand acres of undeveloped farmland in southern Michigan to establish a town. This new community, Harmony Springs, would be a sanctuary for queer individuals, artists, and free spirits alike. He intended to allocate the bulk of his inheritance to a trust designed to support the town, calling on his community to elect a board of ten members who would manage the funds and advocate for the town's brand new residents.

The Christmas origins of the town's foundation became the scaffolding of Harmony Springs' lore. A place where Christmas was for everybody, at any time, and the idea of holiday spirit as a fleeting thing that visited people in December was waved away as preposterous. From its founding to the present day, many of Harmony Springs' residents had missed out on holidays due to rejection or estrangement from the families that raised them. So, as Harmony and his board saw it, there was much festive time to make up for. To this day, while Harmony Springs dazzles extravagantly at Christmastime, the essence of the season–with a distinctively queer flair–permeates the town all year.

Harmony and Colin lived into their late nineties, with Harmony passing away in 2006. They never stopped advocating for the overlooked and the underserved, and their passion and fortitude paved the way for Harmony Springs to be a pioneering township for statutes on gay marriage, Pride month, drag performing, and trans inclusivity.

Of course, just because a place is founded on queer ideals doesn't mean everyone who lives there is queer. But allyship was the norm growing up in a place like this, which my parents always impressed upon me as a privilege that was not a given in other towns. Because of that privilege, I feel certain I had an easier time coming out than the majority of other lesbians around the world. I was fifteen, but I had known that part of me for years and no one had ever made being gay seem weird or uncool. So many of my local friends' parents and relatives were queer that coming out was almost passé or redundant in Harmony Springs. If anything, it was the straight kids that felt the need to come out.

Sitting on the bench beneath the mural of Harmony and Colin on their wedding day in the town square, watching the sun rise over the freeway, I harness calm for a fleeting moment. I'm resilient. I'm unafraid of challenges. I can handle an egotistical business mogul and figure out a way to get something productive out of this mess of an arrangement. All I need is a vat of bean juice to boot up my kickass mode.

WHEN OUR RENTAL car pulls up to the town's coffee shop, Sugar Daddy's, I can't help but laugh–and not because of the name. Being a female CEO in tech is a complicated line of work. You are expected to perform above and beyond the men in your field, otherwise you're a failure. You're also expected to be a celebrity, upholding that untouchable level of chief executive maintaining a multibillion dollar corporation, while being unavoidably tied up in the drama of fielding off paparazzi and fake tabloid stories.

Which is exactly the sad sight that stands between me and my morning brew. Two local suspects loiter outside the shop's door with their phone cameras out, awaiting my approach. Max is a fine enough bodyguard to handle these two. I slide on my sunglasses and bury myself in my phone, bracing for these backwoods wannabe paps pre-coffee.

"Gentlemen," I say as I waltz past their recording devices.

"One smile!" one of them pleads. I easily ignore; that whole 'smile, sweetie' thing men do doesn't work on me anymore.

"Are you in Harmony Springs to repair your sinking reputation?" the other zings.

I've had a lot of practice in this arena, so I'm able to take a sharp, wintery breath through my nose and exhale my way into the warmth of the shop, ignoring his question. The inside smells too much of freshly baked goods and not enough of espresso. I haven't actually been in a coffee establishment in ages–Max always does these errands for me–but when I have, I'm used to lengthy lines of Los Angeles latte lunatics. The shop here is totally empty, save for the teeny-bopper standing behind the register.

"Welcome in! What can I get you?" she chirps.

As I'm about to order my Gibraltar, the door jingles open and Max jumps around to shoo off the paps.

"None shall pass!" they shout, right into the face of a twenty-something girl whose haircut and septum ring scream 'I'm transitioning out of my emo phase.'

"Whoa," the girl says, remarkably chill after nearly getting knocked on her ass by a bloodlust-y former dungeon master.

"Sorry," Max exhales. "Thought you were those guys." They point outside to the sad excuse for press, checking their photo rolls for 'the shot.'

A woman enters the coffee shop and the emo girl waves her over. She's slightly taller than me, which is especially rare in my heels, and sports the most Midwestern flannel I've ever seen. Her hair is tucked into a messy bun that she probably slept in and her cheeks are rosy from the cold.

"A Gibraltar, please. And whatever Max wants," I turn to Max, getting another glance at Bobby Flannel in the process. She's sneering, like she knows something I don't.

"Uh," the teen behind the counter stammers.

"It's like a Cortado," I say, totally unhelpful.

She stares at me, like a short-circuiting AI bot prototype from our labs. She points to the menu above her, which reads: COFFEE and GAY HOT CHOCOLATE.

"I thought gay people loved coffee," I sigh. "A coffee with oat milk."

"We've got 2%." The woman behind us lets out a snort. "Black."

"And definitely a gay hot chocolate, whatever that is," Max giggles.

"Coming right up!" the teen assures.

"You're not in Silicon Valley anymore, Ms. Garcia-Greene," the woman snickers behind us. *Of course she knows who I am.*

I snort as I turn to face her. "That much is apparent. And it's Silicon Beach, not Valley."

"You're here to–" the emo girl beside her starts. But the woman cuts in.

"Planning to sprinkle some of that *Silicon* magic on us, are you?" she asks, smirk broadening.

"Actually, yes. I'm here to save a photography business that's currently being purposely run into the ground by a stubborn buffoon." I bat a Christmas streamer out of my face. "It could use a little less Christmas kitsch and a little more innovation–something this entire town could apparently benefit from."

"Ah, trying to save us from our quaint ways?" She chuckles. "Very altruistic for a tech mogul."

I lean in, my words clipped. "No matter how you slice it, I'm doing that business a massive favor."

She steps closer. "Here's a newsflash–you might find we're quite attached to our ways here in Harmony Springs."

My smile thins. "Nostalgia is a delusion worshiped by cowards afraid to face the future."

"Or maybe nostalgia is the wisdom to understand new isn't always better," she fires back, eyes flashing.

"I've witnessed more depth in emoji reactions."

"Emojis probably feel profound to someone who's never had a genuine human interaction," she quips darkly.

The barely-barista hands me a soggy paper cup with a rainbow-striped candy cane stuck inside, already polluting my coffee, then gives Max the gayest, most elaborate hot chocolate creation I've ever seen.

I take a sip of my watery-mint concoction and grimace. "This place is stuck in a cursed holiday Groundhog Day."

Max nudges me, their gaze fixed on the ceiling above. I look up and see a tiny, rainbow-berried weed hanging from the ceiling. I squint. *Is that...?*

I jolt back from the strange woman. *Rainbow mistletoe?!* What will this town think of next?

I turn back to her, expecting another contemptuous glare, but what I get is much worse. She's covered from face to waist in my lukewarm black coffee. Outside, the paps eye their phones with glee.

"That was not my fault," I nearly shout. The coffee drips off her face, right along with that smirk. It's too bad; I sorta liked someone giving my level ten snark right back to me. Instead, she takes a deep breath through her nose like I do when a moment of rage-xiety comes over me.

"Not a problem," she says, sputtering through the coffee on her lips. "I have wipes in my truck."

She hands the girl some cash and glares at me one last time. "Welcome to town, Ms. Garcia-Greene. I'm sure we'll be seeing each other." She walks out the door.

"I thought this town was called *Harmony* Springs," I mutter as Septum Ring steps up to the cashier.

"The ushe," she says.

"I–I didn't get your names." Max tries to assuage the situation. "Let us pay for that." They elbow me.

"Sure, let us pay." It's the least I could do, I suppose. Not trying to come to this town and pick fights with random strangers.

"You better," Emo Girl says, smug. "I'm Emma, assistant to the photographer. That's Jo. I think you can guess what she does."

I follow her gaze outside and see Jo opening up the back of a multi-colored monstrosity–*The Photo Truck*. Emma grabs their bagels from the cashier and swiftly takes her exit. We stare after her, slack-jawed.

"Ohhhhhhh, she's–"

"Yep. Got it, Max."

I CAN'T DECIDE whether I'm more pissed off or triumphant. Sure, my vintage Strokes tee is permanently stained, but oh, the sweet, sweet schadenfreude of watching Ava Garcia-Greene's perfect poreless face contort in realization was so delicious I could skip lunch.

Emma, in the passenger seat, seems unsure of what stance to take at the present moment, probably picking up on my own flip-flopping emotions. But I can't rant internally, so she's getting the full monty of my inner monologue.

"And her *face*, like, is she using a real-life AI filter? Where are her pores? Is she wearing fake skin? It's insane."

Emma snorts. "I think you're deviating a bit."

"And I think she deserves more pores, morally speaking. That's all."

"Uh-huh." Emma side-eyes me. "I'm impressed you can cop to her attractiveness when you're seeing red."

"I'm a pissed off *lesbian*, I still have eyes," I retort. "But listen, just because she's... you know... etched by the golden ratio, it doesn't mean I would *go there*."

Emma leans forward in her seat. "Hmm. Do you think *she's* ever been to Ladyland?"

Growing up in Harmony Springs, surrounded by every subgenre of gay person imaginable, has actually overwhelmed my gaydar. It's like a circuit overloaded with too much data, ultimately frying the delicate wiring that fine-tunes one's ability to discern sexuality. Nevertheless, I sit with Emma's musing question. Not because I'd ever date Ava Garcia-Greene, but as a totally neutral, inconsequential thought experiment.

"I get the sense she doesn't like *anyone*, even platonically. She's as much of a corporate robot as her AI Hate My Family Generator."

"I mean, there are people dating chatbots these days, I'm sure there are gay robots out there by now."

"Well, I'm not robosexual, so it's a moot point." I say. "Em, why did I ever agree to this?"

"You're stubborn as an ox but you're not a complete fool."

"Thanks for setting such a high bar, person who works for me."

"No problem, person who can't afford to give me a raise."

"I would if I could!" I insist.

Emma folds her arms. "And I'm not complaining, I'm making a point about why you agreed to this. Chrissy needs help. Your ego will survive, this business might not."

"But can Ava even do anything? It's pure hubris that she thinks she can save a business that is literally suffering because of the app that *she* made!"

"I've been thinking about it, and I think you can use that to your advantage."

My curiosity is sparked. "Oh?"

"Well, it was her hubris that led her to make that promise on a national radio program. Everyone is watching. She doesn't have any choice but to help us; her job at the app that's ruining our business is on the line."

"Where are you going with this?"

"Let her fail."

"What?"

"Let Ava swing her big fat ego around until even she's exhausted by how impossible the task at hand is, and then, right before Christmas, you can convince her to write us a big blank check to make up for how much she botched it. At the end of the day we need a cash infusion, right?"

"Why don't we ask for a blank check now, so she can go home?"

"Her pride could never."

Emma's not wrong.

"Okay, so we let Ava flail, prove to her that her big corporate strategies don't apply to The Photo Truck, and once she's desperate to have anything to show for all her big talk, we corner her and demand money?"

"Egos are like Chinese finger traps. The more you try to go against the grain, the more stuck you'll get. Let her be hoisted with her own petard or whatever."

"Hoisted..? What?"

Emma is defiant. "I read Shakespeare, okay? I love language!"

They say a photo speaks a thousand words, so I'm a reader in a sense, too, but whatever mumbo-jumbo Emma is spouting is not actually English. That being said, Emma is also spouting pretty high-level strategy at the moment.

"I'm on board. I guess. Let's hose the bastard."

I can feel her eyes roll without even looking over.

I pull up to Emma's place and park.

"Jo, come inside for a second. Duke hasn't seen you in ages and he's devastated."

Well, that's one individual who has never failed to make a good impression on me. Or, I should say, a *great* impression. Duke is Emma's Great Dane mix rescue, a hulking himbo of a dog whose heart and soul far outsizes his already massive body.

"I can't be responsible for ruining my father's legacy *and* devastating Duke in the same week. Let's go."

As soon as Emma unlocks her apartment door, a tornado of affection and slobber tackles me to the ground. I'm not exaggerating in the slightest. But I'm not only unbothered, I am thriving. I said the murals were my sanctuary, but in some ways, being pinned beneath a 180-lb breathing weighted blanket has a similar effect on my overstimulated psyche. I am the recipient of pure, unadulterated, unconditional love and I can't help but be hyper-present in the moment.

"This is definitely what the doctor ordered," I say from beneath the beast, my stomach rumbling.

"The doctor hasn't ordered us food, unfortunately, but we should."

"Gulab Jolly?" Yes, even our favorite Indian place in Harmony Springs is still Christmas-themed. Anjali and Nisha could serve their korma sauce in wine glasses and I'd drink it, that's how good their spot is.

"You know the drill."

"I'm on it." I re-order our usual online.

Emma and I definitely like our routines. We get coffee together every morning, even when we don't have a shoot, like today. And since we both live alone, we always text good night as a little check-in at the end of each day.

Lena and I haven't always been the closest, so in many ways, even though we aren't blood relatives, Emma often feels more like a sister. At least in the way I always wanted one.

Emma's dad and my dad were best friends since birth. I was raised calling her father Uncle Gene, and to her, my dad was Uncle Roger. They both grew up in Harmony Springs, next door neighbors, and they were inseparable up until my dad died. When he passed, Emma was still in high school, and she leaned on me emotionally. It gave me a sense of purpose, somehow, to set aside my own grief and work to assuage hers. It's probably not healthy, but it's the truth.

Because I'd inherited the truck, she started hanging around, fiddling with cameras and lenses, learning the ropes while unofficially shadowing me. Once she got to college, she worked out a way to get credits toward her film degree by interning at The Photo Truck, and the rest is history. She's the reason the truck even half-exists today, and that's part of why I'm taking her plea to entertain Ava's charitable bid to heart.

We sit on the floor beside her coffee table, our Indian feast laid out before us, Duke resting his giant head on my foot. I scoop up a mouthful of aloo gobi and moan. Food is awesome and also, I forgot to eat breakfast and have been awake since god knows when.

Emma picks up the remote. "Bravo?"

"Bravo, Bravo, fucking Bravo."

I'm grateful we have each other to share in these small but perfect moments amidst all of the hullabaloo. Would that it could last for longer than midday *Real Housewives* and curry.

The next morning, after our coffees–and mutual bitching about the carbohydrate stupor we landed ourselves in yesterday–we drive the truck over to the North side of town for one of the few shoots that hasn't yet canceled on us. I'm savoring this booking for multiple reasons–namely, it's a booking, but also, this is my final day of work before the Ava train comes hurtling into the station.

The Olafson clan pile into the truck and I start my usual holiday photoshoot spiel while Emma makes last-minute tweaks to the lighting setup. I'm flipping through my book of poses when I glance up and see that Karl, the father, is fully across the studio, his nose pressed to the glass window.

"...Karl?"

"Wow, she's... wow!"

Either Mrs. Claus and Santa's flying reindeer blessed Harmony Springs with a cameo, or the Wicked Witch of the West just landed.

CHAPTER 11
AVA

MAX PULLS the rental car up to The Photo Truck, parked at yet another intersection of Gay and Christmas. Jo and I may have gotten off on the wrong foot yesterday, but I'm here to do a job: repair my image.

Which is precisely what Max and I were berated about on a six a.m. wake-up call this morning from Jason, who already caught wind of those second-rate pap shots of me spilling coffee on Jo. Huffing through his pre-sunrise CrossFit session in LA, he spewed a jumble of idioms about thin ice and striking hot irons. My desperation to get him off the phone overrode self-preservation and I found myself agreeing to get a head start on smoothing things over.

I've got to speak with Jo, move us past any bad blood, and make sure everything we capture for the Board and Aspen is as gay and harmonious as Harmony Springs itself.

"Looks even worse up close," I say, examining the truck's peeling exterior.

"It's... charming!" Max attempts.

I pull my sunnies down the bridge of my nose and shoot them a glare.

"Charmingly hideous," they amend.

I push my sunglasses back up, knowing I was correct in my assessment. Not that it brings me great joy when someone else's business is tragic, but the thrill of being right never gets old.

"May I make one suggestion?" Max peeps, as soon as I'm about to step out.

I raise an eyebrow–permission granted.

Max holds out a Gramsta-branded tee. I stare at the shirt in their hands. I highly doubt Jo is going to want anything to do with this peace offering, but it's more than I thought to bring.

I take it. "Wait here."

I get out of the car and make my way to the side door of the colorful truck, but before I can knock, I see the face of a middle-aged golden retriever of a man peering out the window at me. I'm not taken aback by this; it happens a lot with tech fanboys. They drool all over my creations and speak to me as if I had not been the one to invent them myself. It's kind of adorable in a pathetic way–like they're toddlers trying to impress me with their knowledge of the ABCs.

Before dog-man can wipe the drool from his chin, Jo pushes past him with a feigned courtesy that evaporates the moment she sees me.

"What are you doing here?" Her tone is icy.

"Lovely to see you again, too." My reply drips with sarcasm. If I couldn't tell from her voice alone, the annoyance is written across her face.

"Ms. Garcia-Greene, I thought we agreed over email that we'd meet tomorrow."

"Please, call me Ava," I offer, though her glare tells me she's not buying the friendly act. "Our first meeting yesterday was–"

"Messy?" she interjects.

"Yes, and not because I... tossed coffee in your general direction." I still stand by that not being my fault. The idea that gay mistletoe can be hanging above your head at any moment in this town is truly haunting.

"You did a lot more than that," she snaps, accusatory. She's clearly been brooding over our encounter. "I have a shoot happening, so I need to get on with it."

"Wait–" I say, smoothing out the wrinkled shirt in my hands. "I wanted to… start off on a better foot."

She examines the shirt, her gaze fixed on the oversized Gramsta logo.

"For the other shirt… that got…" My words falter, my usual eloquence deserting me in her cold stare.

She turns dismissively and heads back to the truck.

"Wait!" I call out, desperation creeping into my voice.

She stops and faces me again, arms crossed.

"I'm–I'm sorry, okay?" I blurt out the apology, cringing at how clumsy it sounds.

"Apology accepted," she replies curtly and turns away once more.

"Wait! Again," I exclaim. "I was hoping… I could see your process? Be a silent observer during your shoot?"

"You? Silent?" she scoffs, her skepticism palpable.

"Ooh, got me. Feel better?"

The man's face reappears, smooshed against the window like a pup who's learning how glass works. "When do we get to meet Ava?!" he whines.

Jo glares at me, overwhelmed. She lets out the deepest, most intentional sigh I've ever heard.

"Stay out of my way," she commands, dismissing me with a wave of her hand.

Emma hands Jo her camera as I take in the… erm, sights. The truck is cute, cuter than I thought it would be, but dated as all get out. The computer is a relic, the first generation of Mac desktops without a tower. Various items are haphazardly held together with Christmas-colored duct tape. And the driver's seat? Flat as a pancake and stuck that way. Hidden behind Jo's makeshift backdrop, these flaws are not immediately visible, but they scream amateur hour to anyone taking a closer look. I snap some photos to document and Emma glares at me.

"All right, who's ready for a family pyramid?" Jo sing-songs with grating enthusiasm.

"Pyramid? Isn't that a little... jejune?" The words slip out before I can stop them, earning me one of Jo's now-infamous glares. I zip my lips shut.

She poses the family as I poke around the truck's antiquated tech. Definitely old, definitely needing repair, but not completely unsalvageable.

"I'm sorry, I can't ignore the tech genius in the room," the dad swoons. "It's soooo nice to meet you, Ms. Garcia-Greene." *Like, buddy, chill, your wife is right there.*

But he reaches his hand out to shake mine, and I can't deny the man his dreams.

"Please, call me Ava," I say, leaning down to him at the bottom of the pyramid and shaking his hand. The family pyramid shakes and I retract. "I'm here as an invisible observer, though. Pretend like I don't exist!"

"How could I do that? I'm a day one Ava stan!" His son cringes. My superfan searches his pockets for his phone. "I still have the original filter pack on my Gramsta."

The pose wobbles even more.

"Honey," his wife huffs. "The first rule of the truck is no phones, remember?"

"Mom's right, phones away, please!" Jo cuts in, a hint of a strain in her voice. "They spoil the Christmas magic. I promise as soon as we get this pose–"

Jo raises the camera to take a photo.

"All right, all right, but this is something else!" the dad gushes. "I used to dabble in dev myself. My issue was I was never any good with the backend, just had big design ideas."

"That'll get ya," I reply. "Gotta have a talented tech team to make the magic happen."

Jo's frustration mounts. Every photo on the cracked computer screen is of the dad talking.

"That's great, now I need to make *my* magic happen over here, thanks," Jo snaps. *It's not my fault tech bros are obsessed with me.*

I retreat to the corner, attempting to take up less space–something I haven't been able to do in years, thanks to the macho world of tech. I watch as Jo tries to get the perfect pyramid picture, but my attention can't help but wander over to the monitor which jiggles with every step. I poke it and it wobbles even more.

Jo turns toward me and points. "Don't touch that." She turns back to the family. "Everyone say 'don't touch that!'"

"Don't touch that?" the family puzzles as one. The photo displays on the monitor–a fail.

I can tell Mom is growing tired of having the kids' knees drilling into her back. "Can we try a new pose?" she says, exasperated.

"We can get it," Jo insists, determination flaring.

I step away from the monitor, my hands up in submission. As she takes another photo, I accidentally slip my raised hand in front of the flash. The photo that pops up on the monitor appears as if half of it has been consumed by specters. But no, that's a shadow of my body, and Jo is growing more livid by the second.

"Ava, you're in my light," she bites.

"I didn't–"

"*Please.* Sit."

Reluctantly, I squat in the corner, no chair in sight. Jo doesn't seem to care as she nails the perfect shot at last.

"Great!" she beams. "We're done with that. Let's do individuals. Who wants to go first?"

Mom leans down and attempts to get her youngest to go first, but I recognize the *CAMERA SHY* written all over her little face; it mirrors my own from years past. Though I still feel that way, fame has compelled me to push through it, one forced smile at a time.

"Hey, that's okay," Jo coos. "Maybe Mom goes first?"

"Oh, I don't–" the mom starts. But Jo nods to her as if to say *I've got a plan.*

The mom sits on a stool Emma places in front of the backdrop as Jo kneels down to speak to the daughter. "You, my friend, have been promoted to assistant camera."

I don't know where Jo is going with this, but a double-chin photo of Mom from the perspective of a three-foot munchkin will be, at the very least, hilarious. Jo instructs the girl to peer through the viewfinder and click the button, and sure enough, a terrible photo of Mom appears on the screen.

"Look at that beautiful photo you just took!" Jo undeservingly compliments. I strain to see the artistry as she continues. "Are you ready for me to take one of you?"

The little girl nods, suddenly enthusiastic. She clambers onto the chair and strikes a pose. Jo, now fully in command of the shoot, is in the zone, immersed in a flow state that's familiar to me. It's almost... respectable. Yes, that's the word. Respectable.

Ultimately, though, all Jo did was fool a six-year-old (or however old she is, I don't grasp children's ages) into doing what she wanted–not that hard. And while the picture she got out of it is shockingly good, what I previously assumed stands: she *still* doesn't understand how to run a business, and I've *still* got my work cut out for me.

CHAPTER 12
JO

AVA'S OUTSIDE THE TRUCK, scribbling an autograph on Karl's bare chest. I may not get the hype, but that doesn't make the hype any less pervasive.

"I'm surprised you didn't knock her out with a C-stand," Emma observes as she zips lenses into their cases.

"I'm trying to avoid spending Christmas in federal prison, thanks."

"Who's going to prison?" Ava materializes behind us.

Emma fixes me with a look. "Not Jo."

"That's good because you weren't half bad behind the camera," she says to me. "You got them out of their shells."

Emma pipes up. "Jo's got all the tricks. Straight from the Roger Fisher Academy of Fine People Skills."

Ava scrunches her brow. "Roger Fisher?"

"My dad." I don't elaborate and Ava doesn't push it.

Instead, she starts futzing around the studio, flipping through my wall calendar, touching flash bulbs, and generally molesting my truck.

"Can I help you?" I ask, acidic.

She actually chuckles which annoys me even more. "I think that's my question for you."

I do not like how pleased she is with herself. "Did you not just say how impressive I am behind the camera?"

"I said you 'weren't half bad' but you can run with that." She picks up a packet of vintage Polaroid film and inspects the expiration date. I bite back a defensive retort about how expiration dates are irrelevant when it comes to shooting on expired film, that's part of the magic. She'd delight in my defensiveness, so I hold it in.

"Anyway," Ava continues. "You've got artistic talent, I'm not going to deny that. But I also wasn't wrong about making improvements to your *business*."

She strides over to my Mac desktop at the back of the truck.

"Is this a computer or is it technically a slide rule?"

I scoff. "It's not even that old."

Ava blanches like I told her the computer had leprosy. "You're putting files on there and not backing them up. You're playing Russian roulette with an ancient processor that one day is gonna straight-up eat your entire portfolio because it overheats."

My stomach clenches; she's probably right, but her words land as a personal attack. My dad's business has rested on my shoulders for the past five years, and I've fought to keep it afloat. When she says I'm putting that at risk, I can't help but feel I'm being accused of dishonoring my father's legacy.

Emma pipes up before I can formulate a retort. "We welcome a cash infusion to replace our hardware!"

"Glad you'll welcome it, but that's only the tip of the iceberg," Ava says.

I sit down with a thump atop a Pelican case and try to massage the crease out of my forehead. I'm painfully aware of how poorly I'm masking my annoyance. "Pray tell."

"I need more time to observe and investigate, but off the top of my head, you need to implement more automation throughout your business, update your tech, stop being complacent about outreach to new customers because it's a small town... get a real online presence. Come into the twenty-first century. Etcetera."

This woman cannot help herself from adding a thick layer of snark to every time she speaks.

"Etcetera?" I am a glutton for punishment.

She comes to stand over where I'm seated and folds her arms. "*Etcetera* means there are lots of specifics I can't conjure up out of thin air without first digging into exactly why this business isn't working."

Our gazes lock. I thought she had blue eyes but the green of her suit highlights little aquamarine flecks around her pupils. *The color of a pool full of chemicals.*

"Doesn't helping The Photo Truck kinda go directly against your vision for AI to replace all photographers?"

Ava blinks and our staring contest ends. "Don't worry, the success of your single vehicle business does not threaten my empire. And anyway, I happen to think we could coexist and serve different purposes. Gramsta is hoping this whole... excursion... to Harmony Springs will demonstrate that."

I snort. "'Coexist and serve different purposes'? Is that the company line? Very kumbaya language to describe the myriad jobs being hemorrhaged by AI."

"We're *creating* jobs with AI. The more popular our AI services on the platform, the more engineers and data analysts and project managers we hire."

I hold up my hands. "If that helps you sleep at night."

I swear she flinches but it's so subtle I can't be certain. *Good.* She's in need of a wakeup call from one of us blue-collar plebes in the trenches of her totally altruistic robot revolution.

Emma jumps up from her place at my alleged slide-rule of a computer. "Upload complete!"

I stand up from my seat and clasp my hands together, searching for the perfect hint to get Ava out of my personal space so I can get some editing done without her judgmental hovering. But it turns out this corporate girlboss can occasionally read the room without an assist.

Ava tucks a piece of hair behind her ear and purses her lips. "I need to catch up on some work at my hotel."

I offer her a tight smile as a reward for her momentary perceptiveness. "Thanks for dropping in. Unannounced. A day early."

Her lips twitch. "You are sincerely welcome."

I walk her to the door of the truck. She steps down and my chest begins to untighten for the first time in hours. As I'm closing the door, Ava turns around.

"Christmas is in two weeks. We don't have much time to do what needs to be done."

I don't disagree. "You've got your work cut out for you."

"Glad we're on the same page," she chirps back, already deep in her phone. "I'll have Max make us a dinner rez tonight so we can tackle our first official day tomorrow."

My mouth opens and closes like a goldfish as I grapple for an excuse that will get me out of this, but Ava has needled me into a tight corner where I'll be a hypocrite if I do anything but go along with her suggestion.

Emma pops up over my shoulder. "Send us the deets!" And then she reaches around me and shuts the door on Ava.

I whirl around to face her. "You're supposed to be on my side!"

"That woman is playing 5D chess. Chinese finger trap, remember? Go to dinner. I'm sure it'll be somewhere nice, and she's definitely paying."

We make our way to the front of the truck. I get into my broken driver's seat and turn the key in the ignition. The engine sputters but eventually gears up. I grimace.

"Play the game," Emma tells me. "And play it to your advantage."

I pull out of the lot. "Where did you become such a savvy businesswoman?"

"Where everyone learns anything these days."

I suspect she's talking about a certain monopolous social media app, so I side-eye her. We make the rest of the drive to Emma's place in relative silence.

We pull into the complex. As she gets out, Emma playfully punches me on the arm.

"Jo? For the love of all things Christmas, wear something other than flannel tonight. At least look spiffy while you're ripping Ava a new one."

Occasionally, Emma has decent advice.

I STEP out of my rental in front of the nicest restaurant in town, which isn't saying much. It's a two-story building that looks like its interior was sucked straight out of 2014 LA, but it'll do.

I pull down my vintage Prada LBD and adjust it according to my reflection in the shiny car. This may be a work dinner, but I pride myself on being the best-dressed CEO on the planet at all times. Unfortunately for me, it's also approximately thirty-seven degrees outside.

I throw on a blazer Max draped over the passenger seat–they know me too well. I gave them the night off from chauffeur duties to do some more brand reconnaissance, aka interrogating the hotel staff for everything about Jo, Emma, and all things The Photo Truck. Max loves when I assign them sneaky tasks; they live for going undercover and using their charm to squeeze information out of unsuspecting prey. If they didn't also love to gossip, they could probably be a massive asset to the FBI.

I search for the valet, car still running, when the *beep* of a lock sounds behind me. I turn to see Jo approaching in a collared shirt tucked into flowy pants. It's so... effortless. Something bubbles up from my stomach. Jealousy? Nerves? I'm not entirely sure.

"You just gonna leave that there?" she says, nodding toward my car.

"The valet is missing," I report. "I was about to go inside to–"

"They're missing because they don't exist. This is the Midwest; we park our own cars."

"Right. That's embarrassing." I gesture to her outfit. "You..."

"Look nice?"

"I was going to say 'aren't in flannel,' but sure." She rolls her eyes.

I'm nailing this whole image recovery thing.

We're seated at a table on the first floor. The vibe is moody and a little more date-y than I had planned, but I'm pushing ahead with tonight's agenda because I don't have a choice.

"So, tell me more about the truck," I say. "Your internet presence was a little... lacking." Sure, there is some information I could (and did) dig up, but I want to hear the story from the horse's mouth.

She huffs. "That's because the entire town already knows the story. My dad started the business in the eighties, taking pictures for Christmas cards–"

"Christmas? In this town?" I jest.

She doesn't bite. "I was always my dad's helper, then I took over when he couldn't do it anymore. I've been running it with Emma as my assistant ever since."

"So, unpaid intern?" I jab.

"I pay her!" she retorts. "What I can."

"And I'd like to help with that."

"How could you possibly–"

I can tell she's about to rip me a new one, but then she stops and takes a deep, intentional breath.

"What's your pitch?"

Now we're talking.

"I've done a deep dive on your business operations thanks to Gramsta AI." I catch her wince at the mention of artificial intelligence. "The truck is an all-year business like you mentioned, but has most activity during the holidays?"

"Hence why her name is Chrissy, yes."

"The truck… has a name?" I swear, this town can't get any more sentimental.

"Chrissy. The Christmas Truck," she laments. "Dad named her."

"…Cute," I say, unsure of the proper response to this sort of statement. I forge ahead with my pitch. "I'd like to take a look at your cash flow, but I'm certain the truck could be much more profitable at other times of the year by expanding your business in a few areas."

"Expanding?" Jo's skeptical. "Folks here are simple. They're not like people where you're from."

"What does that mean?" I don't mean to be defensive, but I love my sprawling city, filled with packed freeways and the vague smell of marijuana everywhere you go.

"With all due respect, people in Harmony Springs don't need photos of themselves for Gramsta holding the latest fit tea they're trying to sell to their followers."

That is *actually* cute; fit tea was so 2016.

"I suppose you're right about that," I concede. "But I had bigger things in mind. Would you follow me?"

I guide us up the stairs and out to a vast patio overlooking the parking lot. Even though management had closed it off due to the freezing temps, Max worked their magic and convinced them to open it up for us. The setup is classy yet simple. Dare I say, I'm actually a little impressed?

"Sure you can handle the cold, beach babe?" Jo catches me shivering before I even notice myself.

"Oh, I'm a babe now?" I laugh. "Better than being a monster, I suppose."

"I never called you a monster," she says.

"Everyone else does," I tell her. "And I'm aware you probably feel that way, based on our first conversation."

"I don't like to judge people until I actually know them."

"I call big, *big* bullshit."

She laughs. "Okay. You're the glaring exception."

"Let me show you something," I say, leading her to the roof's ledge. Her big gay truck stands out, but not by much. The whole town has at minimum one rainbow bumper sticker per car. "To all my designers' chagrin, I broke out my old sketch skills and made a mockup of what the trucks could look like. Can I show you?"

"Trucks, plural?"

She has no idea what's in store. I take out my phone, pulling up digital mockups of a sleek, high-tech truck. Tooting my own horn here: they're good.

"Whoa," is all she can muster.

"I'm a little rusty," I say sheepishly. But I'm not. I'm actually insanely talented, but I've learned over the years that a little pretend-humility can often work in my favor.

Jo studies the designs. "There's no Christmas anywhere."

"Yup!" I say. "If you're going to be a year-round business, we've got to treat you like one."

She crosses her arms. *Tough crowd.* "You might think Christmas is 'garbage' but the people here don't. Most of the permanent businesses in Harmony Springs have a holiday theme."

"You say that, but your business is stuck in a rut. You need to accept that your vision might need to change in order to adapt. You're holding yourself back."

She groans. "You sound like my family."

I let her scroll through more mockups, hoping she'll find something that pleases her in the deck.

"What is *that?*" She pauses on one of my personal favorites: a truck with her face printed on the side.

"One of the glaring issues of your company is that you don't have a face for the brand. No one for potential customers to connect with. Plus," I offer, "you're nice-looking. So people will connect with that."

She narrows her eyes at me. *Was that a weird thing to say?*

"No more Christmas theme is one thing. *That* is not happening." She turns to the truck in the parking lot, like she's checking to make sure I haven't already desecrated it.

"You don't need to be that overt, but if you want to grow you need to step up the personality marketing."

"I'm not going to be the face of this company," she hands back the phone. *Touchy.* "It's not my place."

"Not your place? Jo, it is quite literally your place. Don't you want your business to thrive? If you cleaned up your branding and stuck to a growth model, you could franchise your photo truck nationally." I'm struggling to grasp how she can be so resistant to a trajectory of wild success.

"The truck isn't about any of that," she says. "It's a family business, not meant to be corporatized. People come to feel comfortable and open and themselves, not... that." She nods to the phone again.

Okay, flower child, point taken. I put it away.

"This is hard for me," I say. "But, I'm going to put my ego aside–"

"The whole thing?"

"Ha *ha*," I deadpan. "It's clear I have a lot more to learn about Chrissy." She smiles at my use of the truck's Christian name. "Book me for an all-day shoot tomorrow. Being a client will show me a lot about your... user experience."

"*All day?*" I thought she'd be grateful for a lengthy booking in these trying times, but my Jo-dar is off. "I can't just clear my schedule for you. I have clients."

"They can reschedule," I insist.

"They can't."

"They *can*."

"They *can't*."

"Oh, but I think they can." I hand her a check. A *big* check. She scowls.

"Do you get how fucked up that is?"

"Yes," I say. I want to think she enjoys my frankness.

"Ego aside?"

"Ego aside," I assure her.

"And no helping me." She does air quotes around 'helping.' "You're there for photos."

I nod.

"Eleven a.m. Sharp."

She turns and walks back down the stairs.

It's not much, but headway is headway.

CHAPTER 14
JO

I HATE how easy it was for me to snatch that check for ten grand out of Ava's perfectly manicured fingers. When I deposited it via my bank app this morning, Chase actually called to verify it wouldn't bounce–I've never made such a large deposit before. That shouldn't make me embarrassed but it does. Money is money, and even though I'm happy to bleed Ava and Gramsta dry, I can't quite accept that me or Chrissy actually earned those funds. But, as Emma pointed out over our coffee run, better to be in a shame spiral with ten thousand in my checking account than be in a shame spiral and broke. Guilt and shame aside, this money still barely scratches the surface of what the business needs to survive even another few months.

At least I have some tricks up my sleeve for today to reestablish dominance in this battle of wills. Ava signed on to be a client, which means I get to be in charge, and I have every intention of exploiting that dynamic, however fleeting it may be.

My phone alarm goes off. T-minus ten minutes until Ava descends on this truck. I survey our setup for the photoshoot.

I've dug out every piece of queer Harmony Springs Christmas memorabilia in my possession–treasures first gathered by my father and then added to by me. Together, Emma and I have artfully arranged trans flag-dyed wreaths, rainbow-berried mistletoe, a nativity scene featuring members of MUNA, and more paraphernalia into a colorful backdrop. I'm aware it might read *slightly* garish, but that's *slightly* the point.

Emma bustles past me, arms laden with rainbow tinsel. "You did say the theme was 'Santa's Christmas card if he was a gay bear with a cocaine problem.'"

"Mission accomplished?" I ask.

"Well, what's the reaction you're hoping for, exactly? She asked neutrally."

"She certainly did." I understand Emma has the best of intentions. "I think Ava is a little inauthentic. Whether or not she started out that way, she's this perfectly coiffed corporate prototype."

"Fair."

I continue, "And Harmony Springs was founded on radical authenticity. If she wants to swoop in here and tell me how to do business, she needs to understand and embrace the principles of the community I'm trying to do business in."

"So you're..." Emma gestures at our set, "...challenging her to a cringe-off in order to unlock her most authentic self?"

"That's one way to put it."

She nods. "Honestly, a very Gen Z approach. I approve."

We spend the next few minutes pinning up the last of the rainbow tinsel, with a split second to admire our handiwork before we hear Ava pulling up.

Ava and Max pile out of their rental car and I have to stifle an actual gasp, because...

"What is she *wearing*?" Emma mutters.

Don't get me wrong, if anyone is going to pull off a fitted pinstripe two-piece suit tailored to the gods, it's Ava Garcia-Greene. But she appears even more out of place than she was yesterday in her cashmere sweater and pencil skirt.

If I had to guess, Ava's mostly been assigned photoshoots for big glossy magazines lauding her winning combination of youth and power. It's hard to imagine her sitting for a cozy Christmas card, which is exactly why I've orchestrated today the way I have.

Strutting across the fresh powder of snow in six-inch stilettos and Beetlejuice's wardrobe, she waves at me cheerily.

"Morning!"

I'm thrown by her peppiness. It almost makes me resist calling out her stuffy corporate attire, but today is about being authentic, right?

"This is what you're wearing to spread holiday cheer?"

She straightens out her jacket. "Holiday cheer? I'm here for headshots."

I open The Photo Truck door for her, and as she slips past, a whiff of her perfume–a woody, complex scent–momentarily envelops me. I find myself wishing for another moment to savor it, to decipher the familiar notes it stirs in my memory.

Ava gawks at the over-the-top set dressing. "What is all *this* about?"

"I've got you booked for a Christmas card session, and unfortunately we can't accommodate last-minute changes. It messes with our bottom line. I'm sure you understand."

Ava scoffs. "I paid handsomely enough for this shoot to be whatever I want it to be."

"You actually paid the going rate for canceling another client's session, which is a thing The Photo Truck has never done once before in its decades of operation."

I catch Emma and Max exchanging a look. I'm glad our bickering is entertaining to someone.

To my surprise, Ava picks up a rainbow Santa hat from one of the prop bins and turns around, mugging for the camera that's not yet there to capture her smize.

"Happy?"

I kind of am. Seeing her in a goofy hat, I can almost picture a younger Ava for a split second, unburdened by public relations and dry cleaning. But I won't be copping to that.

"Not particularly."

Ava squints at me. "I'm not picking up on the people skills I've been hearing so much about."

I relent a little. "Listen, you want to experience what I do for my clients. I want to take your Christmas card photo because that's what this truck was built on. This business put down roots in Harmony Springs because the queer people here needed what my dad was offering: a space to form new traditions during a holiday that had previously been a strained time for many of them."

For once, Ava doesn't snit back at me. "Fine. So what now? You lead, I follow."

I'm momentarily speechless. "Seriously? I mean, great. Yes. Okay!" She's enjoying watching me stumble. *Pull it together, Jo.* "Well, a good Christmas card is cozy, like how people want to feel this time of year. So this–" I gesture at her starched suit, "is not going to put the recipients of your cards at ease."

Ava bites her lip. "I'm not really an athleisure gal, Jo. I have my work clothes and my workout clothes." She mulls for a second. "And I sleep naked, so I don't own pajamas."

My heart thuds loudly. Did she seriously just throw that out there? *Do not picture her naked in bed, do not picture her aquamarine eyes blinking up at you from a pillow, do not picture–*

Do. Not. Picture.

"Thank you for enlightening us. Um." Wow. I have completely forgotten what the original game plan was, much less my own middle name. "Harriette."

She blinks at me. "What?"

Oh my god, my middle name is Harriette. *What am I doing?* "We have a group errand to run and only half of us have a car that is not a photo studio, so... Max? Can I give you directions to where we're going?"

If Max has clocked all of the mental chaos currently brewing beneath my surface, they don't acknowledge it. "Let's hit the road, glam squad."

The bustling Harmony Springs Mall is decked out to the nines for Christmas. Like the majority of business institutions in this town, it is much more than a shopping center. Alongside clothing stores, soft pretzel kiosks, and a quintessential faux-marble fountain from the 1980s, the mall's expansive atrium doubles as the town's premier event space. School choir concerts, community theater musicals, drag queen story hour, and the annual Thanksgiving town banquet–free and sponsored by the city's endowment–all take place right here. As such, the walls of the mall are home to countless framed photographs of the community events that have been hosted there.

Ava is taking it in with a bemused expression. She nudges Max's arm. "Toto, we are *so* not at the Grove anymore."

I've observed a closeness between her and Max that transcends the typical relationship you'd expect between a bazillionaire CEO and her executive assistant. It doesn't strike me as romantic intimacy, rather it reminds me of my dynamic with Emma, which I never could have initially predicted.

Emma bounds over to the wall beside a kids' toy store. "Ava! Max! You gotta see this."

I already know what awaits us: eight-year-old Jo, dressed as all three wise men in the school nativity play.

Ava actually *grins*, flashing perfect white teeth (of course) that I haven't seen yet. She leans in. "Jo, are those shaved My Size Barbie heads on your shoulders?"

I snort. "Good eye."

"How'd you land that role?" Max asks me.

"The other two wise men got the flu that year," I explain.

Something wistful drifts across Max's face. "And no one gave you shit for being a girl playing a wise man? Or three?"

"It was standard in school that casting was gender-blind. The superintendent felt it kept things fair and equitable. Nobody got boxed into playing any specific gender."

"That's nice." Max's voice sounds hoarse and they turn away momentarily.

There's a subtle movement in my periphery and I see Ava place her hand reassuringly on Max's shoulder before turning to me. Her eyes meet mine, and I understand we need to move the show along so that Max can take a minute.

"Glam squad?" I address our crew. "We've got a Christmas CEO to outfit."

Emma salutes me. "Where to first, boss?"

Now it's my turn to grin. "There's only one answer."

"Hurry up," Ava calls back to us from three storefronts ahead. The woman could power walk through a mall with the best of them.

"Does she always do this?" Emma pants.

"Yeee-up," says Max.

"Hey! I heard that," Ava shouts, now walking *backwards*.

"Where's the lie?" they laugh.

"Now you're trying to make us feel inferior," I yell. "How do you keep up with her?"

"I ask myself that every day."

I'd like to do the same.

Nope—no. I exile the thought from my brain as I see Ava about to miss our turn. "We're here!"

She spins around and I can almost hear her surprise as we

enter what I consider the inner sanctum of the Harmony Springs Mall: Murray's Mistletoe *M*Porium.

We catch up to her, now standing in awe. "Is this... what I think it is?" she asks me.

"Do you think it's a year-round, multi-level Christmas sweater emporium?"

"Year-round?"

"I've been telling you–this town has a Christmas spirit that thrives even in the heat of July." I say. "Murray's even stocks SPF 50 Christmas rashguards for watersports."

Ava throws up her hands in surrender. "I've never denied that certain market insights can only be gained on the ground."

A squeaky unmistakable voice pipes up from behind a rack of Chappell Roan 'She's got a sleigh' hand-knit cardigans.

"Market insights? You're not with the IRS, are you?" a nervous Murray Sanderson pokes his head out to peer at Ava. "You look familiar... we already got audited last year!"

Max jumps in. "This is Ava Garcia-Greene." Off of Murray's blank face–"The CEO of Gramsta?" I'm gonna guess Murray hasn't even joined Facebook yet. "Well, she's not the IRS."

Murray visibly relaxes. "Nothing to hide! But you hafta say you're with the IRS if someone asks."

Ava's brow furrows. "I'm not sure that's–"

Murray turns to me. "What can I help you with today, Jojo sweetheart?"

It's not an exaggeration to say I've gotten at least five Murray's sweaters a year since I was in utero.

"We've got a Christmas photoshoot today with Ava here, who has definite narc energy but is not–as far as I know–involved with any federal agencies," I tell him.

Murray lets loose a wheezing yelp of laughter. *"A narc!* Imagine!" He gathers himself. "What do you look for in a holiday sweater, dear? We've got every section imaginable. Irony, Pop Culture, Dad Puns, Queer Niche, LED, sustainable knits… and my husband Arnold's annual Hanukkah collection."

Ava chews her lip. "Um. I'm not sure I've ever shopped for a Christmas sweater before?" She looks like she just admitted to a crime, and perhaps she's not wrong in recognizing how foreign her life experience is to this veteran Harmony Springser. But for all his tax neuroses, Murray is a mensch at heart, like Arnold always says. He's not one to let anybody feel less-than for not being acquainted with his level of Christmas spirit.

He beams at Ava and I watch her apprehension melt away. "Lucky you! Welcome to the first day of the rest of your life, doll."

And with that, we spend the next hour following Murray from section to section, piling pullovers, crewnecks, and other holiday knits into a massive shopping cart pushed by the ever-dutiful Emma. Eventually, we roll up to the dressing rooms.

Murray clasps his hands excitedly. "I've got to fold some rainbow stockings but give me a holler if you need me to weigh in!"

Before she can stop him, Murray wraps Ava in a bear hug–or maybe it's a cub hug when he comes up to her shoulder? Either way, I watch her stiffen, then relax into it, giving him a tentative pat atop his shiny bald head.

Murray skitters off, and Ava steps into her dressing room, shutting the door firmly behind her. Emma, Max, and I stand together in silence for at least five minutes. I think each of us fears breaking the spell of Ava's agreeability by saying the wrong thing, but after another five minutes pass, Max knocks gently on the door.

"Aves?"

There's a muffled reply from inside.

Then the lock quietly clicks open.

Max slowly opens the door, revealing Ava deeply tangled in a heavily tasseled Christmas tree sweater.

"Imsthguckspehfa."

Max whistles. "Oh goodness, okay, stay right there, I've got this." They go to work on their straitjacketed boss, untwisting strands of alpaca yarn from her mussed-up glossy hair.

Let the record show, I am watching this Marx Brothers slapstick comedy unfold very respectfully. It is through no lascivious fault of my own that as Max disentangles the final tassel and begins to lift the cursed sweater off of her, I catch a glimpse of a disturbingly defined ab sculpted into the sliver of stomach that flashes my way. I avert my eyes... turning them head-on into Emma's knowing gaze. She doesn't say anything, just smirks. *Dammit.*

"Crisis averted," Ava announces sheepishly. She took her heels off in the dressing room, so she's even shorter than usual beside me. I peer down at the top of her hair, still askew from the sweater debacle.

"Find any pieces that didn't try to off you?" I ask.

She rummages through her pile and pulls out a dark green pullover embroidered with a rainbow reindeer clutching a wad of cash, beneath the phrase "Make It Rein."

"I don't hate this one," she offers.

I'm caught between commenting on the distinctly gay vibe of that reindeer and making a snarky remark about how the CEO picked the most capitalist sweater in the entire emporium. But I don't get a chance to voice either, because Emma cuts in.

"It's perfect, Ava. Still you, but... soft, too."

Emma's observation would bother me, but it seems to roll off of Ava. "Can you help me put the rest of the sweaters in the cart?"

"Oh, Murray will put them back," I inform her, but she waves me off and begins walking to the register.

Max and Emma follow her with the loaded cart, and Murray comes bounding up to the checkout.

"Did you find what you needed?" he asks, taking Ava's card.

"Totally. Can you pack this separate from the rest?" She hands over the money-grubbing reindeer.

"Course!"

I watch in confusion. "I thought you only liked the one. You're buying all of it?"

"I assume Harmony Springs has a women's shelter or something I can donate to?"

"Oh. I—yeah, of course. Emma's mom actually volunteers there."

Emma brightens. "I can take your donations over after work!"

Ava signs her name on the receipt. "Perfect."

Murray smiles at Ava with a newfound admiration. "For someone who's never owned a Christmas sweater, you've got Christmas spirit to spare."

Ava shakes her head. "I've got more to spare in general. It's not a big deal."

Murray frowns. "You can be humble, but you should realize that selflessness is a rare quality, no matter your net worth."

Ava's discomfort is palpable. "Merry Christmas, Murray. Thanks for all your help today."

"Take care, darling."

And with that, we head back into the labyrinth of the mall, arms weighed down by shopping bags and minds burdened by a disquieting suspicion that there might be more to Ava Garcia-Greene than meets the eye.

We're almost to the food court when I tune out of Max and Emma's heated debate on Christmas and capitalism long enough to realize we've lost Ava.

"Hey, hold up."

We begin to retrace our steps, rounding a corner to find Ava standing in front of the window display at Jingle Belle of the

Ball, fixated on the drapey red velvet gown at the forefront. She notices we've joined her and glances at me.

"It's probably... too stuffy for a Christmas card?" she asks hesitantly.

"Stuffy is not the word I'd use," I say. She's still quiet, so I add, "If it speaks to you, you should try it on."

"Hm." And with that, she strides into the boutique.

We follow her inside. The saleswoman, Shirley, unpins the dress from the mannequin and guides Ava to a curtained-off area in the back to try it on.

Emma gestures for Max to join her at a display featuring her favorite local jewelry designer, leaving me alone at the back when Ava pokes her head out. She scans the room, searching for anyone but me, but eventually relents.

"Can you zip me up?" she asks.

I approach the curtain, and Ava turns her back to me. I'm still mentally kicking myself for stealing a glance at her six-pack back at Murray's. Determined not to stare this time, I reach for the zipper, trying to be as unobtrusive as possible. It backfires. A strand of her hair gets caught because I'm not paying close enough attention.

"Ow ow ow," she winces, tilting her head back.

"Oh my god, I'm so sorry." I pinch the hair while wiggling the zipper back down.

By necessity, I allow my eyes to focus on the task at hand. I carefully disentangle each strand, and my fingers accidentally brush against her. Ava shivers. I watch as delicate goosebumps bloom across the bare skin of her back, trying to keep my breathing in check as my heart gallops.

As I free the final strand, I catch a glimpse of us standing together in the mirror. We look more familiar with one another than we actually are, like a convincing stock photo of an attractive couple.

"Are we good?" Ava breaks my reverie.

"Yes," I say, a little too quickly.

She reaches back to sweep her hair away so I can zip her up. Her fingers brush against mine and there's a zap of electricity. I swear her touch lingers for a moment, and I wonder if she felt it too.

I watch the elegant column of her spine disappear as I rezip the dress.

"All done," I murmur, then take a step back... walking right into Max. *0/10 spatial awareness, Jo.* Emma is on the other side of them, and the three of us watch in unison as Ava turns to face us in her gown.

The dress drinks up every single curve, the rich deep burgundy red contrasting with Ava's coloring perfectly. Oh, my.

She smoothes the front down. "Is it okay?"

Emma and Max's eyes are trained on me, awaiting my answer. *Be normal, be normal, be normal.*

"Uh, yeah." I clear my throat, "It's okay."

Emma elbows me hard, then addresses Ava. "She means it's stunning. Very you, very Christmas."

I'm grateful for the save until I notice Emma and Max exchange their own private look of amusement. I'm not loving the alliance brewing in the peanut gallery today, but there's not much I can do about that with Ava staring me down.

Ava nods at Emma's reassurance, yet her gaze lingers on me a moment longer, as if she's piecing together a puzzle in her mind. If she has more to say, she keeps it to herself. For that, I'm thankful, because I'm at a loss for how to explain my flustered state. It's tough to remember she's the opposition when she's effortlessly cracked my lesbian attraction nuclear codes.

Max and I pile two trays with every Christmas treat imaginable at the food court while Ava and Emma lay claim to a table for the four of us and our many shopping bags. As I shake extra cinnamon sugar over an elephant ear, Max speaks softly.

"She might not realize it, but this is exactly what she's needed for a long time."

I'm surprised. "Oh yeah?"

They give me a crooked smile. "I'll never admit to having said this, but she lives in a bubble. A corporate CEO snow globe of her own making. It's safe in there, to some degree, but it also keeps the world out."

I appreciate their unexpected candor. "My lips are sealed."

Max uncaps Ava's coffee order. "Wrong creamer. Be right back."

I balance our trays and make my way over to where Ava and Emma are deep in conversation, slowing as I approach. I'm not being a snoop, I'm doing... what did she call it? On-the-ground market research.

"You're cooler than I thought you'd be," Emma is saying.

Ava shakes her head. "Not hard when you're routinely decimated in the press like me."

"But you gotta admit, you stoke the controversies, too," Emma points out.

"Being a female CEO is no walk in the park, especially when you're constantly trying to push for innovation that challenges the status quo."

Emma nods. "I can respect that."

"Besides, if I don't stand up for myself, who will?"

I can feel myself starting to empathize with Ava's need for a tough exterior, so I decide it's time to wrap up my focus group of one. I step up to the table and begin to lay out our Christmas carbohydrate feast.

Ava holds her stomach. "I'm gonna be bloated in my Christmas card!"

"Jo's camera angles are very forgiving," Emma reassures her.

I'd like to point out Ava's abs are sure to demolish whatever effect our fried banquet would have on any regularly-built human, but instead I tell her, "There's nothing to forgive, trust me."

Perhaps it's the fluorescent Christmas lights strung across the food court playing tricks on me, but I swear my comment causes her pretty cheeks to pinken. I file the moment away. For market research, of course.

CHAPTER 15
AVA

"WE'RE GOING to leave you to it." Emma nudges Max and they escape out the back door of the truck before I can even get a word in. The women's shelter closes to donations soon, and Emma wants to be sure they get there with time to spare. God knows the residents of this town need this kind of attire to fit in, so I don't protest. I usually heavily depend on Max in situations like this shoot, not only to do my bidding, but to put me at ease with that classic Max attitude. Now, it appears, I have been left to Jo and her literal devices.

She puts her final tweaks on the lighting setup for my Christmas card. I would've preferred to keep it simple, because that's usually how I like it, but I'm finding myself reluctantly enjoying the camp of Harmony Springs.

The flash suddenly goes off in my face. "I blinked," I spew, immediately self-conscious in my slinky red dress.

"That was to test the light," Jo assures me, but it doesn't make me feel better. She must catch me eyeing the photo because she leans over to the computer and drags it into the trash. "Fresh start."

She raises the camera and I tense. She lowers it and I relax. She does it again, and so do I, and goddammit, she *laughs* at me.

"I didn't peg you as the type to get nervous over a photo," she says. "Ava Garcia-Greene, poster girl of... everything."

"Why would I be nervous when you're simply peering into my entire soul?" I mutter.

"It's not so bad!" Jo encourages.

I let out a sigh concerning enough that she announces she's got to bring in the 'Christmas big guns.' She leans behind the backdrop to the front of the truck, her flannel brushing up her back to reveal the soft skin across her hips. A twinkle of music plays through the truck speakers: the horrifyingly classic intro of Mariah Carey's *All I Want for Christmas Is You*. My sigh turns into a groan.

"Not into Christmas music, eh?" She makes her way back to her spot in front of me.

"Are you surprised?"

"It *is* very controversial these days." She readies the camera. "Clients either love it or they want to claw their ears off when they hear it."

"Can't say I love it," I say casually, as if I wasn't just about to flee the country to avoid it entirely. She laughs a truly infectious laugh, which makes me crack a smile, too.

Jo sneakily snaps a photo, which is an improvement from the trash can shot, but she can definitely still tell my ears are bleeding internally.

"What about something a little less... Mariah?" she suggests.

"You can try," I grumble. She chuckles again and changes the song.

"How's this?" *Feliz Navidad* blasts.

"Some would argue even more grating," I shout over the music. She goes to change it. "It reminds me of my childhood."

"Yeah?" She turns the volume down to hear me, amused by my remark.

"But not because I'm Puerto Rican. I mean, I am, but we

never celebrated our heritage," I admit. Jo's eyes probe me deeper than her camera lens and I lose my train of thought.

Oh, right, yes, Feliz Navidad. "Remember the *Sesame Street* Christmas movie?"

"Do I remember *Christmas Eve on Sesame Street*... Who do you think I am?" She jokes. "They show it every year at the local theater."

Of course *they do. What's gayer than Bert and Ernie on ice?*

"I'd watch that scene with Big Bird and the little girl ice skating on repeat," I tell her. "So much so that I remember the tape disintegrating in my VHS player."

"No way," she laughs.

"Way. I desperately wanted to be good at ice skating."

"Were you?"

"Never skated a day in my life," I say, pulling the new sweater over my head.

"What?! We have to go while you're here!" She stops, remembering she doesn't like me. "I mean, if you want."

"Don't you think it's a little too late for me to live out my *Sesame Street* dreams?"

"Absolutely not." She grins and catches me off guard with another flash of the strobe. The picture pops up on screen.

I'll admit it, she's good.

"So I get the sense you're not a huge Christmas fan?" she says slyly.

"What told you that?"

"You're missing out. Christmas rules."

"Christmas *rules*?" I mock.

"Yes!" she says, sincerely. "Even if you don't 'believe.' It's the perfect time to spend with family. To be grateful for the year. To take advantage of the world slowing down."

"Which neither of us are presently doing."

"Speak for yourself." She takes another picture, this time catching me making a most offended face.

"Delete that!"

"Rule number one of the truck: never delete a memory that precious," she simpers.

I guffaw–no way that 'memory' is anywhere near precious.

She sneaks another smiler, this time where it looks like I'm laughing off into the distance like one of those Women Eating Salad memes. Honestly, it's more *me* than any photo Annie has ever taken of me (yes, *that* Annie).

"So who are you going to send this to?" she asks.

This photoshoot was more of a reconnaissance mission for me, a chance to suss out the user experience of Jo's business. I wouldn't be caught dead sending people Christmas cards.

"I have to think about it," I say after a moment.

"Besides millions of followers," she laughs.

"Yeah, but does that even count? That's all fake," I shrug.

"The inventor of modern social media herself admits it."

"Yeah, yeah." But I'm still stuck on who I could possibly send this to, and she notices me spiraling.

"And I'm assuming that's why you're anti-Christmas?" She digs in.

"Christmas hasn't been all bad," I concede. "Mom always kept up the traditions the best she could. My dad wasn't around."

"Oh." Her face falls. "I'm so sorry, I didn't know."

"It's okay." Because it was. Would it have been great to have a father figure in my life? Yes. Would a bad one probably do more damage in the long run? Yeah, it's, like, statistically why so many people are fucked up.

"You have a good Christmas memory, though? With your mom?" she asks.

"Hmm..." I think. I don't want to break her little Christmas-lovin' heart, but it's been a bleak time of year for me for a minute now. I would literally do anything to escape it.

But then a memory comes to me. It's not like my nightmare

from the plane. It's unexpectedly warm. "One of our last real Christmases, my mom got me my first computer. I mean, it was ours, but I hardly ever let her on the thing. That changed my life."

"See? Christmas. Rules."

I go to smile at Jo and she quickly snaps a candid. The photo appears on the screen and is what you might consider *the one*. I stand to get a better view of my relaxed–dare I say–*smize???* leaping off the screen.

"Wow," I muster.

"You look… kind." She appraises me, as though she finally sees something she likes about me.

"You are good at your job then." I motion for her camera. "Your turn."

"Excuse me?"

"You heard me. It's your turn." I take the camera from Jo and point her to the seat.

She resists. "Rule number one of being a photographer: the photographer does not get her photo taken."

I sneer playfully. "What, you think I created Gramsta and wasn't a photographer myself?"

"Really?" She's surprised at first, but recovers quickly, and with that classic Jo annoyance says, "What haven't you done?"

"Jill of all trades. Master of… also all trades." Sometimes it's impossible to feign humility. But she laughs again.

"Do you see what I'm wearing?" she says, still trying to evade the camera.

"Isn't that what you always wear?" *Jeans? Check. Flannel? Check. Platform Docs? Checkity check check.*

She rolls her eyes.

"Don't worry, remember? I like a challenge."

She shoves me playfully. People don't tend to, well, touch me, so my face must've given that away. She backs into the chair.

"Uh, sorry, I didn't–" she stammers.

"We're even now," I say, forgiving.

"All right, what do I do, Ms. Photographer?"

"To the left a little…" I tell her.

She turns.

"Perfect right there." I snap a photo. I'm a little rusty behind the camera, but it's not bad. I adjust the flash a hair to remove some of the shadowing from her already-defined jawline.

"What about you? What's your favorite Christmas memory?" I ask.

"Using my own tactics against me, I see." She pauses, like she's deciding whether to trust me or not. She picks at her thumb and looks up at me through her thick lashes.

"Every Christmas after we opened presents, my dad and I would drive the truck around and take photos of the community," she says. "But the best part was sitting up in the passenger seat on the way home, listening to him belt his heart out to The Beach Boys' Christmas Album."

Jo casts her eyes down, swallowing hard.

"Oh," is my dull response.

Yep. Dead dad alert.

"I'm sorry, I didn't mean to…" I sputter.

"No, no. I love thinking about my dad," she says. "He was stubborn, but such a kind, creative soul."

"Runs in the family."

"Which part?"

"All of it?" I offer.

She laughs. "Any idea of who you're gonna send your card to yet?"

"Honestly?" I exhale. "No."

She looks at me; like genuinely takes me in.

"I have something to show you. For truck knowledge purposes."

"And that is?"

"You'll see." She shoots me her trademark grin and hops to the dilapidated front seat, cranking the key in the ignition.

For two seconds, heat blasts from Chrissy's air vents, beginning to warm up the front seats, and then with a wheezing sound, the air turns off completely. Jo doesn't even blink from her perch atop the broken driver's seat.

"Guess we'll be adding that to the list." We drive off, shivering into the night.

CHAPTER 16
JO

I'LL ADMIT IT: I'm secretly relieved that Emma and Max had to rush off on their charitable donation errand. Their absence spares me from any more of their expressive silent judgments about my latest (frankly indefensible) off-script turn of events.

As I park the freezing cold truck in my mother's driveway, I peek at Ava in the passenger seat. She's back in her pantsuit but with the reindeer sweater pulled over the top. After letting her hair down during our shoot, she's tied it back in a messy bun. She notices me staring at her.

"Is this what you're showing me? Suburbia? I've seen it on television, you know."

I unlock the truck doors and we step out. There's a light flurry of snow coming down, landing on both of our lashes. "Suburbia with a you-look-starving heaping portion of overbearing Midwestern mom."

"Also as seen on TV."

"Not like this." I hold my arms out. "The Fisher estate!"

Please don't ask me why I brought you home to my family. I'm not sure I have a good enough reason without some serious internal reckoning.

Maybe the good karma of Ava's earlier sweater donation

rubbed off on me. In spite of this golden opportunity to question my actions, Ava doesn't bat an eye.

That said, her lack of interrogation leaves dead air, which I brilliantly fill with, "Pasties."

"Sorry?"

"Pasties. My mom is making Pasties tonight. It's a Michigan thing. They're... transcendent. Figured you could use a home cooked meal?" I'm aware I'm asking it as a question. *Please save me from myself, Ava Garcia-Greene.*

"Pasties," she ponders, like she's tasting the word itself. "Okay then."

In the same second as she flings open the door, my mother has already embraced Ava's slight frame in a crushing hug. I gave Carol approximately fifteen minutes' lead time, texting her that we'd have a dinner guest moments after my impulsive pitch to Ava, but you'd never know because she's acting like Ava has just returned home from war.

My mom's intensity can drive me up a wall, but hearing Ava had no idea who to send her Christmas card to pierced me like an arrow labeled *Carol Fisher*. Ava could benefit from that same level of overwhelming care and concern that I often find suffocating.

Carol takes a step back from hugging Ava, still clasping her upper arms. "I'm Carol, Jo's mom. Welcome to our home! And Merry Christmas Month!"

"Ava Gar–Ava. Thank you for having me, Carol." *Is she... nervous?*

My mom ushers us into the living room, where Lena and Matt are seated on one of the sofas. Lena has her swollen feet up in Matt's lap and he's giving her a massage. She waves to us.

Ava and I sit on the couch opposite them while my mom bustles around the kitchen.

"I'd get up but then I'd start panting again. I'm Lena, my footman is Matt."

Matt gives a friendly grunt, then goes back to the task at hand.

"Hot chocolates!" Carol bursts back in, handing the first steaming mug to Ava before plopping a mega-mallow in.

"Thank you." Ava goes to take a sip and before I, a Fisher hot chocolate veteran, can warn her that the water boils hotter in this household, she's burnt her mouth. She winces, then catches herself and plasters on a brave smile for the family.

I nudge her with my knee. "It's basically a rite of passage to start Christmas in this home with a scorched tongue."

Ava relaxes a little.

My mom chortles. "Jolene is telling the truth! It still happens to me half the time. That electric kettle was a wedding gift and I swear it has some 1980s cocaine in its little engine, the darn thing heats up so fast!" A beeping sounds from the kitchen and she bounds away. "Got to check on the pasties!"

Lena snickers. "Speaking of cocaine in the engine, may I present our mother, Carol Fisher?"

Ava laughs, and settles back into the couch, blowing on her mug diligently.

"So Ava, how do you know Jo?" my sister asks.

Ava silently gives me the floor.

"She's consulting on The Photo Truck. Whipping us into shape for the holidays."

Lena's surprised. "You can afford that?"

"It's pro bono," Ava interjects.

Matt's head pops up. "From U2?"

"No, my love." Lena wiggles her feet at him. She studies Ava. "Well, that sounds very generous of you. Jo could use the help."

I try not to let my sibling's words sting, but defensiveness quickly swells within me. *If you knew I needed help keeping Dad's legacy alive, why haven't you stepped up?* I recognize it's not fair to think this way. She doesn't owe me her time and energy because I've chosen to shoulder this burdensome business–a business that can barely sustain itself, yet is inseparably tied to my sense of self and my connection to our late father.

"I'm actually learning a lot from Jo in return," Ava tells Lena. "I do a bit of work in the photography industry and I get a lot out of seeing talented creatives in the zone."

Color me flabbergasted. Did Ava compliment me of her own free will, *and* lightly come to my defense with my sister? Before I have time to relish this utopic Twilight Zone we've entered, my sister's husband emerges from his own zone, the Lena's-feet-zone, because he suddenly blurts out:

"Wait. Ava as in *the* Ava Garcia-Greene?"

Ava freezes, and I watch as her entire demeanor transforms in a split second. It's as though she tightens from within, instantly sitting straighter. "That would be me."

Matt rises from the couch and walks over, shaking his head in awe. As he gets closer, his glazed red eyes make it clear why he's been so slow on the uptake this evening.

He extends his hand, but fortunately, Lena intercepts with a quick, "Honey, that's a foot-hand."

Nevertheless, he towers awkwardly right in front of Ava, mesmerized. "Dude. You're like, a mega super celeb."

She's not as smug as I would have expected. "Oh, thank you."

Lena looks at me curiously, mouthing *Gramsta?* as I nod. She leans back, impressed. Matt rejoins her.

My mom reenters at that moment, taking in the vibe shift. "Did I miss something?"

I open my mouth, feeling weirdly protective of whatever fleeting anonymity Ava just had yanked away from her, but Ava intercepts. She turns toward my mom with a poised smile.

"I'm helping Jo with her business and Matt recognized me from my role at Gramsta."

A mix of confusion and curiosity plays across my mother's features. "Well, I never heard of a Gramsta, but I'm glad you're helping Jo."

"It's a company where I have a bit of a public role," Ava explains.

"That's wonderful," my mom replies warmly, her gaze shifting back and forth between us. "Anyone who helps my Jo is a friend of mine." She clasps her hands. "Well, follow me to the dining room, little chickens! Pasties are on the table."

We spend dinner laughing and talking and feasting on my mother's impeccable cooking. I occasionally catch Matt slipping stoned philosophical questions about the nature of celebrity to Ava between bites, but the focus of the evening is my mom. She captivates us with a rollicking story about juggling drag queen drama while producing the community theater's nativity play twenty years ago. Ava is more at ease than I've ever seen her.

After dinner, Matt lights up a joint–and the living room fireplace–while Lena pours us thimbles of sherry, a winter evening tradition passed down from my great-grandma Beth.

Ava sits beside me, sipping her sherry, her skin a bit flushed, either from the fire or the alcohol, or both. "Thank you so much for the delicious meal, Carol. I haven't eaten home cooking in… Lord knows how long."

My mother beams with pride. "My pleasure, dear. You've got a lovely way about you. You're welcome here anytime."

"Th-thank you." I can tell she's searching for something to take the attention off of herself. She spots a framed photo atop a cabinet and walks over to it, picking it up. My mom goes with her.

"Mm," Carol remarks, "That would be the day Roger bought the truck. I thought he was being a damn fool."

Ava traces the photo through the glass. "Chrissy used to be a milk truck?"

My mom laughs. "At the time, I thought Chrissy should *stay* a milk truck." She's lost in thought for a moment, then crouches down to open the sliding door of the cabinet. She pulls out a thick leather-bound photo album and brings it over to the couch. Ava sits back down with us.

Mom turns to the first page, where there's a second print of that framed photo, and a few other shots from Chrissy's early days–shots of my dad hanging drywall and hardwiring the back of the truck for the studio.

Ava studies the album as my mom flips through the pages.

"How did Roger come up with The Photo Truck?" she asks.

"Roger always dreamed of becoming a photographer," my mom begins. "After college, he moved to New York to apprentice with a renowned fashion portraitist. His talent was apparent, and the competitive environment took advantage of his hard work. He was so run-down that whenever he came home to visit, Jolene's grandma Helen would put him on bedrest."

A knowing look crosses Ava's face. "I think I might have needed that kind of intervention at times."

"Oh, I believe many of us could," Mom chuckles softly, patting Ava's knee reassuringly. "When Helen got sick, he moved back to Harmony Springs permanently, though he thought it would be temporary. He was completely broke, so of course, that's when I locked him down!"

Ava laughs, stealing a glance at me. My heart jumps.

"He eventually saved up enough from freelancing to buy that old milk truck. Roger was handy and he converted it into a mobile studio all by himself. He became the town's go-to for Christmas cards and eventually expanded into weddings, babies, headshots, you name it. That Chrissy isn't just a studio; she's a testament to his resilience."

Ava is visibly moved by the story. "Inspiring," she murmurs.

Mom nods. "He was. Roger believed that everyone deserved beautiful memories, regardless of their means. And that's exactly what he gave them, year after year. Forty, now."

"The truck has been around for forty years?" Ava asks, baffled. "Starting a truck business in the eighties is visionary."

"Oh yes," Mom smiles to herself. "He was ahead of his time, Roger."

"Thank you for sharing all of that, Carol," Ava says, unusually solemn.

Unbidden tears suddenly well up in my eyes. Grief is such a peculiar creature. I can spend months talking about my dad in everyday conversations, seeing his photo daily in the truck and plastered all over the walls of the backhouse, and be fine. But then, out of nowhere, a single poignant moment hits me like a gut punch, and suddenly the well of grief becomes an endless abyss, leaving me wondering if I'll ever find my way out.

I sharply suck in a breath through my nose, trying to force air into my belly. My mom is caught up poring over the photo album, but I see Ava glance my way in my periphery. I turn my face to mask the swell of emotion currently playing out for anyone to see.

Ava stands up abruptly. "Carol, I think the sherry is heating me up a bit too much. Would you excuse me for a moment?"

"Of course, dear."

Ava begins to walk out of the room, then turns around. "Jo? I fear if you don't join me I'll be wandering suburbia the entire winter trying to find my way back here."

I kind of doubt Ava Garcia-Greene could ever truly get lost–heck, she's probably microchipped–but a brisk walk sounds ideal right about now.

We step out into a magical December snow globe. Thick pillowy layers of snow have smoothed the edges of every hedge and curb. The delicate flakes that coated our lashes earlier have turned into a heavier snowfall. The world around us is on pause, caught in the stillness of the evening. Neighborhood Christmas lights cast a soft red-and-green glow as we walk, our crunching footsteps the only sound.

Ava breaks the quiet, her breath puffing out in front of her as she speaks. "Can I ask you more about your dad?"

I'm surprised because most people treat my dead father like The Game we all played in the early 2000s–acknowledgement is poisonous (also, you just lost The Game).

"Sure."

"Well, I mean… what happened?"

"He got sick five years ago. He was open about it–he didn't believe in adding to his own suffering by trying to hide it from loved ones. So in some ways we had a lot of time to prepare for what was coming." I push through despite the swell of emotion. "But after he passed, I realized there's no such thing as being prepared for someone dying. It's a sort of finality that I think we can only feel when it actually happens. You can't pre-feel those feelings."

Ava considers this. "You can't prepare for a reality you've never known."

"Exactly." I peek at her. She's already gazing at me, her eyes full of something… foreign. I'd like to search her eyes for longer, but I feel a pull to keep telling her about my father. "Toward the end, he couldn't even pick up a camera anymore. But he was still so in love with that truck. I'd drive him around for as long as he could manage. On one of those drives, he told me that Chrissy was mine and to take care of her for him. He died a couple days later."

I sneak another glance at her and am instantly in shock because Ava's eyes are shiny. Rather than sad, she's fiercely angry.

"It's so unfair." She dabs at her eyes with the belt of her coat. "I would totally sue God on your behalf if that was a thing."

I choke out a laugh because it's such an absurdly Ava thing

to say. "Nobody needs to sue God. I think that's the nature of life. Grief and death are part of the mix, the reason everything else gets to exist–joy, life, birth."

We walk in silence for a bit, Ava's gait quickening. She's ten paces ahead of me before she realizes I'm no longer by her side.

"Why do you always have to walk so fast? You're supposed to be enjoying this," I laugh.

"Oh. Sorry. I didn't even..." She trails off, toying with the chunky gold ring on her left hand. "You're a little bit wise, Jo Fisher."

"I mean, I *was* once all three wise men, Ava Garcia-Greene."

Her laugh is light and twinkly like a sleighbell.

"So," I press her, "how was your first pastie?"

"Divine. Your mother is a divine cook. She's like... an Easy-Bake Oven Mom."

I huff. "What does that mean?"

She shakes her head. "I dunno. I guess, like, she has all the standard mom ingredients and they got baked at an appropriate preset temperature and she came out... fully formed."

I blow rings in the fog. "Trust me, she can be a lot."

Ava laughs. "Oh, don't worry, I picked up on that."

"What's your family like?" I ask. "Who's missing you for the holiday?"

Ava pauses. "I've spent the last ten Christmases alone or with Max. Growing up, it was me and my mom, and we had a falling out right before Gramsta took off. On Christmas Day, actually."

I can't imagine how lonely the past decade of Christmases must have been for her. "I'm sorry. Christmas shouldn't be spent in isolation."

"I'm a tough cookie. I've been alright."

I can't hold back. "Unsolicited advice from someone who truly knows nothing? It might be worth having a talk with your mom. Someday you won't be able to, and winning the argument won't matter then."

She's silent for a moment, then nods.

I scoop a handful of fresh powder off of a neighbor's half-height brick wall as we walk past and begin to subtly pack it into a snowball. I let her stride a few feet ahead of me, and then lob it at the back of her coat.

Ava whirls around, her face filled with surprise. "You did not. This is cashmere!"

I laugh. "And this is frozen water!"

But my laughter is quickly stifled by the look of outrage on her face. "Okay, wait, I'm sorry, I know nothing about luxury knit–"

SPLAT. Without warning, a hastily made snowball collides with my face, leaving me sputtering and blinking through snow.

"Okay, you've got an arm on you, Gramsta!"

"You thought people were only afraid of my personality?"

"Bring it on, then," I challenge her, already scooping up my next snowball.

She sprints away from me, laughing as she dodges behind a tall oak tree. I charge after her, my boots crunching in the thick snow, my breath forming clouds in the cold air.

Ava peeks out from behind the tree, her eyes glinting mischievously. She slings another snowball, which whizzes past my shoulder. "You're going to have to be faster than that!" she calls out.

My adrenaline kicks in. "Oh, it's on!" I declare, packing another ball tightly. I make a feint to the left, then sprint to the right, releasing my snowball. It arcs beautifully through the air and taps her shoulder as she tries to make a break for another hiding spot. "Gotcha!" I shout, triumphant.

Ava stops and scoops up a handful of snow, her movements quick and precise. "Nice shot, but you're still one behind!" With a playful snarl, she launches a counterattack, her snowball hitting me square in the chest.

We run through the snowy landscape, the friendly fire of our snowballs writing a temporary truce in the winter air. Every hit brings a burst of laughter and mock indignation, every miss a promise to aim truer next time.

We battle all the way down my mom's block, ending up at the small playground I grew up going to with all the neighborhood kids.

Stopping to catch our breath, Ava packs another snowball, but doesn't throw it. She holds it up. "Truce?" she asks, a slight pant to her voice.

"Truce," I agree, nodding, too winded to continue. But instead of dropping her last snowball to the ground, she impulsively slings it at me from a foot away and I stumble backwards, landing flat on my back.

Winded, and staring straight up at the night sky, Ava looms over me, peering down, a slightly guilty expression on her face. "I occasionally have poor impulse control."

I extend my arm toward her. She reaches down with her manicured hand to help me up, but her delicate Pilates-toned muscles are no match for my arms, conditioned from hauling fifty-pound Pelican cases around like they're featherweights. With a playful tug, I pull her down instead and she lands beside me with a yelp.

"That was fair," she admits.

"You've got much to learn about the tactics of a snowball fight, my friend," I tell her.

She lets out a little snort. "We're friends now?"

I move my limbs up and down in the snow. "Well, at least our snow angels are."

Ava mimics my movements. "I've never made a snow angel before."

The stillness of the night recloaks us as we catch our breath, laying in the imprints of our angels. I turn my head to her, on the ground next to me. She stares back at me, her expression barely readable. Challenging, almost.

It could be an illusion of the falling snow, but I swear she bats her eyes at me.

Our faces are close enough that the mist from our breath collides in the space between us. Despite the freezing temperatures, there's an electric charge in the air, a magnetic pull that draws my head closer to hers.

For a moment, time slows, and we're the only two people in the world. Our eyes lock, and there's a silent question hanging between us.

I watch in real time as her pupils dilate. She's staring at me so intensely it's like I'm really seeing her for the first time.

As our lips almost touch, Ava sucks in sharply and I snap out of whatever bewitching wintery spell I was under. She awkwardly fiddles with the ring on her finger as I draw back, unable to look her in the eye.

The cold seeps into me, commingling with the fluttery anticipation of our almost-kiss and I shiver.

"We should head back. Warm up," I suggest, standing up hastily, still avoiding her gaze.

Ava quickly gets to her feet, pointedly ignoring the hand I offer. Her expression is as closed-off and professional as it was the day she spilled coffee on me.

"Reality beckons!" she declares with forced cheer.

What have I done?

I CRASH into my hotel bed, perplexed by my kind-of-almost-maybe-not-kiss with Jo. Am I...? I can't be attracted to her. It does not compute.

It was probably the sherry. That's it. I've never been great at holding my liquor, even a little. I like to keep a clear mind, and that is not what we were doing tonight. Perhaps the lack of oxygen, too, from running around throwing snowballs at each other like a couple of kids.

No, I'm a good liar, but I can't lie to myself. Her lips were so close... beckoning me in... then my stupid SyncCircle went apeshit due to my fluttering hummingbird of a heart, and Jo pulled back. It's a good thing she made that call, although a small part of me–okay, maybe not that small–still stings from her rejection.

I've never experienced this sort of raw magnetism toward anyone before, much less a woman. I thought I was attracted to the men I've been with, but at the same time, the sex always fizzles out once the thrill of the conquest subsides.

My sparse dating life has led the press to speculate that I'm asexual, and at times I've questioned if there was truth in that. In my early years on the internet, a 4chan message board led me to wonder if I might be sapiosexual, attracted to highly intelligent people. But it's not just about the smarts for me. Otherwise the CTOs and CFOs I've had flings with, Ivy League degrees hung in their offices, would have been doing more for my libido. In my experience, men are too fucked up by societal measures for me to connect with them in the deeper way I yearn for.

Ew, *yearn*? What is this town doing to me?

I admit that I have maintained a locked room, deep within my ice-cold heart, in which lives a faint idea of the person I've always imagined to be *my* person. Someone with personality, humor, soul. Sappy for me, I know. As far as I can tell, this heart of mine is like a glacier: frozen over, but huge, and likely only capable of thawing due to a global climate event.

Max is the one person who melts me a little, more like family at this point than the one I was born into. I'm closer to them than anyone, and not just because they're aware of every intimate detail of my existence. I was able to support them through their transition—in fact, Gramsta became the first major corporation that supported gender-affirming surgeries, all because a young Max sobbed in my arms about how they felt so out of place in their body.

So... a global climate event, or Max. And now Jo? She's unlocking feelings in me that certainly no man has ever made me experience.

I've been closed off for a long, long time. My relationship with my mom was the beginning of the end of my being open to anything like love. I got a lot of good things from her—my work ethic, my passion, my fashion sense. But I'm also stubborn as hell, and I will definitely be blaming that on one Ms. Garcia.

Despite the distance between my mom and I, I unlock my phone, the conversation with Jo swirling in my head. *It may be worth having a talk with your mom. Someday you won't be able to.*

I pull up my mother's contact card, featuring a photo of us

decorating a Christmas tree. I must've been around seven or eight in the picture, long before we had our falling-out. As someone who grew up outside the often narrow interpretation of 'American,' my Puerto Rican mom always encouraged me to keep my head down, focus on my work, and avoid drawing attention—just like she had to do. "Try to be normal, Ava," she would tell me.

But those docile qualities are (obviously) not in my nature. As a kid, I would fail math tests because I came to the answers too easily and would spend the designated time finding ways to make them more difficult, never actually finishing. I used to challenge my teachers on textbook interpretations, arguing that while calling mitochondria the cell's powerhouse sounds catchy, it oversimplifies cell biology because ATP production isn't exclusive to mitochondria, making this metaphor a way to dumb down cellular functions—and, more broadly, science itself—for kids.

Shockingly, I was not a pleasure to have in class.

I'm sure it wasn't easy for my mom to deal with me, but that pressure to behave a particular way pushed me in the opposite direction.

Before my eighteenth birthday, I had already developed what was to become Gramsta, and through a programming class at school, was able to pitch my work to a local web developer. That developer was worth his salt and recognized the potential my creation had, so it got passed up the chain, somehow ending up in the laps of some of the most high-powered tech financiers at the time. I wanted so desperately for this to work, to bring me and my mom money that we'd never had. My mom, tired of seeing my unconventional choices backfire throughout my childhood, put her foot down, and forbade me from pitching the app. But I saw the vision when she couldn't.

I made the decision to go behind her back, flying up to San Francisco by myself right before Christmas, and signed a document I had no business signing. I was a smart kid, but I was naive, and the investors clocked that. I was so desperate to make something of myself that the legalese didn't even concern me. Why would someone take advantage of me, a young, impressionable woman? *Ha.*

When I returned on Christmas Day, she was furious I had disappeared. I explained that I didn't tell her because it was the right choice, even if she didn't agree. I told her about the contract and the money I was about to bring in, expecting her to be, for once, proud. She wasn't.

After our blowout fight, I left home and never came back. She never reached out either–not until after Gramsta took off. She sent a phony congratulations text that made me furious. *Of course, after all this time,* I thought, *she contacts me to get the one thing we never had: money.* So I sent her a check and haven't spoken to her since.

Despite the awkwardness with Jo, I was having an okay evening, but the mere thought of my mom ruined it all. I carry my resentment of her around like a sack of unwanted White Elephant gifts, and I'm not yet ready to lighten the load.

The only thing I know right now is this: I am Gramsta. And whatever it is I'm feeling at this moment, I cannot let it get in the way of the one part of me I am sure of.

We sprawl out in the snow as I stare into Jo's deep brown eyes. Time slows, and we're the only two people on Earth.

My ring vibrates as my heart rate peaks, but this time, I don't let my hesitation stop me. I go all in as my lips meet hers.

I climb on top of her, my boldness catching her by surprise. My face is cold, but she is warm. She brings my temperature up, up, up. I can barely stand it.

We taste each other and our fiery passion melts the surrounding snow, turning it into an endless ocean. My ring continues to buzz as we float through the water together, propelled by the electric current between us.

I awake in my hotel room to Max banging on the door. "Ava? Ava, it's time to go!"

Shit.

I climb into the rental car examining my 69 sleep score on my SyncCircle. All of my mom and dream drama has me late, running on fumes.

"Usually I can't crack a B, but this is even more dismal," I complain to Max. "How do I break the threshold of sleep excellence?"

"Not be a CEO," Max deadpans.

"Research that for me?" I ask, pulling up my calendar for the day. "We're heading back to the same spot to watch another one of Jo's shoots. It's actually her sister. She's super pregnant. Ooh, and we can stop for some coffee. You loved that Gay Hot Chocolate. Maybe I'll try one, too. Can't burn my mouth again. Oh, wait you weren't there. We can get them for everybody! Great idea."

Max waves their hand at me. "It's giving… high-strung."

"I'm always high-strung, Max." This is the truth, but Max is picking up on something I am not ready to put down.

They eye me suspiciously, like they know I just had a wet dream about Jo.

"Drive?" I chide. They're not getting anything out of me.

On the truck, I watch as Jo fluffs Lena's hair. I'm in the corner on fan duty, because even very pregnant people deserve to look like Beyoncé at SoFi Stadium. It's been awkward between Jo and me today, and we've been exchanging only micro-pleasantries—

something that, in the short time we've been acquainted, is *so* not us.

I'm not used to being rebuffed. There's a boiling pit in my stomach and I couldn't even get my coffee down–which is fine because I'm already amped from this cocktail of confusion and rejection. I am usually so quick to read people, and her pulling away from our almost-kiss was the last thing I expected last night. It hurt; it still hurts. Toiling over this has me distracted, but I'm a multitasker: I can be insecure, resentful *and* a bright-eyed assistant, all at the same time.

"I know I needed a big belly for these shots, but god, I'm exhausted," Lena grumbles.

"You look great," I try. She's got that pregnancy glow, despite her overly swollen digits.

"Aren't you supposed to be mean?" Lena glares at Jo. "You said she was mean, but what I've seen so far... cold and socially awkward, sure. But not mean."

Can't knock her for calling it like she sees it, but Jo sighs. It's like she told Lena not to say anything but was prepared she would anyway.

"I didn't say she was *mean*, I said she was *stubborn*. There's a difference."

Jo reddens from her shit-talkery, and the pit in my stomach has officially turned into a black hole. They must've talked last night after I left. Lena must know what happened. And worst of all, Jo is *embarrassed* by me.

"Pot, meet kettle," Lena snickers.

"Shut up and look pretty," Jo ribs. Lena roars with the same adorable laugh as Jo, who nods at me–still avoiding eye contact–and that's my cue to turn on the wind machine in my lap.

Lena basks in the fan. "That actually feels so good."

Jo clicks her camera repeatedly, triggering the flash over and over, nearly giving me a seizure.

But when the images of Lena materialize onscreen, I can't

help but gasp. They're stunning. And not only because Lena is beautiful, but because everything about the photos is perfectly imperfect. Her hair is messy, but in a way almost impossible to achieve without a stylist, and her smile is a genuine expression of some of the purest joy I've ever seen photographed. You can't fake this kind of moment.

I turn back. They're both staring at me.

"What?" Jo says, concern on her face.

I recover myself from the literally breathtaking photo. "Oh, sorry. It's just…" I start to bake my humble pie. "I see what you mean. About the photos."

Jo's expression reads like she doesn't believe the words coming out of my mouth. I probably wouldn't either, especially if she believes I'm that stubborn, which I am. Which I am *allowed* to be.

"Oh, good, that means we can be done," Lena sits with a thud.

Jo and I laugh.

Our eyes meet for the first time all day.

"Wait!" Emma shouts from the truck as Max and I head out. "Do you all have dinner plans?"

"I do. I have plans," Max blurts. "But Ava doesn't!"

"Max, what–"

"I have plans, too," says Emma, "but you don't, do you, Jo?"

"I don't think–"

"Guess you two should get dinner! Together!" Emma shouts.

"Great, I'll put it on her calendar!" Max points to their phone and slides into the driver's seat. I hop into the car after them.

"What was that?" I ask.

"Just doing my job," Max says, the smuggest of smiles on their face.

I MISCALCULATED the threat posed by the peanut gallery's burgeoning alliance. Unless Ava divulged our almost-kiss to Max, I doubt our assistants realize what's already transpired, which makes their blind scheming all the more reckless and maddening.

Ever since our lips almost touched, Ava has adopted a cold, overly professional demeanor that has led me to second-guess the entire day at the mall and the dinner at my mom's. I find myself rewriting each moment in my head, trying to convince myself that every longing glance and unspoken moment of connection we shared was a figment of my imagination.

Either she's in the closet and in denial, which, no thanks, been there done that (see: prom queen Wynnie), or she genuinely didn't recognize the signals she was sending. If that's the case, then I'm utterly mortified. Don't mind me scrambling to walk back any response I made to what I perceived as signs of her attraction.

Where does that leave us? Seated across from each other at the four-star restaurant Max booked us into, poking at our pastas and trying to fill the air with polite conversation.

Somehow our cordial exchange is more painstaking to endure than the barbs we traded on Aspen's radio show.

"When is your sister due?" Ava asks me, twirling linguini around her fork.

"Imminently," I tell her.

"Cool." She sips her water.

Silence.

"How's your bolognese?" I ask.

"A little spicy," she admits.

"Want me to call the waiter over?"

She hurriedly shakes her head. "No, it's fine… the spice, um, builds character."

I'm surprised; I never pegged her as someone too timid to send a dish back. But pointing that out would mean acknowledging the fire in her that appears to have been extinguished approximately twenty-four hours ago. I'm not ready to dig into that.

Instead, I watch her grimace and take another heaping bite.

I rack my brain for something else inoffensive we can discuss to pass the time.

"Jolene Bean!" *Thank goodness.* Jamal Clements, one of my good friends since high school, strides over to our table in his maroon apron, saving my ass.

"And who's this lucky lady…?" He sees Ava and I watch the recognition land. Thankfully he's got enough upscale dining finesse (and self-awareness) not to call her out.

"Ava," she offers, sputtering a bit.

"Ava!" he exclaims. She gives him a weak smile. "Well, Jo and Ava, I'll be your server the rest of the evening, Kellan has clocked out for the night."

He refills our glasses. "Would you like to see the dessert menu?"

Ava and I scramble to say no simultaneously and Jamal

chuckles. "I take it you've got better plans than our chocolate soufflé?"

"Not exact–" I begin.

"Okay, well," he leans in conspiratorially, "I've got a couple of extra tickets to The Jingle Balls party tonight. I have it on good authority that Captain Ho Ho Hooker will be debuting her first holiday performance of the season."

Our local drag shows are one of the best parts of Harmony Springs, a realm of pure unadulterated queer celebration. Yet, it's hard for me to imagine Ava fully immersing herself in such a flamboyant and unrestrained environment.

The contrarian in me runs with that thought experiment and before I can stop myself, I hear myself saying out loud, "Hand those tickets over, we'll be there."

Ava almost chokes on her pasta but she covers it up by chugging water.

Jamal beams. "Gorgeous! Ian says we need to stay in and catch up on wrapping presents tonight, so I'm glad they're going to a good home." He fishes two tickets out of the pocket of his apron and slaps them down on the table before sashaying off.

Ava stares down the two tickets like they're going to bite her.

"You don't have to come with me," I tell her, suspecting that the challenge in my voice will speak to that defiant edge within her.

"I don't?"

"I mean, it's fine if it's not your… scene," I stumble.

Something–annoyance, maybe?–flickers across her face. "It sounds like a Harmony Springs institution. I might as well continue immersing myself in the town… *scene*."

"Great."

"Great!"

Great.

. . .

The Jingle Balls is Harmony Springs' drag house, and I've been sneaking into their events since I was a sprightly sixteen-year-old baby lesbian. I wasn't even there to drink, I simply felt at home amidst the artistry and the 80s glam and the musical soundtracks and the high camp. The queens' jubilant embrace of otherness made me feel at home in myself even when I didn't feel like myself at home.

The bass is thumping from around the block as we approach the party. I'm thinking about the fact that neither of us is dressed right for the venue–not that the queens will care–when Ava unbuttons her cardigan and ties it around her waist, exposing her toned back and shoulders in the silky black spaghetti-strap top she's got on underneath. My breath hitches from the sight.

A short-statured queen dressed like a sexy Tiny Tim in a Victorian-style coat over Christmas lingerie tips her beret at us. "Welcome to our holiday ball! I'm Tiny Tease, from Charles *Dick*-ens' A Christmas Carol, which you'll be seeing drag variations on all evening!"

As soon as I hand over our tickets, another queen, Ebenezer Screwed, leads us down a pitch-black hallway reverberating with the sounds of the party deeper within. Before she allows us in, she leaves us with her parting wisdom:

"There is nothing in the world so irresistibly contagious as laughter... and serving cunt."

She pushes open a set of double doors and we're blinded by the flash of strobe lights and disco balls. A remix of Pansy Division's *Homo Christmas* is pumping, and queens and partygoers alike dance on the stage and catwalk that extends out across the center of the room.

It's too noisy to speak, so I motion toward the bar and Ava nods. It's hard to read her expression in between strobes, but she hasn't sprinted out of here yet, so that seems promising.

We order our respective drinks of choice–a dirty martini for me, an old fashioned for Ava–and make our way into the thick of the crowd. It's a relief to not need to make conversation. The music is loud and the bass is as intoxicating as our cocktails.

There's a lot to take in and it feels safe to stare at strangers for once within the clipped flashes of light. Ava's eyes roam the space as she sucks on the thin black straw of her drink. There are people of all genders grinding on one another, making out, dancing by themselves and in conga lines. A hauntingly good Jacob Marley queen dances with chains on stage as the music builds even further.

"I girded it on of my own free will, and of my own free will... I wore it, hennyyyyyy!"

The bass drops.

"YASSSS, HUMBUG!!" someone screams behind us.

Ava downs her drink. She shakes her empty glass and nods toward the bar. *Fuck it.* I sling back the rest of my martini and we march to order our second drinks.

"How are you liking it?" I ask her.

"WHAT?" she responds.

"HOW ARE YOU LIKING IT?" I yell.

She gives me two thumbs up as the bartender hands us our cocktails.

"I love your app!" they shout at Ava over the bar. "Don't let the haters get to you!"

She beams at them as they line up a rack of tequila shots. Behind us, Tiny Tease drops out of the ceiling from a swing.

"God bless us, every one!" she hollers, popping the end of her crutch open, turning it into a confetti cannon. *POOF!* The crowd goes wild.

Ava picks up her shot, spilling a little. "To our haters!" she shouts. Ava, the bartender and I cheers, throwing back our shots. I watch the tiny pieces of paper flutter down into her silken hair as she squinches her face.

"Sorry it's not top shelf," I laugh.

"Here." She hands me a second shot from the bartender who nods our way. *Another one down the hatch, I guess.*

Maybe it's the alcohol, but the music gets louder, the beat taking root in my hips until I'm no longer content standing amidst the throng. I need to dance, and honestly, Ava probably does, too.

I lean in toward her, realizing this is the first time I've needed to put my face so close to hers. She smells like Santal 33 and fresh baked bread. Or maybe this is what two martinis and two shots do when you only eat half your pasta at dinner. Either way, it's time to dance.

"It's time to dance!" I shout, probably louder than needed because she flinches.

I clamor up onto the catwalk and crouch down, holding my hand out to her. She takes it, climbing up beside me and starts to move her body, and fuck, what the hell did I just speak into existence?

Watching Ava dance is pure torture. When she's dancing, she's not arguing with me, so that's nice. But also. *Also.* The rhythm of her movements. The masterful sway of her hips. The way she closes her eyes to the music, her lips parting ever so slightly, lost in a sultry trance–I'm captivated by this version of her. I want desperately to hold her. To dance *with* her, not next to her, to touch her hips and pick up her pretty little hands and hold her face between my fingers. In the blur of drunkenness, I can fleetingly admit these desires to myself.

But I can't touch her, so I channel all that electricity into my own dancing instead. The music pulses around us, a throbbing heartbeat that matches the one in my chest. We're lost in it, hands and elbows and thighs brushing accidentally. Each contact sends a jolt through me. *Fuck, I have got to get a hold of myself.*

I widen the space between us and scan the dancefloor, desperately seeking a distraction to soothe my longing for the unattainable. A pixieish redheaded femme in a leather corset and mini skirt snags my roaming gaze with their penetrating one. Crooking a smile, they push through the crowd toward me with a confident stride.

"Gemma, she/her," she shouts over the music. "You're hot."

I give her a flirtatious once-over. Behind me, I can sense Ava's gaze. I'm not sure why she's watching me so eagle-eyed, but my bruised ego sees it as a cue to perform, to show her how swiftly I can move past her rejection.

I extend my hand, Gemma uses it to pull me closer. "I'm Jo. Same pronouns."

She's so close I can see the tiny rhinestones she applied over her winged eyeliner. "You're hot *and* you look like a steampunk wood nymph," I tell her.

Gemma throws her head back and laughs, her top riding up to reveal a belly-button ring. She brings her lips close to mine, then pulls back teasingly. She loops her arms around my neck and begins to move to the rhythmic thumps of the bass.

I steal a glance toward Ava, only to find her... completely gone. I whip my head around, causing Gemma to take a step back.

"I'm so sorry, I need to find my friend." I excuse myself and attempt to navigate through the throng of dancers, my head on a swivel searching for Ava. As soon as I start to move across the room, I realize I'm tipsier than I thought when I was swaying in place on the dance floor. But I've pushed through drunker nights and harder tasks, so I forge on.

After a mildly dizzying search indoors, I spill out into the chilly night air, scanning the street until I see her standing on the dimly lit sidewalk. Her cardigan is back on and she's holding her phone aloft in a futile attempt to catch a signal.

"Going home?" I venture.

She turns around, startled. Her face clouds when she sees me. "Yeah. It seems like you've got your night figured out." She shivers as she checks her phone again. "One Uber in this town and it'll be at least forty minutes, or so my app said before I lost reception."

I crack a slight smile. "Then you're having a truly authentic Harmony Springs night out."

Her expression doesn't soften in the slightest. "You were, too."

"Do you have a problem with that?" I shoot back.

Not even a flinch. "You can go back inside, Jo. I don't need a babysitter."

"Why are you leaving?" The alcohol emboldens me to speak my mind. "Does it gross you out, two women kissing?"

Ava scoffs. "You've got little Tinker Hell in there waiting to blow your mind. Why do you care that I'm leaving?"

I'd rather not get into *that* answer, so I forge ahead with my single drunken talking point. "You won't answer my question. Do I have to ask it a third time?"

Annoyance flickers across Ava's face. "No, I do not have a problem with it, nor do I find it *gross*," she says quietly.

Jeffrey pulls up in George's car, his glaring headlights cutting through this weird, tense moment. He waves through the rolled-down passenger window. "Evening, ladies! My next rider canceled, so the George-mobile is all yours. Did that queen of mine pull off his number tonight?"

Ava offers up a compliment about George's drag performance but I'm not listening. I'm frozen on the sidewalk in indecision as Ava opens the back door and slides in, slamming the door shut behind her without so much as a goodbye to me. After this exchange with Ava, I want to call it a night. And my place is on the way to her hotel, would it be the *worst* thing if I just...

"Can I get a drop-off at mine?" I blurt out.

Jeffrey, thankfully oblivious to any tension, beams back at me. "The more the merrier! Hop in, love!"

I sit in the passenger seat, ignoring Ava in the back as the car makes its way across the snowy midnight roads of Harmony

Springs. I make small talk with Jeffrey, only half-listening to his responses, the rest of my mind devoted to the confusing swirl of annoyance and frustration churning within me.

You didn't want me, and then you're gonna make me feel bad for being wanted by someone else? I believe Ava knows she's *supposed* to say she doesn't find girls kissing to be gross or weird, but I don't trust that she means it. I already humiliated myself laying in the snow beside her, moving in for an unwanted kiss, so why does she need to twist the knife of rejection any deeper? My brooding sobers me up faster than an IV drip.

Jeffrey pulls up in front of my mom's house. I thank him and get out, not looking back. I begin to walk briskly up the snowy driveway toward where Emma parked Chrissy after she shooed Ava and me off to dinner.

There are footsteps behind me in the snow. I whirl around to see Jeffrey driving off, and Ava standing in front of me, wide eyes, face flushed, expression wild.

"What are you–" I start.

Before I can process what's happening, she pushes me up against the side of The Photo Truck and presses her warm plush lips against mine.

The moment she kisses me, my overactive mind short-circuits. Any resentment I had is drowned out by lips on lips. I try to remind myself to *focus, focus, focus,* to capture whatever fleeting bliss is being offered to me so I can savor it.

Her lips part ever so subtly, and I take her invitation to slip my tongue into her mouth, tasting her sweet orange-whiskey flavor. I caress my hand over the side of her head, flexing my fingers over her glossy hair. I'm not sure breathing is necessary if it means breaking this kiss even for a moment.

Ava is pressed up against me, her urgency spoken through her fingers twisting in my hair, trying to pull me deeper in every way. My hands move downward, tracing repeatedly over the swell of her hips from her waist, holding her as she squirms desperately. Our mouths still plastered together, I can *feel* her moan, and that unravels me. I don't care if it's the worst idea I've ever had, or if I can never have her again. I'm letting this animalistic lust take over, because life is too short not to take whatever she will give me tonight. Dignity, business, heartache be damned.

I break our kiss. Ava's pupils are so blown out her eyes look black. "Shall we do this somewhere warmer?" I ask, my breath fogging the air between our barely parted mouths.

Ava doesn't respond. Instead, she starts walking toward the backyard.

When I don't follow, she turns around. "You said you had a backhouse."

Do I? Nothing seems real right now, so I nod and let Ava Garcia-Greene lead me to my own home, where she has never been before. I might be useless, but she's the most competent tipsy person I've ever encountered.

"Key?" she holds out her hand.

At the very least, I can unlock the door myself, so I do.

I try to calm my racing mind. *I do this all the time. I take women back here plenty.*

Ava steps inside, taking in my space, studying the artwork on my walls. She leans forward, studying my cyanotype portrait of Emma. She strolls over to an oak console and picks up the ship in a bottle my dad and I built together one summer. I have to look away.

I was wrong, having Ava in here is different. I'm exposed. *Is my art stupid? Do I even have taste?* I busy myself, turning on lamps for ambiance. *Oh god, ambiance? Who am I?*

"I'm parched," she states, squinting at an O'Keeffe print that has never appeared more yonic.

I fill two water glasses and hand one to her. She gives me a *hm.* We're past pleasantries, duly noted.

I walk over to my vinyls and thumb past Jeff Buckley and

Leonard Cohen. Sexy, but more cry-after-sex sexy than hot-one-night-stand sexy. *Is this a one night stand?* I wish she would kiss me again and force-quit my racing thoughts.

My fingers land on Janelle Monae. Les-bingo. *Dirty Computer* fills the backhouse. I'm grateful for something to drown out the voice in my head telling me that this is a bad idea.

Ava comes up behind me at the record shelf. She sets down her glass of water. I turn to face her and she unabashedly checks me out, head to toe, for once not trying to hide it at all. My stomach flutters, then drops through the floor when she very slowly and deliberately lifts her silky camisole up and over her shoulders, revealing what I've suspected all night–no bra and the two prettiest, perkiest, perfect-mouthful tits I've ever seen. *Force-quit, achieved.*

"Oh, fuck," I murmur. She looks smug. I can't hold back. I kneel on the ottoman right beside the record shelf and get to work, tonguing and teasing her taut nipples with gusto.

Only when her hips begin to move desperately, seeking something more, do I pull back.

She's offended, and I huff out a little laugh at her frustration because it's *so* not warranted. I take her hand and lead her to my bed.

"Lay back for me," I instruct, and shockingly she obeys without hesitation, her hair fanning out on my pillow.

I caress the waistband of her pants. "May I?" I ask teasingly. She nods. I hook my fingers in and pull them off, revealing her lacy red thong.

Lying mostly naked before me, Ava's eyes catch mine and then flit away. "Jo. I..." she trails off. Self-doubt twinges in my gut.

I lay down beside her, my face next to hers. "We don't have to do anything you don't want."

She shakes her head. "I want *you*." She says the final word so softly it's practically a whisper. "I'm just... new."

She seems almost disappointed in herself, and I can't allow that. I lean in, offering her my lips as reassurance. She meets them halfway, her mouth trembling as our tongues start their dance again. I pull back to say, "Let me do my thing," which elicits a tiny laugh and the cutest little blush from her. Who knew this stoic goddess could *blush*?

Time to wow the CEO of Gramsta with everything I've got.

I begin working my way down her body, peppering her with kisses on her collarbone, the round of her shoulder, the space between her breasts, each nipple, then the smooth warm skin of her belly, abs flexing beneath the surface as I run my tongue across it.

I arrive at her red panties and I inhale her intoxicating scent. I don't take them off, opting instead to continue planting kisses over the fabric, making her squirm, desperate for friction.

"Mmm, Jo, please..." her eyes are closed and her hands are making circles on my head.

I press the flat of my tongue over her pussy through the red lace and apply pressure. I'm teasing myself at this point, too. I'm hungry to fully taste her, to hear her lose speech and go wild for my tongue. But I also want to draw this out as long as possible. I suspect this will be my one and only chance to have Ava in this way, and I selfishly want to drive her so crazy that she thinks about this night—and me—for years to come.

She's so wet the panties have practically melted away, so I get rid of them. I pull the fabric to the side, exposing her glistening pussy and swollen clit. I swipe my tongue quickly over all of it, once, twice, three times, then plant a kiss directly on her most sensitive spot.

Ava's hands roam my hair, twisting and pulling hard enough to hurt, except right now my pain transmutes into arousal because she simply can't help herself.

I draw her clit into my mouth and suck ever so gently while she uses her hips to press herself against my face, asking for more. I give her what she wants–a harder suck, for about ten seconds–and she starts to moan and shake. Right on the edge where I want her. I pull back again, then drop another teasing, pecking kiss onto her pussy while she wriggles beneath me.

She's frustrated, eyes dark, face flushed.

"Tell me what you want me to do," I coax. I could be pressing my luck, but I can't *not* indulge the part of me that needs to hear her vocalize her desire.

She gives me another moan and raises her hips toward me but I shake my head. "I want words."

"Unnnnngh," she whines, "I need, I need…"

"You can do it." I give her pussy an encouraging little kiss. I can't deny that stealing her power of speech has me feeling good about myself.

"I need your mouth. All of it. Please." So polite.

I lick a stripe across her slit. "Like this?"

She squirms. "Mmmm."

I think I've drawn out as much verbiage as I'm gonna get, so I relent and dive into her pussy, running my tongue around her opening, suckling her clit, riding the waves of her mounting pleasure with (dare I say) expert rhythm.

Soon her hips are rocking to a beat of their own, and I'm chasing the orgasm with her. When her hands begin to tighten my hair into such impossible knots that my eyes are leaking tears, I know we're arriving, so I keep my tongue consistent and firm.

The sweetest jus floods my mouth as she cries out, letting go of my hair to hold her hands over her face as she cums beautifully for me.

I kiss her pussy three more times, for good measure, and then I army-crawl up the bed to lay beside her. Her eyes are closed, but she snuggles up against me, nestling her head under my chin.

We lay like that for a while, entwined, until I notice her breathing getting deeper and heavier.

I whisper her name. "Ava?" No response. She's escaped into dreamland, sated and snuggled up with me.

I stay awake for a long time after, holding her as her chest rises and falls. I wish I could capture this euphoric peace and save it for later. But as sleep overtakes me, my final thought is that, come the morning light, will it all be ripped away?

CHAPTER 19
AVA

THE FIRST THING I hear is my phone vibrating like an earthquake on the nightstand next to me. The first thing I *feel* is my brain pounding against my skull. This is why I don't drink in excess. Always in control.

Until now, apparently. I so desperately wanted to let go last night and be me for once.

I reach my hand to silence the vibrations when I realize where I am. I squint my aching eyes as the quaint backhouse comes into focus. Jo stirs next to me, arm reaching over my bare chest. Flashes of the night before come flooding back.

Jo and I definitely hooked up.

And, I can't speak for Jo, but I definitely liked it.

A little projector flickers to life in my mind, displaying images of my childhood bedroom. While other girls my age were swooning over Hanson, I had posters of Sarah Michelle Gellar as Buffy and Liv Tyler from *Lord of the Rings* plastered all over my walls. I convinced myself I was celebrating girl power as I dreamt of their heroism. But now, I wonder: was it really about admiration? Was there something more to those daydreams?

I put a pin in my sexual awakening as I catch a glimpse of Max's picture on my home screen. I slip out of Jo's snuggly embrace and slip on last night's cardigan before sneaking outside.

"Max?" I say, brushing the sleep from my eyes. "I blame you–"

"Ava. This is bad."

I become alert. "What? What's going on?"

"Get to the hotel. Now."

If Max is acting serious, then this is *serious*.

Stepping back inside, I throw on my clothes and steal one last glance at Jo. I feel bad for ditching, but look at her–she's gorgeous. She probably does this all the time. And I've got a job to do, which, if Max's tone is any indicator, I have endangered.

I make my way out to my Uber–of course, it's George.

"How are you this morning, Ms. Ava?" he asks slyly.

Tech Times news alerts pop up on my phone. *Ava Garcia-Greene Wants You to Think She Cares–Here's Why She Doesn't.*

Fuck. I am unwell, George.

I sit on the edge of the hotel bed next to Max, the article pulled up on their laptop for a full, non-mobile version of my shame. A picture of me and Jo, sweaty, face to face, dancing, tops the headline for the world to see. Just by acknowledging the way my eyes are locked into hers… you *know*.

I've had less than an hour to process my first lesbian encounter and therefore the entire conceptualization of my own sexuality, and here it is for the entire planet to perceive. They say a picture is worth a thousand words, but in this case, I think it may be three. Those three words are more powerful than an entire dictionary. Those three words are what so many people fear saying their entire lives. And they were mine to tell whenever I was ready, whenever I felt sure that I was, in fact, queer.

Welcome to my life, I guess.

I'm used to my personal business being blasted, but now I'm

also being presented as someone who's partying on the company dime, not doing what I came here to do. I don't think my ancient cis-het all-male Board could understand my sexuality, and hopefully they don't really care, but they do care what the quality of my character appears to be to the rest of the world. And right now, that's *not good*.

"I'm so sorry, Ava," says Max.

"Has the Board seen?"

"It's only a matter of time." Max holds my hand. I take a deep breath.

It doesn't help.

CHAPTER 20
JO

WAKING up to find Ava gone stings, even though I should have expected it.

What catches me off guard is the article Emma sends me–a blaring headline sprawled above a photo of me and Ava dancing together. Though the image captures nothing more scandalous than our dance, the implications won't sit well with Ava. Her reputation, fragile enough for our radio spat to send her to Harmony Springs, is not equipped for this kind of exposure. The suggestion of partying on the job is one thing, but I am certain the deeper, unspoken implication of her dancing closely with another woman is likely to send her into a tailspin.

Why am I so certain she's spiraling? It's been two whole days since I've heard from her, and either her phone is off or I'm blocked, because neither Emma nor I have been able to reach her. Max also won't pick up, which I can tell is bothering Emma enough to make her check her phone every two minutes as we sit across from each other at Sugar Daddy's.

"What if she's not having a big gay freakout?" Emma pitches. "Not every 'straight girl' loses her mind when she switches teams."

"Sure, only every straight girl I've hooked up with," I say bitterly.

"Hadn't you hooked up with exactly *one* straight girl prior to Ava?" Emma reminds me.

"Yes, and she was already one too many."

"Ava's getting dragged on TechTok, Elon Schmuck tweeted he wants to buy Gramsta, and the AvaGG subreddit is run amok with 'Gayva' rumors even if the general public didn't read that much into the pic." Emma takes a pointed sip of her drink. "Maybe it's just 33% gay freakout. The rest could be… sheer existential chaos that has little to do with you."

I cradle my face in my hands. "This is all my fault."

"Hey. Hey. Breathe. We're scrappy. We'll figure this out, we always do. We can stretch that $10k pretty far. Far-ish. Far adjacent?"

In spite of my stress, my disobedient mind is fixated on a much different issue, one which comes into focus as I close my eyes and try to breathe. The issue of Ava's soft thighs resting on my shoulders. The issue of Ava's moans echoing in my ears. The issue of my incessant need to taste her, to hear her, to touch her.

"Earth to Jolene." Emma is snapping her fingers in my face. "Lost you in the breathwork, buddy."

I rack my brain for something helpful to contribute that isn't a montage of Ava's squirms. "We might as well start spending that $10k. It's too bad we didn't get to alleviate Gramsta of more cash, but that check might be able to cover the seat, the heat, and some updated finishes."

Emma shoots back the rest of her hot chocolate. "Sounds like Mikey's lucky day."

Emma had no way of knowing how apt her prediction about Mikey was. A couple hours later, we're standing in his office at the repair shop. I'm sure all of the blood has drained out of my face because Mikey actually pulls out a chair and beckons me to sit.

Mikey is heavily tatted and pierced up the wazoo, with a calming, dad-like energy that would normally put me at ease if he wasn't also telling me it would be–

"Twelve *thousand* for the repairs?" As if things couldn't get worse. Without further support from Gramsta beyond the initial $10k, there won't even be a business left to require a running truck.

Mikey is sympathetic but firm. "These aren't any ol' fixes, Jo. With a vintage truck like Chrissy, you're dealing with unique parts, most of which are out of production. For something like the seat and the heating system, it's not a simple swap."

He pauses, ensuring I'm following. "For the driver's seat alone, we're talking custom fabrication or hunting down on eBay. And the heat needs an overhaul of the HVAC, which, for this model, is like finding a needle in a haystack."

I wish my dad was here to tell me what to do. I bury my head in my hands and try to conjure Roger's wisdom, but there's nothing but static in my mind.

Mikey puts a hand on my shoulder. "I admire what you're doing with the truck, okay? I want you to know that," he says solemnly. "If I'd been able to chase my dreams, maybe I'd be wielding a camera instead of a lug wrench."

Mikey leans back. "I can't tell you what to do, but I can tell you this: these are two relatively small fixes," he clasps his hands, "But long-term? It's going to be a continuous expense."

I let out a slow breath.

"Right." I gulp. "Well, we're about two thousand dollars–and my sanity–short, but we will… get back to you."

Mikey rubs his beard. "Jo, I can't recommend that you continue driving the vehicle until repairs are made. It's not road safe with the seat like that."

My stomach clenches. Emma senses my panic is reaching

Defcon 1, so she steps in. "Heard, chef. Don't suppose we can hitch a ride back to my place?"

I lay on Emma's living room floor with Duke flopped out like a weighted blanket over me while Emma reads job postings from Craigslist.

"Ooh, someone is having a unicorn party! They're looking for a clean-up crew. That's probably not too bad, like glitter and some polyester mane hairs to vacuum up?"

If my life wasn't literally over, I could muster up a laugh. "I don't think it's that kind of unicorn, Em."

"Oh."

Duke licks my face, marvelously unaware of the downward spiral my existence has taken.

Emma clicks another link. "Okay, wait, how about boudoir?"

"I could do that."

She leans closer to the laptop screen. "Nevermind, it's boudoir photography for pets."

I groan. "The sad thing is, I'm not sure we're actually above any of these right now."

Emma shuts her laptop. "Okay, that's it. We need a full-throttle reset on–" she waves her hand at me on the ground, "–all of this."

"How do you suggest we do that? Murder-suicide?" I posit wryly.

"Gosh, you get dark fast. No, dude, we make cinnamon popcorn and watch *You've Got Mail* and in about two hours, life will be infinitesimally more hopeful again."

I'll give it a shot before taking my first suggestion.

You've Got Mail is one of my favorite low-key Christmas movies, and yet, as we watch, I get angrier and angrier. By the time the credits roll, I'm seething.

Emma looks at me worriedly. "I'm sensing this didn't help but I'm not sure why?"

I chew on a popcorn kernel. "You think it's romantic, but no. Tom Hanks totally screws over Meg Ryan and puts her mother's store out of business and he never so much as apologizes? 'That's business'?"

Emma mulls this over. "You're not wrong. I dunno, maybe he apologized to her off-camera and we didn't see it?"

"If something happens in a movie, then it happens *in* the movie," I insist.

"It does feel like a bad sign that even Nora Ephron has pissed you off today," she cops.

I sigh. "No kidding."

I'm about to suggest we revisit the murder-suicide when Emma's phone on the coffee table starts vibrating. MAX AVA HOT lights up on her screen.

"You did not see that," she snaps as she picks up the phone. "May I ask who's calling?"

I don't hear Max's response so all I have to go on is a "Hm" followed by "I'll text it" from Emma before she hangs up without so much as a goodbye.

"Ava and Max are on their way over."

I scramble up from the couch, suddenly panicking again. "Here? I look like shit. I've had your dog on top of me for the better part of three hours and I haven't showered since yesterday morning!"

She studies me. "If I didn't know better, I would say you're the one having a big gay freakout."

I don't have a strong comeback so instead I march straight toward Emma's shower. "I don't want to hear it!" I shout behind me as I shut the door to the bathroom. "Also I'm borrowing a clean shirt."

I take the fastest shower known to womankind, steal a spritz from Emma's bottle of Light Blue and pull on her Bnny shirt. Then I go stand by the door, trying to avoid Duke's all-encompassing love so as not to immediately require another shower and change of clothes.

Emma goes to her kitchen for a seltzer. "Do you want a pickle or something?"

"Absolutely not, thank you."

Three sharp raps at the front door. I swing it open to see Ava for the first time since our tryst, with Max beside her. If Max got the dirty details, their face reveals nothing as I greet them.

Ava's hair is slicked back into a tight bun and she's in a new variation of that tailored pinstripe suit she wore on our mall excursion. Her camel coat is impeccably dry-cleaned, and I'm not mad that it's about to be coated in Duke hair. She's back to the corporate distillation of Ava, all of her sincerity locked away under that same impersonal smile she gave me in the coffee shop on the day we met.

"May we come in?" she asks regally. I step to the side but not fully, forcing her to brush past me to enter.

Emma, eating a whole pickled carrot, comes out of the kitchen. She nods at Max and Ava. "Gramsta." *No names. Cold.* "Have a seat in our... office."

Our corporate guests take their place on Emma's sofa. Duke hops up to squeeze between them, which I can tell is testing the composure Max is fighting to maintain.

"So," Ava starts. "We hit a little hitch."

"Is that what they call it?" I shoot back, but get no reaction from her.

"There was a lot to figure out with the Board, hence the radio silence." She pauses, like she's waiting for me to sign for delivery on the history she's rewriting. "But the good news is, they think the best course of action is to press onward with revitalizing The Photo Truck. If we can document my revamp of your business by Christmas like I promised, then all this noise about how I haven't *walked the walk* will be irrelevant."

I'm not buying the nonchalant way she's spinning this; there's no way the Board didn't rake her over the coals during her two-day absence. Clearly she won't be presenting anything but the version she wants to tell.

"I'm glad this has all worked out so well for you," I tell her flatly. I want so desperately to tell her we don't need her help anymore, that she and Gramsta and her soft thighs and cold demeanor don't belong here in Harmony Springs, much less my life. I've suffered enough at the hands of a closeted woman to realize this does not end well. Even if we never kiss again, that old pain of mine will linger in every subsequent encounter. I'll be forced to repeatedly face another chapter of my life that ends with me being used and discarded by a confused straight woman.

But I'm in no position to say anything close to that. Instead I channel my resentment into driving a harder bargain. "It does sound like you need this."

Ava's eyes flit to mine and then away. "I think it's mutually beneficial."

"From where I'm standing, 99% of our problems could be fixed with a big fat check."

Ava's gaze holds a flicker of resolve. "That may be partially true," she starts, her voice steadier, "but merely writing a check won't quiet my critics or satisfy the Board. I need to be actively involved, not only in refurbishing the truck but in reshaping your business approach." She glances uncomfortably to the side. "And documenting it for PR," she adds.

I fold my arms. "The money might seem negligible to you compared to your precious reputation, but it's not negligible for us. I want an unlimited budget for the projects we handle this month, and a cash infusion to set us up for success in the year ahead so that we have a safety net for testing whatever strategies you're implementing."

She starts to speak but I'm not done. "If you can commit to that, then I'll do what's necessary over the next week to support you, including playing the role of the cooperative Midwest business owner who sings your praises for the press and public."

Ava waits for a moment, like she's anticipating more demands. Then:

"Legally, there's no such thing as an unlimited budget, but you have my word that no expense will be spared. Besides," she looks faintly sad, "you've intuited what I need to get out of this, so I suppose that's a bit of power back in your hands."

I essentially blackmailed my way into everything I've been hoping for for the last five years, but I don't feel very empowered. Nevertheless, I affix a winning smile on my face and hold out my hand to Ava. I sense her split-second of hesitation but then she acquiesces and we shake. Heat courses through me as our hands touch and I try to keep my dumb stuttering heart from beating out of my chest.

"Time to hit the ground running!" I proclaim.

All I have to do now is perform an Oscar-worthy display of composure. *Jesus, Meryl, and Joseph.*

CHAPTER 21
AVA

WE DECIDE to divide and conquer since we have limited time. Max and Emma break off to revamp the truck's social media presence, despite Emma's obvious annoyance with both Max and myself, while Jo and I head to the local mechanic to pay for the HVAC and seat repair on the truck. Covering it is the least I can do–and the most, too, unfortunately.

I sit in the driver's seat of the rental as we ride to the shop. Jo chews on her lip.

"I think we should throw an event," I broach.

She lets a classic Jo side-eye slip. "You mean, your Board thinks we should throw an event?"

Nothing gets past her. "Well–" I stutter.

"Go on." Her gaze flicks down my body then snaps back to meet my eyes. *Is this what being intimidated feels like?*

"We need something to get the word out there that the truck is forty years old, but better than ever," I pitch. "Center our narrative around the fact that Chrissy is a staple of the community."

We stop at a traffic light. "Okay, Ms. Marketer," she says, a slight spark coming back into her eyes. "But we'll be competing with the Chosen Family Festival. That'll never work."

"What's that?"

"Right before Christmas, everyone joins together to celebrate the beginnings of our town," she explains. "It's how the founders came up with the idea to create Harmony Springs. At their own gathering with their dearest friends–their chosen family."

"What if we're part of the festival?"

Jo shakes her head. "Not a chance. They start booking the next festival on New Year's Day and I didn't have the funds to pay for a spot when sign-ups opened last January. We can't just try to join at the last minute."

"We're not *trying* anything. We're doing," I say. "We're not taking no for an answer." I pull into the mechanic's parking lot.

She takes one last look at me, as if she's trying to get a read, but I steady myself. Unfortunately for her, my poker face can contend with the best of them. I can't let my feelings overrun the mission. It's already happened once, and I paid the consequences. Not again.

Twelve grand later, we land back at Jo's. Mikey cut us a decent deal compared to LA mechanics, but Jo still flinched when I put down my AmEx.

"All right, that's that," Jo says, getting out of the car.

"What about the studio renovations?" There's still so much of the plan we need to execute, despite not having the truck, and I am not letting her slack off now.

"Oh." Her lips turn down in surprise. "I didn't think girlbosses such as yourself did that sort of thing."

I laugh, genuinely. I've been called a girlboss as an insult before, but hearing it come out of Jo's mouth tickles me in that boys-flirt-by-calling-you-mean-names-on-the-playground kind of way. Except I never had that until now. *When in Harmony Springs, I suppose.*

"Girlbosses girlboss however they see fit. And right now, I think it's time for us to girlboss the shit out of this truck."

"I suppose that has nothing to do with the fact that it's Christmas break and every contractor in town is too busy to take on the project?"

"Not at all," I fib.

I will never get sick of her grin.

"Come with me to the shed so we can make a list of what we need," she calls out over her shoulder, already on her way.

"Good thing you're not wearing another pantsuit," Jo snickers as we walk down a crowded aisle at Handy Hardware (apparently the owner's last name is Handy, but they embrace the double entendre). The place is a mess, but in an adorable, locally chic kind of way.

"I would never desecrate designer like that," I say, stepping over a Baby Jesus fountain to grab a gorgeous wood sample. "What do you think of this for the floors?"

"I mean, it's beautiful, obviously. It's just so expensive in comparison to the laminate, no?"

"Jo." I literally put my foot down and I don't even mean to.

"Sorry, right." She waves me off. "I'm new to the whole sparing-no-expense thing."

"Well, you better get used to it."

"Oh, yeah?"

I search for a flirtatious comeback but nothing materializes.

Why is flirting with women so much harder?

We keep walking, sample in hand. Jo shakes her head.

"What?" I ask.

"You're... interesting, Ava."

"I'm not doing this to be nice, you know."

"I know," she says.

"I can't have a business I'm associated with looking bad."

"I know," she says again, a sly grin spreading across her lips.

"You two have a minute?" Emma asks me and Jo. While Jo and I spent all of yesterday designing the new interior, Emma and Max continued to toil over the truck's online presence. "We've got an update on the website if you want to check it out."

Max makes a few clicks on Jo's ancient excuse for a computer and reveals a gorgeous Squarespace, fit with a brand new booking system and eye-catching portfolio. It's clean, but still fitting with their larger-than-life brand.

"You two are still on my shit list, but Max is a literal genius," Emma says, matter-of-factly.

Max is good, but to pull that off on this piece of shit?

"You pulled that off on this piece of shit?" Jo gapes.

I chuckle. "So you admit it."

She's not so proud in the face of Max's feat.

"There were moments we both wanted to pull our hair out, but I think we made it work," Max tells us.

"I'll say," I smile, proud of all we've done together. This is the kind of shit I live for. Growing a business. Scrapping everything in my power together to make it work. These are my roots. I hardly knew I missed it.

"Would you all mind getting started on measurements while we… meet with members of the city council?" Jo asks Max and Emma, scratching her head.

"Members of the city council?" Emma raises an eyebrow.

"Yes!" I say. "I contacted Harmony Springs' council to schedule a meeting about featuring the truck at the Holiday Festival. We're chatting with someone named… Wynnie?"

"You're *chatting* with *Wynnie*?" Emma gapes.

"What did Wynnie ever do to you?" I laugh.

"What did she do to *me*? More like what did she do to–"

Emma starts, but Jo silences her with a glare, something I'll be Sherlock Holmes-ing later.

Our chat on the ride over is surprisingly pleasant. I can sense Jo softening toward me. It's nice to think that we can move past our ill-fated fling. Now we can focus on being friends. *That's normal, right?* And friends deserve the scoop on members of the city council.

"So," I say, pulling the rental into the Town Hall parking lot. "What's the beef with Wynnie?"

"Nope. No. Not getting into that." Jo gets out of the car and I scramble to catch up with her as she walks toward the building.

"I think I should be aware. For business purposes," I cajole. "You want me to work my magic in there, I need intel on what we're dealing with."

Jo stops before she reaches the entrance. She takes a deep, *deep* breath, then rapid-fires: "Wynnie was my ex. She's straight. She broke my heart in high school. The end."

Before I can muster a response, the woman of the hour flings open the double doors in all her Midwestern Beauty Queen glory.

"Hiiiiiiiiii! Jooooo! It's so good to seeeeee yoooou!" she purrs.

Is it too soon to say I hate this bitch?

CHAPTER 22
JO

I ALMOST HAVE to laugh at the Book of Job-ian twist of fate that we have to beg Wynnie Tatum to get a spot at the festival. But hysterical laughter is a slippery slope into crying while laughing, a phenomenon my mother has coined a 'goo-goo-eye'. And yes, the one thing worse than laugh-crying is learning at an embarrassingly late age that 'goo-goo-eye' is not a word anyone uses outside your immediate family.

Right this second, the source of many a late-night high school goo-goo-eye is walking up to me, arms open wide, enveloping me in the nostalgic *eau de Wynnie*–two parts fruit-filled expensive perfume, one part Black and Milds smoked secretly in cars and alleyways.

She takes a step back and holds out a hand to Ava. "It's a real honor to have you here, ma'am."

I can viscerally feel how unpleasant Ava finds being called 'ma'am' by an admittedly stunning woman who is the same age as her.

Ava gives Wynnie a quick handshake. "Thanks for agreeing to meet us so last-minute."

Wynnie waves her hand as she goes to sit behind her desk.

"Oh, it's not a problem. Soon as you said it was for Chrissy, I was ready to grease some wheels over here."

She winks at me. I see Ava subtly twist her mouth in annoyance. *Huh*. I'm realizing I have a bit of a home field advantage. Even though I don't love having to hobnob with my high school heartbreak, if I play this correctly I could stick it to Ava a little bit by laying it on thick with Wynnie right in front of her. Remember when I said I was gunning for an Oscar?

I lean over Wynnie's desk, letting my forearm flex right at eye level. Ava tries to hide her discomfort. "That's incredibly kind, Wynn, thank you."

Little pinpricks of blush appear on Wynnie's face. For all her beauty-queen pageantry, she's incredibly easy to fluster. I guess it helps that very few people are aware of her truth, so she's rarely the recipient of same-sex flirtation.

"Now, Jo," she begins to scold, "You understand better than anyone how early folks here start preparations for CFF."

"I do, I do." I strum my fingers on the corner of the desk. Her eyes catch on my hand and her breath hitches in her throat. Ava shoots me an annoyed glare. *Good*.

I carry on with my plea. "Wynn, is there any chance you could get the council to make an exception? The truck is an institution, and we're trying to save it on an incredibly tight timeline. I think the community will want to rally around us; we just have to give them an opportunity."

"I don't disagree, Jojo. I want to help, really, I do." Wynnie leans back in her desk chair. "Let me see if we could rearrange a few booths to make space for the truck. I'll make some calls." She flashes her pearly whites. "How's that?"

I think I've lost the reins of the flirtation I ignited. *What is going on?* "That's, um, that's amazing. Thank you."

Ava steps forward. "Yes, thank you."

Wynnie all but ignores her, instead rising out of her chair

and placing her acrylic-nailed hand atop my strumming one to quiet the motion. "It's nice to see you around. Maybe we could run into each other again sometime?"

She pointedly glances to her left hand and I notice with surprise that she's no longer sporting a wedding ring.

Okay, I get it now. My plot has backfired, but I'm too proud to admit defeat here in front of Ava, so I feign interest in Wynnie's suggestion even though the idea of going back to her roller-coaster of love-bombing and rejection makes me ill.

"Oh, Wynn, that's…wow." I'm not sure if I can get the rest out, but I invoke my patron saint Meryl Streep and push onward. "I'd love to hang."

Barf.

Wynnie looks smug. "I'll be in touch, ladies."

Ava gives Wynnie the slightest acknowledgement before striding out of the office ahead of me. I wave, disgusted with myself, and follow her out the door.

As soon as we settle back into the rental car, Ava stares out the front window like her life depends on it, avoiding all eye contact with me.

"That was a wild success," I remark as she pulls out of the parking lot.

Ava turns back toward me, eyes flashing. "You got over your alleged heartbreak pretty fast once Wynnie started batting those synthetic lash extensions at you."

Okay, she's struck a nerve now.

"For your information, my heartbreak wasn't alleged, it was horrific. It actually fucked me up for a long time, probably to this day."

Ava shakes her head. "I'm just making an observation about what I witnessed."

"You're jealous that an attractive woman was flirting with me and that I flirted back."

She raises her eyebrows. "Is that what you want me to be? Jealous?"

"I saw you looking her over with green eyes. Don't pretend you're in a completely altruistic moral outrage over me flirting with my ex."

Ava scoffs. "Then don't pretend you didn't want to provoke me into this exact confrontation by flirting with your ex in front of me!"

"At least this provoked you into an authentic emotion."

"I'm a human. All of my emotions are authentic."

I hear the anguish in her voice and I pause to recenter. "I'm sorry. I understand you have real feelings. It's just… you may as well have shown up at Emma's with the Secret Service, you were so guarded." I clear my throat. "It threw me, seeing you act like the last place we'd seen each other wasn't… in my bed."

She's quiet, eyes on the road. "I understand. I thought it would be easier not to talk about any of it, to forge ahead like nothing happened." She glances at her mirror and turns down a side street.

She puts the rental car in park. I get the sense we're not pulling over to passionately make out and, in fact, have a sinking feeling it's gonna be quite the opposite.

"Jo," she says, turning to face me. "I have a *big* life. I can't be an individual when I'm a figure, a symbol, to so many. Paps snap me buying Diet Pepsi for lunch and Coca-Cola stock plummets. I don't have the bandwidth, or the allowance in the life I've chosen, to explore something like this. Much less right now, when so much is at stake for the company."

I smile weakly. "It's one of the more logically sound letdowns I've been subjected to," I acknowledge. "I want this truck to be revived, and it makes sense to not let our energies get… entangled." I'm lying through my teeth and I hope she can't tell. And if she can tell, I hope she lets me get away with it.

Ava nods. "But, um, maybe we don't have to fight each other so hard? Like, we could be friends?"

It's such an overused line during a breakup but I can tell from her tentative expression that she's asking sincerely. And because I am a masochist, and also someone who will do anything a hot woman asks of me, I say yes and promptly invite her over for naan pizza and a movie.

No, I have never learned a lesson in my life.

We sit on my couch, a cushion nonchalantly placed between us for safety.

"Have you seen *Happiest Season?*" I ask her.

"You think I would go out of my way to watch a Christmas movie?"

"This isn't any old Christmas movie," I tell her. "It's *the* lesbian Christmas movie, directed by none other than Clea DuVall."

I can sense her hesitation. I didn't even think about the content of the film potentially stoking our fire further. I simply wanted to give her another taste of the Harmony Springs holiday rotation.

Okay, maybe I wanted to torture her a little. Who can resist falling in love with Aubrey Plaza after watching that movie?

She attempts to remain calm and casual. "Yeah, let's do it."

I scroll to Hulu and hit play.

We're halfway through the film and Ava's all snuggled up in my favorite quilt when Wynnie calls. I hop off the couch to answer outside and give Ava room to swoon.

"Who's the best?!" Wynnie squeals through the phone. "It's me. I'm the best. I got you into the fest with a total banger of a spot, right between Stocking Stuffers and Hole Foods Donuts."

"Wynnie, that's great. Thank you so much."

"You got it, Jojo." I can hear her red-painted lips smiling through the phone. "Let's do drinks?"

"Uh, yeah, yeah you got it," I feign. *I'm not trying to burn our bridge in this synchronous moment.*

"Perf," she says. "I'll text you."

I hang up and head back inside, finding Ava fast asleep on the couch. I cover her with another blanket and turn off several lamps around the room. I pause by the oak console, my eyes catching on the bottled ship.

It came in a kit my Uncle Gene gifted me when I turned twelve. My dad, ever the handyman, sat with me in his work-shop in the garage, and for hours, we traded off glue-dotting and tweezer duties until the only thing left to add were the sails. The white linen triangles were nowhere to be found. My dad went into the house and found an old flannel work shirt, and he helped me cut out funky plaid sails instead.

As I painstakingly attached them to the masts, my dad explained Plutarch's thought experiment about the ship of Theseus, a hero from Greek mythology. Theseus' ship was preserved by the Athenians, who gradually replaced its compo-nents as they wore down and decayed. Eventually, every part of the ship that was original had been replaced, to which Plutarch asked: was this the same vessel, or a brand new one?

At first, I was insistent that the ship was the same ship it had always been, it had simply evolved. My dad, whose greatest source of joy was a philosophical debate, lobbed a new paradox at me: what if someone else, while the Athenians were updating Theseus' ship with new parts, had been salvaging the old parts and rebuilding the original ship? If you compared those two ships, which one was truly the ship of Theseus?

His eyes crinkled as I sat over our bottled creation, stumped and frustrated. "It's a doozy, huh?"

But I wasn't willing to give up on having a good answer. In

my mind, something either *was* or it *wasn't*. There had to be a solution.

Over the next few weeks, I was obsessed with thinking about the two ships. I sat in math and drew sailboats in the margins of my notebooks. In the evenings, at our dinner table, my dad would tease me. "Have you solved the centuries-old thought experiment yet, Jojo?"

But at twelve years old, centuries seem somehow negligible. Why shouldn't I be the one to crack the code, expose the truth? The hubris of youth propelled me.

It was in health class when I had my epiphany. Ms. Ball was presenting a lecture on puberty of all things, and I ran home to report the newfound conclusion to my father.

Bursting through the garage door, I announced, "They're all his ships!"

He raised his head curiously. "How's that?"

"Ms. Ball was talking about how we change as we grow, but we're still the same person," I explained, trying to catch my breath. "And I realized, it's like the ship! The version Theseus first sailed, the one the Athenians rebuilt, and even the one made from the old parts–they're all still the ship of Theseus. It's about the idea, the identity of it, not just the wood and nails."

He chuckled, wiping sawdust from his hands. "That's quite a connection, Jojo. You might be onto something. The identity, huh?"

"Yeah," I nodded vigorously. "Like Ms. Ball said, we change in so many ways, but deep down, we hold on to who we are."

He got up from his bench and kissed me on the head. "You're a thinker, Jojo. As long as you keep your mind and your heart connected, you can figure anything out, clever girl." I never saw my dad more proud of me than at that moment.

I wonder what he would think of me right now. I wonder what he'd think about the maddeningly complex woman–my new *friend*–snoozing on my couch. My mind and my heart are currently talking through cup-and-string phones, which is to say, communication is not at its smoothest.

I sit back down on the far side of the couch and let the movie play out. When my eyelids grow heavy, I let an honest thought slip through my mind-heart hotline: *at least we get to fall asleep beside each other one more time.*

CHAPTER 23
AVA

I WALK *along a winding wooden footbridge toward the sea. The gentle waves lap against the pilings and kiss my toes through the slats. I breathe in the fresh Maldivian air as my bungalow comes into view. Max waves in their wetsuit, beckoning me to the sea. I'm finally here.*

Suddenly, the wind picks up, whipping my hair into my face. I jog toward Max, but the bridge begins to sway. I pick up my pace to a run, but Max doesn't get any closer. Concern grows on their face.

I look down, the wooden fixtures waving left and right beneath my feet, before I'm thrown from the path into the churning sea.

I'm fully submerged, unable to breathe, when I feel a tap on my shoulder.

It's Aubrey Plaza, floating like a goddess amongst the stormy chaos.

"You're so gay," she says with a wink.

And then I wake up. Next to Jo. Again. *How does this keep happening?!*

This time I'm fully clothed and on her couch, but somehow it's even more intimate than before. One of her arms lies beneath my head in the classic arm-numbing boyfriend pose that men always complain about (which, for the record, she is handling quite well), while the other drapes over my waist, a small sleepy smile on her lips. I try to slip out from under her arm to take off my suit jacket, but she stirs.

"You fell asleep," she mumbles.

"Appears you did, too," I quip, taken aback by my own peppiness at seven a.m. "What did I miss? Please tell me she ended up with Aubrey Plaza."

Jo grimaces. "You might wanna sit down for this."

My jaw drops. "You're kidding."

"It's basically this century's biggest upset in lesbian media. Maybe all media."

"Well then, I'm glad I fell asleep," I huff.

"Aw, is someone upset her fantasies didn't get fulfilled?" she teases, pushing our boundary. Her flirtiness ruffles me. I throw a pillow at her and she goes to lob one back at me, but it winds up flying directly into the face of her mother Carol, standing in the doorway.

"We—we fell asleep watching—" I stammer, gesturing to the long-gone movie on the TV like a teenager caught in the act.

Carol waves me off and claps her hands together. "None of my business! Who's ready for breakfast?"

Jo gives me an embarrassed 'welcome to my life' smirk. *Here goes nothing, I guess.*

We shuffle into the kitchen after Jo lends me a slightly more casual outfit option of sweats and a Harmony Springs Pride Stride 5K tee. All eyes are on us from the kitchen table. Lena subtly hides behind her coffee mug, eyes wide, while Matt's jaw has practically dropped into the giant stack of fluffy pancakes in front of him.

"Nothing to see here besides my famous pancakes!" Carol says, adding more pancakes to the already-full plate in front of Matt. He leans around the tower of hotcakes, his eyes going back and forth between me and Jo, me then Jo, me then Jo...

"Don't make me force you to sign an NDA," I say, sitting across from him.

It's dead silent, until Lena chokes on her coffee with a chortle. "I love her," she says to Jo, who turns red.

"Me, too," Matt says. "And for the record I would be *honored* to sign an NDA for you."

"Want some orange juice, Ava?" Carol asks.

Just like that, everything is back to normal. I rarely take anyone at their word–I've learned the hard way not to–but here at the cozy Fisher breakfast table, I feel like I can trust new people for the first time in a long time.

I kind of love it.

After a heaping serving of carbohydrates upon carbohydrates, Jo and I walk outside as Max pulls up in the rental car and rolls down the window.

"Ava," they say with a nod.

"Max," I say back. It's the most professional we've ever been, and it communicates all that needs to be said.

"Emma should be here any minute," Jo says as she checks her phone. "What's the plan for today?"

"B-roll!" Max says, stepping out of the car.

"We need footage to capture the full scope of Harmony Springs," I tell her. "Our content needs to make the audience fall in love with the truck, the town, you."

I hear it as soon as it leaves my mouth but there's no way to walk it back, so I keep my face practiced and neutral. "We'll drive around and get some footage of you and Emma interacting with the community, then we'll do a one-on-one interview."

Emma sleepily arrives a few minutes later, giving Max a sideways glance I can't help but clock. I think it's safe to say they both know exactly what's going on, even if I don't.

Jo and I aren't acting like we're just friends–you don't spoon your friends like that. But we're also not together by any means. Lena and Matt were a bit taken aback, but Carol acted as if it was a totally normal occurrence for Jo to bring a surprise guest to breakfast. It stirs something in my stomach. This may be new and confusing and exciting for me, but it isn't anything special for Jo. Which is why, from here on out, we're going to stick to accomplishing what I came here to do, no distractions.

Jo drives the rental car around town, giving us a broader Harmony Springs tour. We drive past the local watering hole–Cheers Queers–down to a beautiful gazebo on a lake. It's white and simple, probably the one thing that fits that description in all of the Springs.

Jo parks and takes out her DSLR to snap photos of a couple of locals eloping by the water. Max films Jo at work while I become enraptured by the vows. Two people who love one another so deeply that they'd wake up early on a Tuesday morning to commit their lives to each other. I've only ever been that committed to my business, and I imagine what it's like to experience that, but with another *soul*–ya know, if those existed. Someone who is looking out for me as much as I am for them. Someone who comes before my business, my work, even me. It's almost unfathomable. Yet here they are, so sure of themselves, so sure of each other.

Snap.

I turn as Jo captures my profile through the 35mm film camera that has suddenly appeared in her hands.

"Where'd that come from?"

She takes another shot of my bewildered face.

"The good stuff is over there!" I shoo her off, pointing to the couple.

"That's what you think." She turns and waltzes back to the car.

"Delete that," I say to Max who documented the moment on their phone.

"Already done," they say, trying to hide their smile.

After a few more hours of roaming the town and collecting footage, Jo is losing steam.

"I'm starving," Jo says. Admittedly, she's been lugging around multiple cameras, switching between heavy zooms and fixed lenses all day, while the rest of us watched on in awe, arms empty.

"Not so fast," says Max. "We've still got to do Jo's interview."

"Where should we shoot since we don't have the truck?" Jo asks.

"What about Rog's old darkroom?" Emma chimes in.

Jo twists her lips, unsure.

"That'd be great, if that works for you, Jo," says Max. "We'll go pick up lunch and you two can interview each other while we wait."

"Can't a girl sit and eat for a minute?" Jo grumbles.

"Not with a deadline like this. Right, Ava?"

Max isn't wrong. Plus we need to prove to the Board we're making things happen over here, not just canoodling in drag bars.

"I'll order on the company card. Anything specific you all would like?" I ask.

"Oh, no no," Max interjects. "*You* are staying to do the interviewing. Emma is coming with me."

"Excuse me?" I am so not an interviewer. I hardly interview people at my own company anymore, so I'm not prepared for this. People ask *me* questions, not the other way around.

"Oh come on, Ava. I remember when you interviewed me," Max reminisces. "In fact, I will literally never forget when you asked me who I was going to be in five years. It got me thinking about my life in a way I never imagined; it's like you *knew* I was living inauthentically. And now here I am, trans as heck!"

"Max, that's very sweet, but–"

"It'll look good to the Board," Max says definitively. And I can't argue with that. The more face time I get in for them, the better. "Plus, I've got *my* company card."

With a couple of finger guns and a flash of the corporate gold, Max and Emma bound off and I ready myself for another one-on-one with Jo. The day has been tame, but now we're about to be alone, together, in a confined space, with so many intimate questions on my mind. I can't be trusted to ask normal questions now. There's one thing I can think about and she's standing right in front of me, waiting for me to talk with her. But to be honest, all I want to do is shut up and *feel* her.

I WATCH Ava adjust the tripod before finding a perch atop a Pelican case we've managed to fit into the confined darkroom. I'll admit, it's a little less magical when you can see the empty developing trays and cold tile floors, but Ava frames me up so it's still visually interesting. I'm fulfilling my end of the bargain by being on this side of the camera again, but it doesn't mean I like it. At least being in my dad's old space gives me a sense of support from beyond. God knows I need it.

Ava studies me through the iPhone she's shooting on. "Maybe less of a grimace?"

I guess I'm not masking my discomfort well. I take a deep breath and try to smile at her in a natural way. She balks. "That's actually not better."

"Well neither were you!" I retort.

She chuckles and walks over to me, running her fingers through my hair to try and tame it. It's for the camera, but I can't help enjoying the sensation like any sensible person with a scalp would.

She stops and moves to the table next to us, inspecting a steel tank.

"That's a daylight tank, it's–" I start.

"Used for processing roll film, I know," she laughs. "Didn't I tell you I have one of these?"

"A darkroom?"

"Yes," she says. "In a spare bedroom. I had it converted. I thought I told you I'm a photography nerd."

I learn something new I like about her every day. *Shit.*

She takes in the small space. "How often do you use this as an actual darkroom?"

"Hardly ever," I admit. "The truck biz is fully digital, I don't usually have a reason to develop film."

"I'd say you do. That cyanotype portrait of Emma in your backhouse is captivating."

Do not think about the naked tango that took place right after she admired your artwork.

"My dad taught me about cyanotypes in this very darkroom," I tell her.

"He must have been a good teacher then."

"The best. He always guest lectured at the community college when he had time."

Ava puts the tank down and returns to her seat behind the camera.

"Take it away." I roll my shoulders, trying to relax.

"So, Jo, tell me about where we are right now. Not only the studio, but the town." Ava's on-camera voice carries a formal tint, but there's genuine interest in her eyes.

I launch into one of my favorite special interests, the history of Harmony Springs. I start with the gold rush and lay out the entire saga, all the way up until the shocking deathbed letter and the founding of the town.

Ava shakes her head in awe. "You don't hear much about queer people trying to live their lives a hundred years ago."

"They existed, but history has been traditionally written by straight white dudes. Harmony Springs stands as a testament to what a place can be when it's founded on principles of inclusion and understanding, rather than bigoted views on purity and assimilation."

I have to hand it to her–she's a natural interviewer, in spite of how acerbic and abrasive she can come across in day-to-day interactions. She listens actively, asking all sorts of follow-up questions, about Harmony Springs' founding, the town's connection with Christmas, and Roger's journey to Chrissy. I lose track of time and the camera, talking animatedly as ever about my father.

"He sounds like he was a great influence on you," Ava observes.

"He was," I affirm, a vivid memory surfacing. "Actually, he was the first person I told I was gay. His support made facing the rest of the world easier."

"Even in Harmony Springs?"

"Even in Harmony Springs."

"Was it difficult, coming out here?"

Nostalgia and a tinge of pain thread through my words. "We're in a protective bubble in this town, but the outside world still permeates. Movies and music and literature are still overwhelmingly straight. Coming out means accepting that your life strays from what most of the world considers the 'norm'."

Ava nods thoughtfully. "I can only imagine."

I can sense she wants to ask more but doesn't, so I keep going. "I was drawn to women before I even had a concept of sexuality. My Barbies dated each other, my Ken dolls stayed in their boxes. And when I was little, like younger than ten, I would go through phases of intense obsession with different actresses. I didn't understand they were crushes, even though that's obvious in hindsight."

"Did you ever watch Buffy?" she asks.

"Sarah Michelle Gellar was a big puzzle piece for me," I chuckle. "Why?"

"No reason." She gets back on track. "You never dated a boy?"

I laugh. "Oh, I absolutely dated a few boys."

She's surprised. "But you knew from such a young age?"

I shake my head. "I knew, but I didn't. Even in a queer place like Harmony Springs, there's still social capital to be gained by playing along with heteronormativity. I didn't think about it consciously, but when a guy asked me to prom sophomore year, I genuinely had never been more elated."

"Really?"

"Like I'd won a competition. A be-normal-and-average contest that no one but me realized I was competing in."

Ava's eyes widen as she digests what I've said. "So what was the tipping point? What broke you out of your hetero reverie?"

I'm not sure I want to answer, but I do it anyway. "I fell in love."

She sits back. "Oh."

"I drove her home from a party junior year because she lived nearby, and before she got out of my car, she kissed me. From that moment on, no guy was ever gonna compare for me." I pause. "And then I found out about her fiance."

"Oof."

"I was shattered. In some ways, that heartbreak was further evidence of my queerness, because it hurt me in places I didn't realize existed. I'd never felt that about any guy I'd dated."

"How did you keep it a secret with Wynnie?"

"We didn't do anything to keep it a secret. That's why I was so blindsided. I think people have an easy time writing off women being intimate with one another as intense friendship until someone suggests otherwise."

She takes that in. "I guess our society kind of can't digest a romantic relationship that doesn't involve a man in some way."

"An astute observation," I tell her, and she sits up a bit straighter. "I think lesbians have been commodified in many ways in pop culture for this exact reason. It connects as well to people questioning bisexuals. If you're a bi man, people assume you're secretly gay. And if you're a bi woman, people assume you're doing it for male attention."

She tucks a lock of hair behind her ear and I get a flash of my hands in that hair a few nights ago. *Leave it, Jo.*

"So after Wynnie broke your heart... did you keep dating?" she asks hesitantly.

I want to take a moment to linger on why she's asking some of these questions, but it seems safer not to analyze any of it right now.

"I mean, that first heartbreak sticks with you, but yeah, I moved on... and around."

Ava simpers. "A gay high school Casanova."

I hold my hands up. "Listen, I'm a lovergirl." That gets a blush. "My dad was a decent wingman. He was quite the lothario before meeting my mom. I think he was kinda stoked that I liked girls. He had someone to pass his knowledge down to."

Ava snorts. "Good for Roger. And you, I guess." She reaches up and turns off the camera. "We can cut the end out."

"Whatever makes sense for your video, just don't use the Wynnie parts," I request.

"Of course." She toys with her lower lip and we fall into silence.

Thinking about my dad, I open my wallet, slipping out the worn Polaroid of me and him that I snuck from its hiding place on the truck. Wordlessly, I hand it to Ava, who studies it closely.

"You're exactly the same," she says.

"Gee, thanks."

"He looks kind," she says after a while, before handing the photo back.

"He was." I slip Roger back into my wallet, a safe spot before I return him home to the truck.

My stomach growls rudely.

"I'm starving as well," Ava assures me.

An idea strikes me as if Roger had shouted it from the photo itself.

"After lunch," I start, "Roger gave me an idea about somewhere to go."

"I'm scared to ask if he's wingmanning you from the beyond," she says.

I can't hold in my flirtatious response. "I guess you'll hafta find out."

Oops. Sue me.

After Max and Emma bring us lunch, I drive Ava to Winter Wonderland, home of Harmony Springs' largest outdoor skating rink.

When she sees the big sign, her eyes widen. "Ice skating?"

"You said you wanted to skate like Big Bird," I say.

The smile that wins out on her lips floods me with warmth.

The rink is hopping for the early afternoon, and two different groups of carollers compete for the ears of the skaters at opposite ends of the rink.

Ava keeps her big sunglasses and knit hat on while we're out, and I understand her reasoning, although I can't fully shake the trigger of feeling hidden.

We find a bench to put on our skates. She watches me lace mine up, nervous. "You're gonna be fine. Hold onto me."

Skates laced, we hobble toward the rink. I step onto the ice first and put my arms out to her. She takes hold, and for a moment we're positioned like preteens in a middle school slow dance. I don't hate it, but I also want her to experience the magical freeing sensation of gliding across the ground, so I turn and offer her my hand instead.

"Trust that falling doesn't hurt *that* bad, and don't lean so far forward that you fall flat on your face."

"My face?" she worries.

"I'm not gonna let you fall on your face," I promise.

And for the following two hours, I keep that promise. To be specific, she never falls on her face, only her ass. She doesn't gain the confidence to let go of my hand for more than a few halting scoots across the ice, but I don't mind at all. Instead, we clasp hands–or rather, she grips mine for dear life and I get what I can out of the numbing sensation. By the end of our time at the rink, she's willing to hold hands with our arms outstretched and I pull her around to the mashed-up caroling of *Santa Baby* and *Jingle Bells*.

I offer her the crook of my elbow as we make our way to the rink's exit, but before stepping off the ice, she stops me. "Okay, wait, I want to see if I can do it on my own." I admire her gumption, knowing how palpable her fear still is.

She takes off toward the middle of the rink, where there's no wall to grab for safety, and I watch in awe as she glides gracefully, confidently. I begin to grasp how she handles running a billion-dollar company every day. She grasps how to coexist with her own fear.

I'm watching with admiration as she turns and waves at me proudly from across the rink. She begins skating back toward me... disastrously crossing paths with a hulking 200-pound ice hockey player I went to school with.

I skate as fast as possible to where she's laying on the ice, shooting daggers at the lug who smashed into her. I offer my hand and pull her up as she winces.

"Are you okay? Should we go to the hospital?" I ask urgently.

She shakes her head but flinches as we skate to the exit. "No hospital but... ice?" Her eyes flit away for a moment, then draw back to mine. "My hotel has an ice machine."

"Let's go then," I say, choosing not to interrogate the inherent acceptance that wherever we go next, we are going together.

MY KEY CARD beeps us into the hotel room as Jo keeps me balanced on my good leg, her other hand armed with a bag full of ice from the machine down the hall. She swings open the door and I hobble inside.

I wince as I sit on my bed. I knew I probably shouldn't have tried ice skating for the first time at the ripe old age of thirty-six, but I couldn't resist Jo's enthusiasm, nay *need*, to fulfill my Big Bird dreams. I've had a lot of people make grand gestures for me over the years, but nothing has ever been so personal and special.

She hands me the bag of ice which I put on my rear, then walks over to the kitchenette to fill a glass of water.

"Do you have painkillers somewhere?" she asks.

"Toiletry bag by the sink," I tell her, desperate enough for Advil not to hesitate about her rummaging through my jumble of meds and tampons.

She brings me two pills, then offers me the water, practically raising it to my lips herself. She's babying me, which I would have listed as a top tier ick up until this very moment. Her overbearing care and concern wraps me in a warm cocoon where I barely need to think at all.

"Do you want the TV on or off?" she asks, her voice laced with concern as she scans for the remote.

"No TV."

Jo looks around the room, at a loss as to her next task.

"Come sit," I tell her. "You've done enough."

She sits.

"Thank you," I say.

"You're welcome."

We sit in silence, her leg a millimeter away from mine. I wonder if her mind is clouded with dirty thoughts about her previous display of artistry between my legs, or if it's just me. Being here in a hotel room, on a bed together, after she took care of my every need like no one has before... I can't stop thinking about how easy it would be to slip back into our sensual dance.

I hold my breath, waiting for her to challenge me like she did before. But she doesn't.

So I go in on my own. I lean toward her lush lips, taking in the freckles dabbling her skin, beckoning me like an astronomer to the stars.

The kiss is electric, sending sparks through my body. Jo responds by parting her lips to allow my tongue entrance. Our bodies have been waiting for this moment, for the connection we're finally allowing ourselves to have.

Jo's hands slide up my sides, her fingers tracing the curve of my spine. I moan into her mouth, her touch like a brand on my skin.

Breaking the kiss, I whisper, "Lie down," my voice brimming with need.

Jo lays back on the bed and I kneel over her, straddling her thighs. My bruise throbs, but the pain is distant, overshadowed by the fire burning within me. I lower myself onto her, the softness of her breasts pressing against mine as I align our hips.

Jo's hands cup my face, pulling me down for another searing

kiss. This time, I grind my hips against hers, eliciting a gasp from her lips. The sound fuels my arousal, making me want to push harder, faster. But I hold back, wanting to savor every moment of this encounter.

"Fuck, Ava," she murmurs against my lips.

I press my forehead against hers. "Touch me," I beg. "I need you."

Jo doesn't hesitate. She slides one hand between us, her fingers finding the waistband of my pants. With a deft movement, she unbuttons them and tugs them down, along with my underwear. I lift my legs, shaky with pleasure, and let her remove them completely before settling back down on her.

I'm bare to her now, and her eyes darken with lust. She runs her fingers along my inner thighs, causing me to shiver.

"So beautiful," she whispers, her fingers brushing against my aching clit. I arch my back, moaning at the sensation.

Jo shifts beneath me, lifting her knee and positioning it between my legs. I adjust myself, pressing my wetness against the hard muscle of her thigh. The friction is exquisite, and I roll my hips, grinding against her in search of more pressure.

"That's it, baby," Jo encourages, her voice dripping with desire. "Ride my thigh. Feel how good it can be."

The dirty talk sends a thrill through me, and I pick up the pace, rocking against her with increasing urgency. Jo's fingers return to my clit, circling it in slow, deliberate strokes. The dual stimulation is almost too much to bear, and I cry out, my body trembling with the effort of holding back my orgasm.

"Come for me, Ava," Jo commands, her voice low and rough. "Let go. Show me how much you like it."

Those words are enough to push me over the edge. My body tenses, and I scream into her shoulder as wave after wave of ecstasy crashes over me. Jo keeps her fingers moving, riding out my orgasm with me until I collapse on top of her, face buried in her neck.

As my consciousness resurfaces, I mumble, "Your turn."

She pulls her head back from me, eyes darkening. "Oh yeah?"

I nod, my desire winning a battle within me against self-doubt. "Show me what you like."

Without hesitation, Jo flips us over, positioning herself above me. Her eyes are wild with passion, her hair falling forward to frame her face.

She reaches down, guiding my hand to her soaked pussy.

I slip my fingers inside her, mimicking the rhythm her own fingers had used on me.

Jo moans, her head lolling back as she begins to ride my hand. "Yes," she hisses. "Fuck, yes. Like that."

I curl my fingers, searching for that elusive spot that will drive her over the edge. When I find it, Jo jerks, her entire body tensing.

"Oh God, Ava," she cries out. "Right there. Don't stop. Please, don't stop."

I don't. I keep moving my fingers, my thumb circling her clit in time with my thrusts. Jo's moans grow louder, her body shaking with the force of her impending climax.

"Come for me, Jo," I urge, my voice hoarse with exertion. "Let me see you come."

Her response is immediate. She throws her head back, her walls clenching around my fingers as she comes apart beneath me. I continue to stroke her, milking every last drop of pleasure from her orgasm until she collapses on top of me, breathing heavily.

For several minutes, we lie there in sated silence, hearts pounding in unison. The moment I catch my breath, I slide up onto my elbow so I can kiss her more, but I'm halted by her finger on my lips.

"We have to talk about this," she whispers. Her stare burns me up from the tips of my toes to the backs of my ears.

"About what?" I avoid.

She laughs a little tiredly. "About what we're doing."

I get the rare urge to shrink in the face of her directness but I try not to show it. "We definitely should," I say with false confidence.

"Great." She looks at me a bit challengingly. "So what are your KPIs for this project?" She gestures between the two of us and I laugh, trying to ease the tight knot that winds up in my belly.

It's hard to see any real path forward for us, despite how much my body wants it. And I can't ask her for the type of patience I'd require to figure any of it out. I try several times to open my mouth and give her an answer, but I find myself mute.

Finally, I blurt out, "Help me out here. I'm not sure what to say or how to say it."

I sense I've said something wrong but it's lost on me as Jo's expression shutters ever so slightly.

"I think we should keep reasonable expectations," she says. "Let's enjoy the time we have, this week together, without pressure. This is all so new for you."

Right. Jo probably doesn't want to be with someone so inexperienced long-term. Which makes sense. It hurts a bit, but it's the truth. I can't knock her for it. If this is what Jo wants, then I'll take what she's giving. I don't have a way to offer her more than that anyway; my life is entirely too complicated.

"Sounds good to me," I say, slipping my mouth guard in. *I'm gonna need it tonight.*

CHAPTER 26
JO

AVA'S GONE before I wake up alone in her hotel room. Even though this time there's a text saying she had a Board call, it still gnaws at my lingering tenderness from our first night together. Last night was incredible, and yet I'm slightly empty in the harsh winter light of the morning. To be so in sync with someone in bed like that, even when the things we were doing together weren't particularly inventive or novel, is blowing my mind.

I'm not saying I'm a Casanova, as Ava so rudely christened me during our interview, but I've romped around and had my fun. And I know I'm slightly pussy-blinded when I say this, but I've never experienced the literal force field of lust and sensation that dances in and around me when Ava and I are naked together.

Touching her, her body suctioning my fingers deeper, her mouth on my nipples, sucking tentatively, I felt complete in those moments. It's only now, alone in her bed, that the hangover of that intensity sets in.

Did I truly not learn my lesson from the devastation of my romance with Wynnie? The aftershocks of her betrayal have played out in my love life to this day. It's a humiliating signature that I seem to only be interested in pursuing the affections of women who can never fully be with me.

So what exactly am I doing right now? I'm fully aware that I am once again someone's secret, no matter how much sense it makes to protect Ava and how deeply entangled my own fate is in this decision.

On top of that, I can't deny that my fear of rejection won out over being totally honest about my feelings last night. Her uncertainty when I asked what we were doing cemented for me that the deeper magnetic pull I have toward her is one-sided, and I scrambled in the moment to preserve my own dignity. *One week*. I try to imbue the shortness of our time together with some positivity.

In the least Freudian way possible, I wind up thinking about my dad. He loved to preserve magic, that's why he loved photography. He was all about capturing fleeting moments, and his early death further punctuated for me the motif of his entire life: nothing can last forever, so you have to treasure it while you have it. Ava is a fleeting moment, and if I can stay present right now, maybe the echo of this finite week can carry me for the rest of my life without her.

I sneak out of the hotel and call George for a ride home. Entering the backhouse, I go straight to the kitchen to scramble eggs in my cast iron when my phone lights up with a text from Jamal: FUGLY SWEATER PARTY TONIGHT 8PM! DIRTY SANTA–BRING A GIFT, GET A GIFT. +1S WELCOME (+2 FOR THROUPLES).

I'm excited–Jamal and Ian throw great parties–but my anticipation abruptly subsides as I realize Ava won't be able to come with me. Given our limited time together, I won't be attending either, so I tap out a regretful response to Jamal.

He calls me immediately.

"Hey," I sigh.

He tsks. "Jolene Bean, what's going on? Fugly Sweater Party is your *thing*!"

I debate what's appropriate to share with him. I can trust Jamal with anything, but on principle I would never out anyone. "Listen, I need your discretion with what I'm about to tell you."

Jamal turns serious. "Yes of course, I'm listening and my lips are sealed."

"There's a plus one I want to bring, but I don't think they'll be able to join me unless there's a no-phone, no-photos policy. And it's super unfair to ask that of you, and the other guests, especially on such short– "

"I'm gonna stop you right there. It's a done deal. We'll take phones at the door and tell folks ahead of time."

"You really don't have to do this."

He shushes me. "Our parties are a safe space for every guest. No one needs to document. If it's okay with you, I'll keep my phone on me in case of an emergency, but you have my word."

"I still don't know if they'll be comfortable, but I'll keep you posted on what they say."

"Anything for you, doll. Kisses."

We sign off and I eat my eggs, a pit in my stomach as I think about bringing up the party to Ava. Will my invitation push her over the edge? Will she be disrespected by the mere suggestion? Will she think I don't get the gravity of her need for privacy? Why does everything always feel like my fault, by default? Freud would have something to say about that, too.

Ava breezes in around one p.m., freshly showered and done with her work calls. Between her ice-skating injury and our late night, I'm amazed she's still glowing with a pep in her step. I hope I'm not about to bring her down.

"The Board said the Gramsta series is performing well, and I hyped them up about the caliber of copy we're about to write for the website!"

She strides up to me, shamelessly eyeing my tits poking out of my tight white sleeveless tank. Yes, I wore it for that exact reason, and yes, I will put on a sweater if I have to leave the warmth of my backhouse.

"Did you miss them?" Her cheeks flush. I pull her toward me by the hips and gently tease her ear with my tongue. "You were such a good girl last night," I whisper.

She shivers in my arms. "You liked it."

I nod softly against the top of her head. "Mhmm."

She pushes away from me, eyes flashing with indignation. "*You* are a siren, and I am a copywriting sailor who's about to get lost at sea!"

I smirk. "You wanna roleplay?"

"Oh my g–I mean yes, but no! We can't right now." She's flustered, and that's all I need for the moment.

I throw my hands up. "Aye aye, captain! Let's write some copy."

For the next few hours, we pore over the website until 'photography' stops looking like a real word. Between discussions of fonts and photo placements, the party nudges at me, a decision waiting to be made.

We take a break and I brew espresso for us in my moka pot. Sipping beside each other on the couch, our thighs touching, I broach the subject.

"So listen. There's something I want to talk to you about."

Her face drops and I have to backpedal.

"Nothing serious, truly, like the least serious thing in the world, in fact. You don't have to go with me, like I probably wasn't even gonna go if you weren't here, and it's dumb."

She raises her eyebrows. "Okay, I'm no longer scared, I'm simply dying of curiosity."

"I already called him and he said no phones, no photos, and

everyone is gonna cooperate, they're all queer and super socially conscious and good people," I stumble over my words.

"I think you skipped over telling me what's happening, babe." It's a sarcastic endearment, but I can't help savoring it.

I stare into my espresso.

"Jamalishavingafuglysweaterpartyandmaybeyoucancomeitstonight?"

"A party? Like a house party?"

I nod.

Ava pauses, her pen hovering over her notepad. The hesitation hangs in the air. "And you think it'd be safe? For me?"

"Jamal gave me his word. So I want to believe it will be." Even though I'd like to give her every reassurance, I can't gloss over the inherent risk.

She mulls it over, then gives a decisive nod. "Okay. Let's do it."

I brighten. "Really? You want to go?"

"Well," she says slowly, "I do have the perfect sweater."

Cash Money Reindeer will be a hit.

CHAPTER 27
AVA

JO and I aren't holding hands, but the electricity between us is palpable. I get stares from queer folks in all sorts of vulgar sweaters as we walk through the packed home's wreathed door. The gaydar in Harmony Springs has already been upgraded from 5G and I'm just booting up.

Music rattles the little house as we squeeze through the hallway. Coming to terms with my sexuality in this wholly immersive context was not on my Christmas bingo card. I can handle brutal back-to-back Board meetings with ease, but being perceived like this? It's completely overwhelming.

Jo waves hello to friends as I head straight to the punch bowl for a distraction from the gay blizzard in my brain.

"You good?" Jo sneaks up behind me in her 'I Prefer Mrs. Claus' sweater.

"Um, yeah," I lie. I definitely can't go into this right now, and even more definitely, not with her. "Lots of people here. You know them all?"

I nervously sip my drink and take in all the personalities that surround us. People wearing humping reindeer jumpers and 'Merry Dickmas' pullovers–so different from the crowd of buttoned up executives I'm used to. For some reason, all of them being so vibrantly themselves throws me. I'm usually the one that's boldly confident, but now I'm questioning if that was even real confidence in the first place.

"Mostly," she chuckles. "If you haven't figured it out, Harmony Springs is a small town." She smiles flirtily at me, but I've nearly forgotten the question I asked. I'm so in my head.

Jo senses something's off and nails me right in the anxiety.

"Being around total strangers isn't always easy, but..." She mulls over her next words. "These are your people now."

And without having to go into it, she soothes me. *These are my people now.* They've all had to experience what I'm going through at this exact moment. Their eyes are not ogling, they're *knowing,* and they have done nothing but accept me during my time in Harmony Springs thus far.

I take a breath. The anxiety fades. For the first time tonight, the waves of the Worry Sea part, and I see the party for what it is: a gay. Fucking. Rager.

After nearly an hour of meeting Jo's (and now my) friends, we all sit in a circle in Jamal's living room.

"Let Dirty Santa commence!" he shouts, awarded with hoots and hollers.

One by one, people unwrap the silliest of Christmas presents, from a lava lamp to a basket full of various Japanese Kit-Kat flavors.

On my turn, I pick a thick, circular package. I assume it's a hefty cookie tin due to its shape, but what I get is so much better. A sleeve of ornaments featuring the faces of several gay icons, including the Babadook.

"I guess I'll have to get a tree for my hotel room," I laugh.

"Not so fast," a tipsy Jo says, taking the ornaments from my hand. "I'm stealing for my turn!"

"How dare you!" I joke, as I go to pick another present. This time I opt for something more traditionally shaped, slightly bigger than a jewelry box. I rip off the shiny paper and my face instantly turns as red as the present itself.

Beneath its disguise of reindeer wrapping is a Santa hat dildo, equipped with a vibrating head and guaranteed G-spot stimulation (or your money back).

I turn to Jo, who bursts into laughter.

"There's always one every year, and this year, it's all yours."

It's past one a.m. when we leave Jamal's, linked arm-in-arm, meandering our way down the shadowy street toward my rental.

There's a giddiness bubbling inside of me that I haven't experienced in... possibly ever? It's childish and naive and *wonderful*. I slide into the car, my knee bouncing up and down, no longer able to channel the woozy glee into my walking. Jo rests a hand to still me, and sparks race up my thigh. *Who needs a treadmill when you've got this?*

"That was fun," I murmur, sensing the curve of Jo's smile in the dark.

"I thought you might enjoy yourself." Her eyes catch mine, her lashes casting fluttering shadows across her cheeks.

Caught in her gaze, the energy in the car amplifies, as if a magnetic current charges the space between us. I can't help the sharp little exhale that escapes my tightening chest.

Jo's eyes take on a mischievous glint. "Could you help me find something in the back real quick?" She opens her door.

"What do you–"

She gives me the eyes.

"Right. Yes." *Duh, Ava. This is flirting.*

As soon as we slip into the backseat, Jo leans in, her lips grazing mine softly. Her touch is electric, sending shivers down my spine.

"Did you find what you were looking for?" I whisper.

For a split second, I can tell by her face that she's forgotten the pretext with which she used to lure me back here. But once my meaning registers, her deer-in-the-headlights gaze transforms into a coy grin.

"Not sure yet..." She comes back in for a kiss, and her roaming hand freezes on the box in my coat pocket. "Is that a Santa Hat dildo or are you happy to see me?"

I laugh. "Can it be both?"

The feeling I have, here in this cramped backseat, windows fogging up, local photographer using her teeth to tear into the elaborate packaging of a sex toy we're about to use, is happiness. And I haven't felt it like this in a very long time.

KEYWORDS: *photography, studio, portraits.*

As Ava and I sit in the quiet of my living room the next day, I watch her squint at her laptop screen. She taps away at the keyboard with a list of important phrases to tailor our marketing to. Her focus is admirable, but I notice the tell-tale signs of strain–a slight furrow in her brow and a frequent rub of her temples. We've spent the better part of the day deep-diving into SEO, a topic she handles like second nature. To me, it's dense as fog.

"We should take a break," I suggest as Ava massages her forehead.

Her eyes glimmer gratefully. "That sounds good, actually."

I think for a moment, aiming to find an activity that can refresh us, somewhere people aren't immersed in discussing backlinks and keywords. "Wanna go to Sweet Foundations? They've got the best hot chocolate in town, and a truly impressive array of gingerbread house-making supplies. It's like a paint and sip but… way better." Off her apprehensive face, I add, "It's good Christmas PR, too, a squeaky clean establishment."

"That sounds perfect then," she says, closing her laptop with a click.

. . .

The air at Sweet Foundations is filled with the scent of holiday spices and icing, packed with confectionary architects working on holiday creations. Leah Betteny, the shop's gregarious owner and de facto mother figure of every foundling that moves to Harmony Springs, bounds over to welcome us.

"Oh, Jolene! Wonderful to see you! And who might this be?" she beams at Ava.

"Ava. Your place is... incredible." She gestures around the shop, whose walls are stacked to the ceiling with bins of candy embellishments for the gingerbread houses.

Leah holds her hand over her heart. "You're too kind. Come in, come in. Make yourselves at home and make yourselves *a* home!"

She tours us around the space, pointing out root beer flavored shingles and every type of chocolate door imaginable, then hands us each an empty cookie tin.

"Fill these up with your accessories. The slabs of gingerbread are already on the tables! I'll be working on my gingerbread menorah over there if you have any questions."

Soon we've filled our tins to the brim with candy embellishments and made our way to the table. Ava lays out several large sheets of sugar glass.

"What's the vision here?" I inquire.

"Minimalist. Modern."

I snort. "What is it they say about glass houses?"

"I think mine can withstand being pelted with a few gumdrops," she retorts.

Ava lines up the sugar glass wall panels atop her gingerbread base. "It's all about the light, you should know that," Ava replies, not looking up from her work. "If I were to build my own house, it'd be something like this. Lots of light, open spaces... not much on the inside to hold me down."

I watch her steadily pipe frosting to connect the walls. "Don't you own, like, a million properties?"

"I've got a real estate portfolio, yes," she laughs. "But honestly, I travel so much for work that there's not anywhere I truly feel at home. When I'm not on the road, I sleep at the Gramsta offices more than my own place."

"That sounds dramatic, except I suspect your Gramsta office is nicer than most people's apartments."

Ava gets a dreamy twinkle in her eye. "I do have a steam shower. That's the base of my hierarchy of needs."

"As long as your needs are being met," I tell her dryly. I begin to slice up a sheet of gingerbread and lay my makeshift logs atop each other, caulked by chocolate frosting. We spend a few minutes working on our homes in silence.

"A log cabin?" she asks.

"Simple. Quiet. Not much on the inside to hold me down."

"Hmm," she muses. "It's looking like you forgot to cut out windows."

"I did indeed."

Her glass house has at least seven walls in place and she's just finished hand-tiling a jacuzzi bathtub with Red Hots.

"You may have hired a better architect than I did," I concede.

She smiles. "I think your log cabin that lets no light in will taste better, though."

"That's very generous of you to say."

Ava cuts an arch into the top of double white chocolate doors for her entryway. "Is it nice living in the backhouse, with your mom right there? You seem so close."

I bite back a laugh because I can tell she's serious. And then I check myself because my family *is* close, and even though they drive me insane, we love each other and we show up when it matters. It's sobering to think that Ava doesn't have that at all.

"It has its moments," I say. "It was the right thing for me to do in this season of my life. But do I look forward to having my own home one day, on some actual property, with some kids and dogs and cats and chickens and cows running around? 100%."

She's cutting out tiny panes of glass to fit into the arched double doors, but I see her concentration falter when I mention kids.

"I've never been drawn to parenthood," she says. "I don't want to put the burden of my existence on another person."

I nod, not wanting to say the wrong thing when she's opening up in a deeper way.

"But sometimes I consider the way I've mentored Max, how protective I am of them, and I think maybe I wouldn't be such a bad mom."

As she clips out windows, one of the glass panes flies across the table at me. I pick it up and help her press it into the final spot on the chocolate door.

"I think the fact that you're worried about messing up your kids is actually a good sign. And it's obvious to anyone who sees you and Max together that they don't only care for you, they feel safe with you."

She's concentrating heavily now on placing the doors upright, but when I sneak a peek at her face, I catch a glimmer of wistful pride.

"I face a lot of people every day, but I live my personal life in relative solitude, aside from Max," she states, not moving her eyes away from her foyer construction. "It's hard to trust."

I get it. After seeing how she's had to hide, even in Harmony Springs, I sympathize. It's like having to be in the closet for every aspect of her life, not just her sexuality.

"It's been... new for me. Witnessing your life in this small town," she continues. "Everyone knowing each other. Caring *too much*."

"Do you think you'd enjoy living here?" I blurt out, immediately regretting the implications. "I don't mean, like, not about– I'm curious if that newness is a negative or a positive."

"It's not good or bad. Just different. A new way of being that I hadn't considered." Ava's eyes heat up. "Sometimes newness is... really good."

I flush.

Leah comes out to check on us, complimenting our creations. Ava's gingerbread estate next to my own is equivalent to comparing the Mona Lisa with the moon emoji. But Leah is equally admiring of both, because that is her nature.

"I'll grab you two a base so you can drive them home," Leah says, bustling off to the back.

Ava glances at her delicate sugar mansion, then over at my sturdy, old-fashioned cabin. "Are these gonna keep? What do we do with them?"

"I've got plenty of room in my fridge," I assure her.

"Funny way to ask me back to your place, but sure." She glances around the room quickly, checking if anyone caught her comment. No one did, but the moment stings.

Leah walks back out. "And what is a gingerbread home without a gingerbread family?!" she says, adding little people to our properties.

We slide our houses onto the base, neighbors until the cookies get stale or we demolish them with our appetites.

When we get to the backhouse, I make space in my fridge for our gingerbread creations. But of course, Ava's mansion takes up all the room, so I leave my cabin out on the counter.

"Mine can weather the unrefrigerated storm; yours can have a cool spot to spend the night."

"Can *I* have a cool spot to spend the night?" She bites her bottom lip, and my mind goes blank.

Keywords: taste, lick, devour.

OUR AUDIENCE of gingerbread people had no idea what was in store for them this evening. We crash into Jo's bed, unable to keep our hands off each other for a moment longer. The passion is as fierce as before, but there's something even more behind the hungry kisses Jo peppers on my neck. We connected on a deeper level tonight and I fear there's no going back.

I'm developing big feelings for Jo, unlike any I've had before, but this is brand new territory for me. Now that I know what she went through with her ex, I don't want to burden her with my indecisiveness about my burgeoning sexuality. I always thought I was straight by default. But am I? I pull off her jeans, her warmth on my fingertips—*nope, definitely not straight.*

I turn to the gingerbread house next to me and take a pass through the icing with my finger. I draw along her stomach, down to her hips, kissing the sweet sugar from her even sweeter skin. I make my way along her hip bone, down her thigh, as I continue to touch her over her gray panties. I want her. I want all of her.

I marvel at how natural being with her has become. Inexperience is not typically something I'm burdened with. The night of our first encounter, I was blind, stumbling in the dark, trying to follow her lead. Yet in such a short time, my night vision has fully come into focus. Reading her body is as innate as my own heartbeat, currently thrumming in my ears.

I trace my fingers along the edge of her panties, heat radiating from her core. My breaths come faster, syncopated with hers as I slowly slide the fabric aside, revealing her glistening flesh.

I have a realization and pout.

Jo sits up. "What is it?" she asks softly, her finger tracing my swollen lips. Her immediate concern warms something deep within me.

"I wish I had my Santa hat right now so I could return the favor for last night."

"Good news." Jo crawls over to the dresser drawer. When she pops it open, I laugh. She's got her own Santa hat dildo, along with jingle bell Venus balls and a reindeer-handled leather whip.

"You have no idea how relieved I am that someone else got the sex toy this year," she confides.

I dig through her trove of toys, examining the whip before putting it back. "We're gonna have to report Santa to HR for hitting his employees."

"Yes, Madame CEO." She salutes me.

"So which is your favorite?" I pry.

"Whichever one you're using on me," she grins.

I pull out a Hitachi Magic Wand. *This* I know how to use.

"After all your time in Harmony Springs, you still have something against Christmas?" she tuts.

"Shhhh," I say, turning the vibrator on. It sounds like it has the horsepower of my Audi. "Think you can handle it?" I ask slyly.

"We should do some research and find out."

I gently push her back into the pillows and tug her panties off, pushing her thighs apart to give me the best access. I caress her pussy lips with one hand, while the other balances the vibrator on her clit. Her body tightens as the vibrations pulse against her, clutching the sheets beneath her in an effort to hold back the wave of pleasure building inside her. I watch, transfixed, as her eyes glaze over, hips bucking.

"Ava..." she moans, and a shudder of pleasure passes through me from hearing my name on her lips.

I slip two fingers inside her and increase the pressure of the Wand, adjusting the angle so I can determine the spot where the sensations are most intense. Jo's moans grow louder, desperate as she tightens around my digits. I'm on the right track.

She begins to writhe and her knuckles whiten from grasping the sheets so tightly, so I crank up the intensity of the vibrator once more. Jo's body responds, her fingers digging into my shoulder as she struggles to stay grounded.

"More..." she begs, her voice breaking.

I obey, pressing the vibrator more firmly against her as her hips grind against the pressure. Her breaths come in short, sharp bursts, each one laced with pleasure. I can sense the tension building in her muscles, the way her legs tremble uncontrollably.

Suddenly, Jo cries out, her body tensing as an orgasm rips through her. Her back arches off the bed, her toes curling as waves of pleasure wash over her. I keep the vibrator pressed firmly against her, riding out the storm until she collapses onto the bed, utterly spent.

For a moment, it's silent, save for the buzzing of the vibrator still pressed against Jo's sensitive skin. She lies there, panting heavily, chest rising and falling with each breath. I watch her, mesmerized by the sight of her completely undone, her vulnerability on full display.

Slowly, I pull the vibrator away and her eyes flutter open.

"It's like you can read my body," she says softly.

In my mind, I make a promise: I'll read every last chapter we have left.

I WAKE up with a sugar hangover and Ava tangled in my arms, her head on my chest, fast asleep. I'm replaying our night together obsessively in my head. It doesn't escape me that Ava continues to take an increasingly active role in our trysts. She *wants* to be the purveyor of my pleasure. The heat in her eyes as she brought me to see stars was palpable. The way she moaned with me, like my completion was equally arousing to her, stirs something deep within me. The intensity of her desire is bewitching; when we're naked together, I see a completely different Ava than the rest of the world does, and that privilege is intoxicating.

The vibration of my phone on the nightstand cuts through the morning quiet, and Ava stirs on my chest. I pick up the phone–it's Mikey.

"Jo? Your chariot awaits!" he chirps, despite the ungodly hour.

"Be there soon," I croak, hanging up.

Ava stirs again, slowly lifting her head to look up at me with glazed eyes. "Mm. Morning?"

I kiss her forehead. "Morning, beautiful."

She snuggles closer. "Sleep more?"

I shake my head. "Chrissy is ready at the shop. I've gotta go pick her up, but you can sleep in here if you like."

She inhales deeply, then forces herself to sit up beside me. "No, no, I'm awake! Let's go get our girl."

Her ability to draw from some hidden reserve of kinetic energy within even at seven a.m. is impressive and I tell her so.

She's humble for once. "It's a blessing and a curse. I'm an over-committer."

If only you could over-commit to me.

Mikey waves us over as we pull into the lot. Max, who possesses the ability to apparate to wherever Ava needs them, no matter the hour, is already standing in the lot. Chrissy's been washed (for $12k, I would sure hope so) and she gleams in the wintery morning sun.

We thank Mikey, and I hand off the rental keys to Max.

Ava and I board Chrissy. I sit in the fixed driver's seat, leaning the chair all the way back and up again, pleased.

With a turn of the key, her engine roars to life, and I test the heat. It blasts full-force, better than I can ever remember it functioning.

"It's perfect," I say. "Thank you."

Ava waves off my gratitude, but I can tell she's pleased. "Don't thank me yet, we've got our work cut out for us."

Chosen Family Festival preparations are in full swing, with banners hung across every major intersection of town. The festive spirit has amped up to a level that only Harmony Springs can achieve.

Ava watches in awe from the passenger seat. "I thought Harmony Springs had maxed out on Christmas spirit, but this festival cranks it to eleven."

I feel a swell of hometown pride. "I've been trying to tell you, CFF isn't any old festival. We go all out. It's like Christmas on steroids with a splash of glitter."

"More than a splash," she laughs.

Pulling into my driveway, I park Chrissy. Everything back in its right place, for now.

Max and Emma pull up, hopping out of the rental car. Max, ever the organized one, pulls out a list that's been color-coded and prioritized.

"Alright, team," Max starts, unfolding their master plan. "We've got a lot to cover. First, Handy Hardware is making their delivery in one hour. Emma and I will handle the installations and painting."

"We will?" Emma quips, glancing up at Max. There's totally a vibe between them, but I'm too caught up in avoiding my own romantic analysis to dwell on it.

Max clears their throat and looks at me and Ava. "Meanwhile, you two need to sort out the photo packages so you can design the flyers and sandwich board."

I salute them, the giddiness of what we're prepping for starting to catch up with me.

Ava and I settle at the wooden table in my backyard, the crisp winter air moderated by the warmth radiating from the outdoor heater. Snow blankets the ground around us, lending a quiet hush to our oasis.

"Max slipped me a package that arrived at the hotel this morning," she tells me, reaching into her work bag. She pulls out a recognizable white box containing the latest Macbook Pro.

"You haven't replaced your slide rule yet," Ava says as she places it on the table between us. "I set up unlimited cloud storage for you, so all your photoshoots can be permanently backed up."

"Ava, this is... I don't know what to say. Thank you," I manage. I'm not gonna lie, I could get used to being spoiled.

"Just doing what I promised. Making sure you have the best tools at your disposal."

My smile masks some of the sadness that bubbles up. "You're turning out to be the best tool at my disposal." *For one more week*, but I don't say that part.

I boot up the new computer, finding she's already installed CaptureOne and every other type of software I could possibly need.

"Where should we start?" I notice myself growing concerningly comfortable following Ava's lead with the business. Her presence enables me to excel in the areas of the truck where I truly shine. I'm trying not to think about taking those other duties back on once she leaves.

Ava shifts into what I've come to recognize as her Gramsta mode–sharp, strategic, and jargony.

"Whenever I prepare for a major event at Gramsta," Ava starts, her eyes scanning the horizon as if visualizing every detail, "I focus on the essence, the core message we want to convey. It's about defining that golden nugget, one single word that encapsulates all of it."

"Like a keyword?" The headache of yesterday's SEO rears its head.

She laughs. "Sort of. This is more in the Jo-zone, I promise. How do you want people to feel when they get their photos taken on the truck? Don't think too hard about it; speak from the heart."

Oh, if I were speaking from the heart, I'd be saying something very different.

"My dad always said it was important the camera captured perfect moments in real time, not just a perfect picture to look at later."

She nods. "That's a good baseline for the atmosphere we're

trying to build inside the truck tomorrow. That can inform what our photo package offering will be." She mulls it over. "Keep talking about your dad."

"He wanted Chrissy to be a place where people felt happy, and accepted, and safe to be themselves."

"Happy. Accepted. Safe. Build from there," she urges.

I'm not sure what witchcraft she's performing, coaxing this supposed golden nugget from me, but suddenly the word materializes.

"Belonging," I tell her. "That's our keyword. For the festival, but also for the truck as a whole. Anyone who comes inside should have a sense of belonging."

Ava's eyes light up. "I told you you'd be good at this exercise!"

I flush at her praise.

She steals the computer from me and begins typing in a Word document. I try to peer over her shoulder and she pushes me off. "Patience!"

She sets the laptop aside and clasps her hands. "Sharks, are you ready to hear my pitch?"

"If I am the plural sharks you are addressing, then yes, by all means."

"What if we extend that sense of belonging to the entire town during the festival? Imagine a massive love letter to Harmony Springs."

I lean in, caught up in her enthusiasm. "Tell me more."

"Anyone who donates can have their picture taken during the festival," she explains. "We then composite all those photos onto a massive Harmony Springs banner that we donate to City Hall for them to display, with each colorful pixel a photograph of community members."

"That's brilliant," I say, impressed by her ability to transform my golden nugget into a literal community movement. "And we could offer additional prints of the final banner for purchase."

"Exactly," Ava nods. "It's by the community, for the community, and Chrissy is at the center of facilitating the project, so everyone gets to know what she's about."

"Well, as the spokeswoman of all of the sharks in the tank today, I would like to fully vest in your proposal. With Gramsta funding, of course," I add. She grins.

As we plot out our designs to advertise the Harmony Springs love letter, a twinge of sadness strikes me amidst the excitement. It's become apparent that Ava has not only embraced the spirit of this town but also the essence of my father's truck. I'm no scholar of the transitive property, but to me, that means she understands me just as deeply. Normally, such a profound connection would terrify me, but right now, I'm grappling with a different fear–the daunting prospect of becoming unrecognizable to myself once she's gone.

WE ARRIVE at the fairground gates before dawn, a light dusting of snow on the ground. Jo pulls the truck into our assigned spot and I help her set up. Emma and Max show up with rainbow Christmas donuts from another stand as we wait for the gates to officially open. The event seems alarmingly low-key, but Jo keeps promising me, "You'll see, you'll see."

Max sets up tripods, preparing to document the day's success. But so far... there's nothing to capture.

At 8:59 a.m., I glance at my watch, anticipating the crowd that's supposedly on its way. I try to tamp down the gnawing anxiety that all we've worked for currently hangs in the balance. If today doesn't go well, my reputation will be shot and I quite literally will never be able to show my face at Gramsta HQ again. *No pressure.*

Nine a.m. rolls around and it's still quiet.

"I thought you said there was an early rush?"

"They may be running late," Jo replies.

I tap my toe, nervous that my big push to get us in here was for naught. Jo had to flirt with Wynnie for nothing, and I had to witness it. And all the renovations... Before I can go deeper into my spiral, Max pulls me out.

"Can you hear that?"

At first, I hear nothing. But the more I strain, I begin to hear singing.

Christmas carols seep into the air, featuring harmonies of at least ten variations. I turn to Max, my fellow carol hater, stunned. I've never heard anything so enchanting.

Through the gates swarms the happiest, gayest, most peaceful *mob* I've ever seen. Hundreds of people walk in together from the main highway, decked out in holiday gear... all holding hands.

Jo must clock my bewilderment because she leans over to my ear as the singing grows. "Welcome to the Chosen Family Festival, Ava." I'm unsure which part gives me more chills.

She takes my hand and smiles. I can't help but smile back.

Several hours later, the party that is the Chosen Family Fest has only amplified. We've ushered hundreds of groups to get their photo taken on the truck by Jo and given out an even greater amount of business cards. My worry that we wouldn't have enough photos to populate the banner seems laughable now. Compliments abound on the new truck interior, from first-timers to old school Harmony Springsers who witnessed the truck when it first began.

"This is the best idea ever!" shouts a kid in glittery antlers.

"Roger would've loved this!" an older woman with rainbow Christmas tree hair exclaims.

"He'd be so proud of you, Jo," says a man who Jo doesn't even know.

She casts me fleeting glances between shots–an acknowledgement of our hard work paying off.

· · ·

The sun fades past the hills and the crowds grow smaller and smaller.

"Is that it?" I ask Emma, ready to pack up from out of the cold.

"Is that *it?!*" she says, bemused. "Did you even do your research, Ava?"

I laugh, because actually, I didn't. For one of the first times I can remember, I didn't do research into what was next. I've been avoiding thoughts of the looming end for Jo and me, and ironically, this evasion has eased my grip on control, not entirely for the worse.

"Caught me," I tell Emma. She's tickled.

"Jo, we'll close up the truck if you want to take Ava."

"Take Ava where?" I ask.

"You'll see," Jo says, grabbing my hand and leading me off the truck.

Jo pulls me across the fairgrounds as I tighten my coat around myself.

"Don't worry, you won't be cold soon."

She picks up the pace to a run as we make our way up an enormous hillside, passing others as we go.

I pant and she cheers me on from ahead, dodging stragglers. "Come on! This hill's got nothing on Ava Garcia-Greene!"

"I'm fit but not *that*–"

I halt mid-sentence, due to the unbelievable view that appears in front of me. The hill was higher up than I realized, and all of Harmony Springs is laid out below us, twinkling in the dusk.

"Wow," I say.

"Just you wait."

I take a moment to soak it all in. Hundreds of people from all different walks of life gather, embracing each other and exchanging gifts.

"Small town life, huh?" I say to Jo.

"Actually, most of these people don't even know each other," she says. "They come from all over the country, the world even, to share in our little found family."

I'm touched by the outpouring of love from total strangers. I've never thought much about my definition of family, but I would have never included this.

It's beautiful.

Almost as beautiful as the firework that lights up the sky in front of me. Max and Emma make their way up behind us, in awe.

"Incredible," Max says as another group of fizzy fireworks goes off.

"It really is." I can't believe where I am. And how little time I have left here. "Mission accomplished, I guess?"

I remember how desperately I wanted to get out of here a week ago, and now I can't even remember why. The Maldives are gorgeous, but they've got nothing on her.

Jo looks back at me, and like she's read my mind says, "Would you join my family for Christmas Eve tomorrow?"

"I've got to pack. To… leave." Saying the word stings.

"Max, you'll pack for Ava, right?"

"I always pack for Ava."

I can't help cracking a smile.

"I would love to join your family for Christmas Eve."

As much as I want to go home with Jo after the festival, I don't let myself. I want her so much it's scary. Alarm bells are going off in my head like some big gay heartbreak warning. *WEE-WOO! You leave soon! WEE-WOO! You can't get any deeper! WEE-WOO! Your heart will perish!*

Yet as I doze off in my hotel room, I can't help but imagine what Christmas Eve with Jo and her family will be like, full of delicious food and storytelling, between little kisses from her sweet lips...

Then like any girl with a crush, my mind wanders further. I imagine a life where I stay in Harmony Springs with Jo and Emma and Max and the truck. We live in a cabin as lovely as Jo's gingerbread house–with windows, of course–and we have dogs and cats and chickens and cows, exactly like she wanted. I even imagine kids for a second. I get to wake up to Jo every day and fall asleep in her arms every night.

But it's all a dream, because despite having infinite access to whatever I can imagine, I can't stay here. This isn't my life. This isn't my home. And Jo isn't mine either.

AFTER DROPPING Ava off at her hotel for the night, I drive Chrissy along the sleepy streets of Harmony Springs, windows down, inhaling the calming crisp cold air mingled with fireplace smoke.

It was both selfish and self-sabotaging to invite her for Christmas Eve. My family will be over the moon to welcome her, and it was meaningful to her to be invited. But at the same time, I question if I'm digging the hole of my heartbreak deeper. The more memories we share, the closer we become, the harder our imminent separation is going to hit me. Yet, I've resigned my heart to total destruction for one more day spent by her side. That's how illogical and all-consuming my emotions toward her have become.

Somehow, going straight home feels defeating. Because once I'm home, I'll go to sleep, and then I'll wake up and it will be the morning of my final day with Ava. Wanting to prolong the inevitable, I drive past my exit and park Chrissy by the stretch of highway off-ramp where the town murals are. I turn off the engine and step out into the freezing night.

I gaze up at Silas in the very first panel. He's a young man, skint and scrappy, eyes wide as he takes in the gold treasure that will change the course of his life. I wonder if he knew that money would corrupt him, and that his corruption would further imprison him in hiding his identity. I wonder what age he figured out he was gay. Did he ever fall in love? Did he ever kiss another man, or did all of his desire stay buried deep within him?

Growing up here, and learning the history over and over in school, Silas seemed to be the villain of the town's origin story. A cautionary tale about what power can and cannot provide you. His redemption came only through his son's noble actions.

But standing here in the middle of the night, staring into the eyes of that scared teenager in the quarry, I am flooded with sadness for Silas. Of course he was desperate to gain some stature and wealth. He started with nothing, even less than nothing if you believe he recognized his queerness early on. He was fighting to belong in the world, but the world offered him the worst versions of belonging. He rejected his son because he was wracked with existential jealousy over Harmony's freedom to choose what he made of his life. But, I realize, given his circumstances and the life he had lived, he chose to do the bravest thing he could allow himself to do by admitting his truth to his heir in the hopes that it would inspire further bravery.

I've spent a long time being furious with the unfairness of what Wynnie put me through. But I hadn't fully digested, until now, that perhaps she, like Silas, was being the bravest she could be. My fury all this time should have been directed toward a world that condones these circumstances where hiding your true self can be life or death, not the victims of that reality. I can't wholly excuse Wynnie hiding her fiance, or ending things the way she did, but I can forgive her for facing a struggle that never should have existed in the first place.

I haven't even broached the subject of Ava's sexuality during our time together. I don't want to put pressure on her to define anything. She claims her precautions in public are about upholding the PR image of the trip, but I've traversed these waters before. I can't help but suspect that those precautions are wrapped up in her fear of being perceived as queer. I can't deny that there is baggage that comes with that, especially for someone of her public stature.

My throat clenches as I consider Ava. I care so deeply for her, and a large part of me wants desperately to divert her entire life path by force, keep her with me, circumstances be damned. But her journey is hers alone, and to commandeer her path is not only implausible, but unfair. She deserves agency. She deserves to choose her life as much as Harmony chose his. And if I can't be a part of it, then that is the life she's choosing and I shouldn't stand in the way.

I nod to Silas. "Take the gold and run with it, buddy. At least you make it onto the gay mural."

I crunch back across the snow to Chrissy, buckling myself into the cushy new driver's seat. I turn the key, and Chrissy rumbles to life beneath me, the familiar hum of her engine filling the air. But as soon as I shift into drive, the truck shudders, a grating, grinding noise cutting through the calm. I press the gas. The engine revs but we're barely moving until suddenly the truck lurches forward.

Then, as quickly as it started, it all stops. The truck shuts off completely, leaving me in an eerie silence. I try the ignition again, but nothing happens.

"Come on, Chrissy, you've got this." I'm running my hands anxiously over the steering wheel, hoping the soothe of age-worn leather will fend off my incoming panic attack. Instead, I have rug burn on my palms as I begin to hyperventilate.

I dial Mikey's number even though it's ten p.m.. His is the singular tow in town.

Thankfully he answers. "Jo? Are you okay?"

"It's Chrissy. I'm stranded by the murals." My voice shakes.

"I'll be right there."

We hang up and I sit numbly in the silence.

Twenty minutes later, Mikey's tow truck pulls up. He climbs out, toolbox in hand, and strides toward me, wrapping me in a tight hug. He doesn't say anything, just holds me for a moment before he walks over to the truck.

"Let's see what we're dealing with here." He opens Chrissy's hood and begins inspecting. I watch anxiously, the cold biting as I wait to hear his prognosis.

After several minutes of poking around and muttering to himself, Mikey straightens up, wiping his hands on his jeans. "Well, Jo, I've got some bad news. It's the transmission–it's completely shot. No quick fixes this time."

"What are my options?" I'm afraid to hear his answer.

Mikey's expression is somber as he leans against Chrissy. "Jo, in my expert opinion, this truck is done. Replacing the transmission, especially with a custom job on a vintage model like this– it's not only expensive, it's a gamble if it'll even take."

The reality sinks in. "How long are we talking if we try to fix it?"

He shakes his head slowly. "Months, easily. But even then, she's a finicky old truck. You might fix the transmission now, but something else will go next. You'll be in a constant cycle of repairs, and depending on the part, fabrication can take a long time for trucks like this."

"Thanks, Mikey," I manage to say, my voice far steadier than I feel. "I guess I have some thinking to do."

"I'll take her to my lot for you," Mikey offers, already moving to prepare the tow. "You take care of the big decisions. I'll handle this. Can I drop you somewhere?"

I shake my head. "I'm gonna make a call."

"I'm so sorry, Jo."

He hitches Chrissy to the back of his truck, and I watch, eyes stinging, as she's carted away.

I hesitate before I press call. Emma is bound to still be awake, and I know she'd come get me in a heartbeat. But I want *her* comfort. Even if it's a fleeting salve.

Ava picks up on the first ring.

"I hope I'm not waking you," I begin.

"What's wrong?"

I'm not sure how she heard it in my voice from that one sentence, but the second she asks, the floodgates open and I'm pressing my fist against my mouth to keep from heaving sobs into the phone.

"Jo?" she asks, concerned, "Are you home? I can be there in ten. Need to get the keys from Max."

"N-not home." I manage to stammer out. "Hold o-on."

I pull the phone away from my ear and drop a pin.

"On my way."

I burst into tears again the minute Ava steps out of the car. She runs up to me, face flooded with worry. "What is this place? Why are you here? Where's Chrissy?"

Ava guides me to the passenger seat, and I sit, shivering, as she walks around the other side of the car. As we wait for the heat to take effect, I quell my crying long enough to relay what happened.

She shakes her head slowly. "It's gonna be okay. We'll figure it out. Let's get you home."

I don't have the energy to tell her that it will never be okay. That Chrissy is a piece of my father, and that this truck dying is a dagger-sharp reminder of the worst loss of my life.

Instead, I let her think that there will be some way to fix this. Better not to devastate her, too, on one of our last nights together.

We drive in silence the rest of the way. When she pulls into the driveway, she turns to me. "I'm coming inside."

When we get to the backhouse, Ava wipes the remaining tears from my cheeks with the hem of her coat.

"Why don't we draw you a hot bath?" There's no room for argument in her voice, only gentle insistence that carries me to the bathroom.

I watch, numb but grateful, as Ava turns on the taps, adjusting the temperature until steam rises in gentle curls from the surface of the water. She adds some of my lavender bath salts, filling the room with their calming scent.

Once satisfied, she turns to me, her hands reaching out to help me out of my clothes. Her touch is careful, reverent, as if she understands that every movement is a piece of the solace I need so desperately tonight.

I sink into the water, the heat enveloping me, soothing the cold that had settled deep in my bones. Ava pulls up a chair beside the tub, her presence a silent pillar of support. I close my eyes, letting the warmth of the bath and her quiet companionship do what they can to ease the jagged edges of my sorrow.

The chair squeaks beside the tub as Ava kneels. I hear the sound of a cap flipping open, followed by her firm, reassuring fingers massaging shampoo into my scalp. Her touch is soothing, each circular motion easing the tension that has built up... and sparking a brand new, much more welcome, breed of tension. All I want right now is for her to help me forget everything.

As she washes the soap out of my hair, I lean back, pushing my breasts out of the water, hoping she'll notice my hardening nipples. I hear her hum a small chuckle, and then her hands glide from my scalp down to my neck, massaging as they go, before slipping into the water to teasingly touch all around my tits without paying attention to the pert rosebuds atop them.

I groan a little, and she shushes me. "Relax. Let me touch you."

I could open my eyes, but I'm enjoying the purity of simply feeling her touch and being subject to her whims without visual warning... something I continue to appreciate when suddenly her mouth descends onto my nipple, suckling gently and toying it with her tongue. I bring my hand up out of the water to play with the neglected nipple as she works over the other one.

Soon her hand splashes into the water further away, and finds its way to my thigh. She pushes my legs apart and the warm water licks up against my spread pussy in the most tantalizing way. I wiggle my hips, trying to entice her to touch me *there* but she takes her time, running her fingernails up and down my thighs and belly until I'm wantonly panting.

When her thumb lands on my clit, she inhales like she won a prize. She rubs it softly in circles, mimicking the patterns her tongue is tracing on my nipple, then dips her other finger into me, pressing upwards from inside.

My orgasm builds as she rubs and fingers me, and I've lost all control of my moans, unable to hold back.

And then my moans are of a much different nature, because suddenly she removes her hands and her mouth from me. My eyes shoot open to find her staring at me, a little dazed, a little nervous.

The orgasm slips away from me, and I struggle to reel in my frustration. It's a good thing I do, because the next words out of her mouth are worth the edging.

"I want to taste you."

I have never exited a steaming lavender-scented bathtub so quickly.

She holds the towel out for me and wraps me up, and we go to the bedroom.

As soon as we're there, I'm holding her face and kissing her deeply while I hastily remove every article of clothing from her perfect, lithe body.

She pulls the towel off of me and points at the pillows, and I lay back for her. She looks me up and down with a raw hunger as she approaches the bed.

And then she's there, on top of me, straddling one of my thighs with her own wet pussy as she kisses her way down my body. Her mouth hovers over my slit and then her tongue laves a flat, wet strip across it, ending at my clit, which she wiggles over, driving me crazy.

She laps at my juices, groaning in satisfaction as she settles over my swollen bud with her lips puckered, sucking gently. She has one hand holding me spread open, and the other testing my entrance, first with one, then two fingers, plunging deep inside me until I'm begging her for a third. Anything to clench onto as my orgasm bursts through me like a wave crashing on the shore, so titanic and earth-shattering that there are aftershocks for a few minutes, all of which she dutifully licks me through.

When I've stopped shaking, I bring her face up to mine and taste myself on her tongue. We grind against each other like teenagers and within minutes, we're cumming together. Of course, then I'm desperate to taste her, too, so I flip her over onto the pillows and take my turn.

I lose track of our orgasms, but the thought weighs heavily on my mind that we're both frantically trying to capture as much of one another as possible, as though that could somehow soften the blow of our impending farewell. As sleep overtakes me, I make a wish that somehow the morning will bring about a brand new reality, one that I can bear.

AS SOON AS I heard Jo's truck was totaled, I was ready to leap into action. It's unfortunate Jo had to lose such an important heirloom, but being the forward-thinker I am, I had an inkling it was going to give out on us at any moment. And as per usual, I was right. Also as per usual, I was prepared.

While Jo sleeps next to me, I sneak a text. 'SEND IT,' I shoot off to Max, whom I also woke up to share the bad news, which in reality is good news, because we get to execute our top secret surprise plan. I can't help but imagine the grin on Jo's face when she sees what I've pulled together for her. Maybe then she will understand how much I care.

At around eleven a.m., Jo wakes up.

"Merry Christmas Eve, Jo," I say, trying to hide my eagerness.

She stretches. "Merry Christmas Eve, I guess," she says with tired eyes.

The empathetic sadness I feel at her gloom must be written all over my face, because I see her work to muster a braver expression.

"No, you know what? Merry Christmas Eve, I *know*." She

leans over and gives me a peck. "Dad wouldn't have it any other way."

There she is.

I go to get dressed, but Jo won't allow it. "Nope, Christmas pajamas *only* at a Fisher Family Christmas event," she instructs, handing me an 'I'm Santa's Favorite' set.

"Anything for you."

We make our way into Carol's living room, everyone's jubilant faces falling as soon as they see Jo's. I explain what happened the night before, that the truck is totaled, and that it's not returning from the mechanic this time.

Carol processes the news, her face hollow, and it strikes me: the truck was their last living piece of Roger, and now that piece is gone.

"We all knew this day would come," Carol says, keeping it together for her girls. She opens her arms to Jo, who snuggles up next to her on the couch.

Lena nods and wipes away a tear as Carol rubs her back with her other hand. "On Christmas Eve of all days," she laughs. "Nice one, Dad."

She sniffs a nose full of snot then stands for a tissue, but winces. "Oof," she grunts. Matt runs to her aid.

"You good?" he asks. "Do we need to go to the hospital?"

She shakes her head. "We don't need to go to the hospital every time I'm in pain."

"Nine months pregnant–you're always in pain," Carol confirms.

Matt hands her a tissue as she sits back down, blowing her nose like if she does it hard enough, all of this will go away.

"Gross," Jo says to her, a tiny smile on her face.

"You're gross," she shoots back. *Sisters.*

I clap my hands together. "We're not gonna let this ruin Christmas Eve, right?"

"No question," Jo says.

The mood lifts.

The rest of the day is better than I imagined. We assemble our own Christmas charcuterie boards, each with a specific theme. We nibble from the plates of meats and cheeses and candied nuts telling stories of Christmases past. Their memories are so vivid, it's like I was there all along.

As per tradition, everyone gets to open one present on Christmas Eve. Lena gets an adorable outfit for the baby. Carol opens the most luscious robe I've ever seen. Jo unboxes a new record player. In a surprise to no one, Matt receives a bong shaped like a candy-cane.

Carol turns to me. "I'm sorry we don't have any presents for you, Ava. Do you want to open one of mine?"

"That's sweet, Carol, but I couldn't," I say as Jo stands.

"Wait," she says, running out to her backhouse.

Moments later, she returns, a crudely wrapped present in her hands. "I want you to have this," she says. "Open it."

I take the gift and peel away the layers of tape and brown paper to reveal a film camera.

"It was my dad's first camera," she says. "You love film, too, so I thought it could be a nice reintroduction to your photography roots."

I'm speechless. She's lost one of the biggest pieces of her father, and now she's willing to give me another? I shake my head.

"Yes," she says, wrapping my hands around the small camera body. "I'm sure."

If I had no idea how she felt before this moment, I know now. She couldn't have given me a bigger piece of her heart than this, and I'm overjoyed. I embrace her and give her a kiss on the cheek.

"I love it," I say. She smiles the biggest smile I've seen all day.

Like magic, I receive a text from Max. 'IT'S GO TIME.'

"Just in time for my present to you, Jo." I grab her hand and lead her to the front door. "I was going to wait til tomorrow, but no time like the present, right? Ha! Present."

"What are you talking about?" she asks. Her family follows us.

"Last night was horrible," I say. "And I can't replace what your dad left you, but I pulled every favor I could think of to make sure you were covered."

I open the front door, and on cue, Max pulls up the driveway in a brand-new, state-of-the-art photo truck. Aspen and his team stand outside the door, waiting for us, cameras rolling to capture reactions.

Lena's jaw drops, and Carol runs out to the truck with glee.

But Jo's reaction is *nothing* like what I expected.

MY STOMACH TURNS at the sight of... whatever this is supposed to be. It definitely isn't Chrissy. Sure, the side of this sleek monstrosity of a vehicle is emblazoned with 'THE PHOTO TRUCK' in giant rainbow letters, but that's where the resemblance ends.

Ava's face beams with excitement, anticipating my delight. "It's your new truck!" she announces, sweeping her hand toward the gleaming hulk. "We rallied to get this ready for you. Isn't it amazing?"

The word 'amazing' echoes mockingly in my ears. "How?" is all I can muster.

Aspen and the crew exchange uneasy glances.

Ava continues, oblivious to my shock.

"Remember the mock-ups I showed you that first night over dinner? I had my team start prototyping a new truck during Chrissy's last repairs, just in case. After last night's breakdown, I pulled every favor to finish it. You won't miss a single day of work!"

"Oh. Great." I can't mask the hollowness in my voice.

Ava frowns, her smile faltering. "Is something wrong?"

I stare out at the cameramen, their lenses focused on the two of us. "I guess this is what you do."

Ava is taken aback. "What is that supposed to mean?"

Bitterness rises in my chest. "You'll wrap anything in a bow once it's served its purpose. This is a happy enough ending for the camera crew, so it'll be enough for Ava Garcia-Greene, too."

Aspen signals to his crew to cut the cameras. My mom is inspecting the new truck, oblivious, while Lena and Matt huddle on the porch, pretending not to eavesdrop.

"I thought you would be happy. I thought this would make your life easier," Ava says, her eyes searching mine.

"You replaced something irreplaceable, and it didn't even cross your mind," I say, struggling to keep my emotions in check. "Chrissy wasn't just a truck; she was my connection to my dad. You can't swap that out and call it an upgrade."

"Chrissy was kaput. Mikey said so. She wasn't safe to drive, how would that be a nice legacy for your dad?" she shoots back, her voice rising.

"You've done a good job of acting like you understood what this business–what *I*–was about. But it's just that: an act." I snap.

Ava's face hardens. "An act? I did all of this for you."

"That's rich," I retort. "You're doing this for your image, for your mission, for Aspen and the cameras, not for me. And once it's all over, you'll leave."

"I thought you knew me better than that," she says.

I shake my head, a cold hollow opening up inside me. "You can't know someone in a couple weeks. You'd understand if you could keep anyone around."

Ava's eyes flash with hurt, then venom. "And you would be able to appreciate what I'm doing for you if you weren't stuck in the past."

Before I can respond, Matt's voice suddenly cuts through our standoff. "Hospital. Now."

Jolted out of the tunnel vision of my anger, I notice that my mom and Matt are flanking Lena as she grimaces through a contraction.

Ava slips into action mode. "Max will drive. Let's go, everyone in the truck."

We pile into the back, my mom dismissing the confused Aspen and crew with a wave. Ava takes the front passenger seat beside Max, not once glancing back at me as she helps them navigate the quickest route to the hospital.

I re-tunnel my focus, this time on helping my laboring sister take deep breaths, and in doing so, I can almost ignore the fact that I have willingly set foot in the abomination that is Chrissy's replacement.

That is, until Carol unhelpfully offers, "As a mother, I'm happy there are finally seatbelts back here."

Then Matt chimes in, "And the heated seats, chef's kiss!"

"I'm actually getting a little hot," Lena huffs.

Ava fiddles with buttons on the dash. "We can turn off your seat warmer and adjust the individual AC unit for the back."

A portable-size fan turns on beside Lena and she begins to breathe a bit slower.

"Ava, you're a lifesaver," she shouts to the front.

Even with the fan on I'm heating up again. *How can they all be so happy?* All these bells and whistles are nothing compared to the memories Chrissy held within her rusted walls. As usual, I'm left to bear the brunt of the grief while everybody around me moves on.

Lena's hand squeezes mine and it brings me back to the present moment. I squeeze back.

Concern flickers in her eyes. "Are you okay?"

I shake my head. "I should be the one asking you that."

She chuckles. "I'm currently not having a contraction, so that's pretty okay."

I lean my head on her shoulder.

I'm not sure there's any comfort to be had for me, but at least I can provide some for my sister as we screech to a stop in front of the hospital.

JO IS fast asleep in the kiddie corner of the waiting room. I watch her brow furrow in her slumber. I have the best foresight of anyone I know, having predicted the success of many startups over the years–even to the point where I was *begged* to be on Shark Tank–but I did not see this coming. Jo's reaction caught me so off guard that I could hardly argue with her in the moment. I was sure that what I was doing for her was right, but her words cut deep. She didn't only accuse me of being selfish; she cruelly laid bare my agonizing inability to maintain close relationships. *Is that what she thinks of me? And is she right?*

The cup of coffee I'm pouring spills over onto my hand as I stare at her. I mutter to myself as I clean up my mess. *One of many.*

Carol walks in from the hallway, kindly pretending that she didn't witness my coffee disaster. Instead, she looks at Jo.

"You did the right thing," she tells me.

"It doesn't feel like the right thing."

"You didn't have a choice, Ava. It was best to start fresh." She pats my shoulder. "I swear, even *you* could've sunk your entire fortune into that thing. God knows Roger did."

"He did?"

"Oh my, yes. He put us into credit card debt for a while," she says. "He went to every mechanic in the county and wore them all out of favors. But he loved that thing to death, so I supported him."

"You're a great partner," I sigh.

"And you are, too, Ava. Jo's just… having trouble seeing it."

"I don't understand why," I say. "I've given her my all. And then some."

Jo stirs in the corner and Carol and I freeze, but then she's back to grumpy sleeping.

Carol ushers me to the hallway. "Come on, they've got better snacks out here."

I follow her down the brightly-lit hall, buzzing with patients and nurses, to two vending machines. They're each poorly stocked with nothing but Cheez-Its and Mountain Dew. I deduce that this is *not* in fact why she brought me here.

"Your and Jo's relationship reminds me a bit of mine and Roger's when we first started out," she tells me. "Crackers?"

"Uh, no thanks," I say. "How so?"

"When Roger moved back to Harmony Springs," she puts some coins into the machine, "I wasn't so sure of him at first."

"No?"

"Nope. I was… dating someone else." The crackers slingshot out of their compartment. "Named Leah."

"Oh." I never even assumed Carol might be something other than straight. And then it hits me.

"Wait, Leah from Sweet Foundations Leah?"

"Lovely Leah Betteny. We were dating off and on for a while before Roger came back to town." She bends down to grab the cheesy treat from the machine. "My story is a lot like yours, but in reverse, if you will."

Oh. "You were…?"

"A full-blown lesbian? Yep."

"Wow," I laugh. I love the way this little town has kept me on my toes.

"When I met Roger, he cracked my stubborn sense of self wide open. I had a clear path set out, and falling for him wasn't part of it."

I sigh. "That sounds somewhat... totally... familiar," I admit. "What did Roger think?"

"My hesitation certainly troubled him," Carol relays, "He wanted all of me, but I was clinging to an old version of myself."

"How did you know the new version of yourself was the right one?"

Carol chuckles. "I realized there's rarely a 'right' in life, just paths we choose. Following my heart mattered more than any plan I had made, and it turned out that gender mattered less than love. Roger loved me more profoundly than anyone before, and reciprocating that was all I wanted."

We start walking back down the hall as I process Carol's story. When we reach the entrance to the waiting room, she turns to face me.

"I think," she chooses her words carefully, "Jo is living in fear. About a few things, if we're being honest, but you're at the top of that list right now."

Carol is trying to help, but she's voicing what I've been worried about this whole time. My presence in Jo's life is a negative one. I've been grappling blindly for control–over my company, my future, my identity–and all I've done is project my inner turmoil onto Jo, who deserves so much better.

Jo still sleeps, the furrow gone from her brow. She seems at peace.

Carol watches me. "All is not lost," she says, like she's reading my thoughts.

Before I can correct her that actually all *is* lost, and that's probably how it should be, a doctor walks into the waiting room. "Fisher family?" she calls.

"That's us!" Carol shouts. Jo starts, nearly falling off her chair.

"You've got a very special Christmas present waiting for you," the doctor says.

"I'm a grandma!" Carol exclaims as she bolts through the doors. Jo brushes off the sleep and follows her down the hall, not even a glance in my direction.

"Are you joining?" the doctor asks me.

"No," I say. "I'm not family."

I stare out the window of the private jet as Max snores quietly next to me.

"We'll be landing in Los Angeles in about fifteen minutes. Skies are clear and it's a beautiful seventy degrees…"

I hate the cold, but I've never wanted anything more than a cold winter's day and my love to cuddle up with.

CHAPTER 36
JO

I'VE BARELY BID adieu to dreamland as my mother shuffles me across the threshold of my sister's hospital room. The cold reality of my fight with Ava sinks in as I notice she's nowhere to be seen. Am I surprised, though? Is this not what we agreed to, and what I expected all along?

In her room, Lena is tired but glowing. The teeniest cry emits from the swaddled Christmas blanket in her arms.

My mom puts her hand over her mouth, eyes filling with tears. "My grandbaby!"

"How was it?" I ask Lena.

A heavy snore erupts from Matt, who is snoozing across the room.

Lena shakes her head. "Exhausting. Exhilarating. I want sushi." The bundle in her arms wriggles and my breath catches as I realize there's a new member of our family in the room.

I take a seat by Lena's bedside.

"Can I hold…?"

"Roger," Lena's eyes shine. "After Dad." She gently hands me my nephew.

Cradling Roger, I'm struck by the fragility and strength in his tiny form–his little limbs moving gently, the fine hairs on his head barely visible.

Tears well up in my eyes. "Dad should've been here."

"He's always here, Jo," Lena replies, her voice steady and reassuring. "In every little thing we do, Dad's here."

When I come home from the hospital, I pick up the flannel-sailed ship in a bottle and carry it to my bedroom. I would give anything for my dad to tell me how to put my mind and my heart back together right now, but instead I fall asleep, rocked on an ocean of my own tears, completely alone.

I'VE NEVER BEEN SO DISTRACTED in my life. The last couple of days at work have been excruciating. The office has been mostly empty, but my mind is constantly racing with Jo, Jo, Jo.

I made the right decision to exit Jo's life before I fucked it up any further, but I can't quiet my fantasies of her shouldering her way back into mine.

Is that her texting me? No, just Jason, congratulating me on my Harmony Springs success (apparently, the Board never doubted me and stocks are higher than ever).

Is that her knocking on my door to kiss and make up? No, just Max, bringing me a gourmet fruit basket from Aspen and team (their Gramsta views are through the roof; what a story).

Is that her from across the hall? No, just the poor intern who caught me staring longingly at the back of her head (I'm her boss so she's too afraid to report me to HR).

Gramsta is usually my safe harbor, but being cooped up here is driving me crazy. I'm haunted by my own ghost in these offices, the Ava who strutted the halls before my trip to Harmony Springs–armored, undefeated. Maybe I'm the ghost, a faint imprint of my former self.

Either way, I need to escape. I drive to my rarely used house in LA, where the remnants of the life I packed away at 18 are stowed deep in its closets. The furniture inside is covered with the dust of disuse.

I think about Jo, religious in her allegiance to the objects in her life that hold importance. Chrissy, her record collection, all the trinkets and artwork she inherited from Roger. I've never allowed myself to dwell on clutter from the past, material or otherwise. My religion has been my relentless drive forward, onward, and upward.

It never even crossed my mind that replacing the truck would devastate Jo, and that terrifies me. *Has my practice of denying my own emotions blinded me to the pain I'm capable of inflicting on someone I love?*

I walk to the first closet I see and begin pulling out boxes filled with high school yearbooks and tech gadgets I never bothered patenting. I'm not sure what I'm searching for, but my anguish is so uncontainable I'm desperate for anything to help me make sense of what I'm supposed to do next in the wake of losing Jo Fisher.

I spend hours in a fugue state, with just the bare bulb of the walk-in flickering above me, until I reach the back of the closet. I swing my arm beneath a dark shelf to check for stragglers and my hand hits a familiar keyboard. I crawl on hands and knees and drag out the most formative Christmas present I ever received.

Looking at the scratched, vintage Mac logo, I'm flooded with sorrow. At first, I think my grief is about the abandoned computer, neglected despite its unfathomable impact on the trajectory of my life. But as I run my hands over its iconic beige chassis and chunky keys, I have a breakthrough. It's not the one I expected to have, but I suppose that's the nature of a breakthrough.

. . .

I pull out my phone and type in three little letters.

AFTER ROGER'S ARRIVAL, Lena and Matt hunker down into their new-parent bubble, with my mom by their side. With the holidays clearing my work schedule, I'm left with a vast expanse of time. Each day dissolves into a gray blur. I seclude myself in the backhouse, blinds drawn, as I surrender to the tidal waves of grief–for my dad, for Chrissy, and for Ava.

Emma, visiting relatives over the holidays, sends her congratulations on my new role as an aunt, but she's too caught up to notice my withdrawal until she returns... and then she calls me about fifteen times until I answer.

"Yeah?" I pick up groggily, my voice hoarse from not speaking for days.

She doesn't even berate me for not picking up.

"Carol called. She told me what happened." Her voice is solemn. "Jo, I'm so sorry. Can I come over?"

"I don't think I'm much fun right now," I croak.

"I don't love you because you're fun, Jo. I just love you." The blunt sincerity reminds me of Ava and my stomach drops. "Please, can I come? Please, can *Duke* come?"

I sigh. "You run a hard bargain. But don't expect any hospitality."

"Don't worry, I wouldn't dare."

Duke goes straight for my salty, tear-stained face the minute he and Emma waltz through the door.

"I brought you coffee and Hole Foods Donuts and a fidget spinner that I found in my car," Emma announces, tossing the pink gadget to where I'm laying on the couch.

I extend my hand. "Coffee. Put her here." Emma hands me a steaming latte and I sit up, patting Duke's head in thanks for his cleaning services.

I admittedly haven't been caffeinating for the past few days. Caffeine would probably get me out of bed, and I've been greatly preferring the isolation of my down comforter to the harsh realities of life that await me outside.

Emma sits across from me, housing a maple bar. "So, Ava's gone."

I thought we were gonna talk about my dad or Chrissy, but I wasn't expecting Emma to address the Ava elephant head on. I hadn't kept her abreast of our ongoing tryst after that first night, but I have no delusions about being able to get anything past her.

"She did what she came to do. She didn't break any promises. She walked her walk. She talked her talk. And then she left."

"Hm."

"Did you see our new and improved monstrosity in the driveway?" I ask her bitterly.

She nods slowly. "Definitely not Chrissy."

"Nope."

Emma tilts her head. "Have you been inside?"

"Yup."

She scoffs. "Pulling teeth like a dentist over here, Joj. How was it?"

I shrug. "There's AC in every seat or something."

Her face scrunches. "That sounds… incorrect. Can we go check it out together?" Duke wags over to her and she smooshes his face toward me. "Can *Duke* go inside? He needs new Hinge pics."

I roll my eyes. "Duke requests lose their power from overuse, Em."

She crosses her arms. "Jo, humor me. I promise to hate it as much as you do, how about that?"

I grab a maple bar for myself. "Duke, we're going for a walk." His ears perk up. "To the driveway, buddy."

At least one of us is stoked.

I reluctantly unlock the back of the new truck and we go inside. I wasn't only giving Ava the silent treatment when we rode in here the other day, but the truck as well.

Duke sniffs around while Emma takes in the pristine walls, track lighting, built-ins for equipment storage, and outlets. She whistles under her breath. "Yep, this is offensive."

My mouth twitches. "Wanna set it on fire?"

"Definitely." She runs her hand over the new eco-leather seats. "Is that a motorized backdrop mount? Disgusting."

I take a seat and Duke rests his head on my knee. "I know it's a nice truck. I get that."

Emma plops down beside me. "It would be crazy for you not to get that, but I love you."

"I felt steamrolled. Like Ava got to do everything her way and never had to deal with the consequences. I didn't even get to say goodbye to Chrissy."

"Jo, I say this with love," Emma says, "but Chrissy is literally sitting in Mikey's lot. You could go say goodbye anytime."

Hot tears threaten to spill over. "Something has died. And I wasn't ready. Again. Things will never be the same."

Emma rubs my back with her hand. "Are you talking about the truck, or about Ava?" she asks quietly. I shake my head, tears falling. "There's gotta be a built-in tissue box around here somewhere."

She gets up and starts to poke around the space.

"Um, Jo?" she calls from the front. "Have you seen this?"

Sniffling and wiping my snot on my sleeve, I walk over to where she is, pointing at something welded into the wall of the new truck. It's the Polaroid of my dad and me, formerly tucked away into Chrissy's sun visor, now protected by plexiglass, with a plaque beneath it that reads:

THEY LIVE ON IN OUR PHOTOS AND OUR HEARTS.
ROGER FISHER AND THE ORIGINAL CHRISSY THE
CHRISTMAS TRUCK
1984 - 2024

"Oh." My heart and my mind careen into each other and all I can blurt out is, "The ship of Theseus."

"Sorry?"

Tears flood. The tight knot in my belly loosens. "Maybe there can be New Chrissy, and there can be Old Chrissy, and there can be parts in common."

Oh god, I was so unfair to Ava. Oh god, I was so cruel.

"I'm not totally following your train of thought, but I think we're in agreement that Ava truly did want to make things better," Emma says softly.

"What do I do, Em?" I wail. "If there was even a sliver of hope for making amends, I burned that bridge."

Emma shakes her head. "You don't know how things are gonna pan out. Don't borrow trouble from the future, right?"

I see my dad's face, beaming in the photograph. He's not here. I think he would do anything to be here if he could. But I am here. I'm alive and I can feel the tears streaking down my cheeks and the thumping of my heartbeat and the touch of Emma's comforting hand on my arm.

A smile forms through my tears and I wipe my face. "The future won't even see me coming."

Emma wraps me in a tight hug. "Let's rise to meet it, then."

And we do.

CHAPTER 39
AVA

DID I pull a bit of a Kylie Jenner flying from Santa Monica to San Bernardino? Perhaps. A two-and-a-half-hour drive was something I couldn't stomach. Apologizing is already difficult enough, and this one... this is about to be the hardest of my life.

My driver pulls up to the front of my childhood California-style home, straight from my nightmares. I step out of the car, my heart racing as I approach the front door. I take a deep breath and knock.

I hear some shuffling and a latch coming undone, and then it opens. There stands my mom, hair silver and long, a familiar unreadable expression on her face.

"Ava. Come in." I make my way into the house.

"Well?" she says.

We haven't seen each other in years, but she still understands I cut right to the chase.

"I'm here to... repair this," I say, uncomfortable.

"Hm," she says.

"Is that something you'd like to do?" I hang on her silence.

"It's something I tried to do a long time ago," she reminds me.

"Did you, though? I recall you asking me for money."

"You sent me a check, but that doesn't mean I asked for it," she rebuts. "I ripped it up the day I got it."

"Well… yeah," I say, taking in the house, exactly the same as when I left. "We hadn't talked for years and then you call up as soon as we go public?"

"It was an olive branch, Ava," she says. "I can't believe you thought I'd use you like that. My own daughter."

"*Everyone* was using me like that."

"I don't know what you want from me. I reached out at a time I thought you'd be receptive. Your work was going so well for you."

"But it wasn't going well between us. It never was."

"I did all I knew to do," she says, exasperated. "Parents are just people. You've always had such impossible standards."

"Where do you think I got it from?" I try not to be on the defensive, but it all comes bubbling back. "You were the one who could've protected me, and you chose not to."

"Chose not to? I'm not the one who picked up and went to San Francisco by herself."

"You gave me no choice!" My voice rises. "You didn't support me."

"Is this why you're here?" she asks. "To fight with me again after all these years?"

"No, but–I want you to admit it already!"

"Admit what, Ava?"

"That you're the reason a group of old men run my entire life. That I don't own Gramsta, the only piece of me that I understand. The thing I've given all of myself to."

I see the anger rise and fall in her eyes. But instead of succumbing to the rage, she wells up with tears.

"I failed," she says calmly. "I failed you and I failed our relationship. I've regretted it every single day since you left. I'm sorry."

I've needed to hear those words for so long. They're freeing, yet a pit of guilt remains anchored in my stomach.

"Look where you are Ava. Don't you see? So you don't own the biggest share of your company… that's a damn shame. But you're here, you're changing the world. What more could you ask for?"

She's right. I've been so focused on my singular goal of *being* Gramsta, that I didn't realize all I have. Jo came into my life, showing me exactly what I needed, and I couldn't get past my own bullshit to see.

"You're right. I'm sorry, Mom," I blurt. The words have never escaped my lips so quickly. "I love you."

"Well, not so fast," she chuckles hesitantly. "I have something to tell you. It's been on my heart for a long, long time. Sit."

I follow her to the same floral couch from my childhood. She takes my hand.

"When you were very young, I suspected your behavior was… different from other kids," she begins. "I took you to the doctor for an evaluation."

"I remember."

"I never told you the results of that test because I didn't want you to feel any more different than you already were. I was trying to protect you," she murmurs. "I've come to suspect that was the wrong choice and I'm sorry."

"What did the doctor say?"

"She said you were likely on the autism spectrum. But it was also the nineties, and she gave me a scary speech about the discrimination you might face from teachers, from your peers, for having that label."

I let her words sink in. *On the spectrum.* In the tech world where I thrive, being neurodivergent is not only accepted but often seen as an asset, a unique lens for innovative thinking. I've always found a kinship among fellow nerds, a social comfort in our shared quirks.

"...Ava?" she prods gently, her expression laden with worry, anticipating hurt and anger.

But instead of betrayal, an illuminating clarity washes over me. Permission to finally understand the nuances of my own nature. I understand why she made the choices she did; she was doing the best she could with the knowledge she had at the time.

"It explains a lot."

She laughs at my bluntness and I laugh along with her.

I can't control my emotions as I hug her. It's been way too long. It was always me and her and I abandoned that for my selfish goals. Exactly like I did with Jo.

Tears stream as she strokes my hair, like she used to when I was a child. "What made you decide to find me?" she asks.

"I wanted to make amends. Before it was too late."

She pulls back. "I'm not dying."

"I know, I–I want to squash this, once and for all," I say.

"Ever since I called, I've been waiting to do the same," she tells me. "I could've done a better job protecting you, and I'm sorry. I... I had no help." Tears form in her eyes.

"No, it's okay, Mom, I would've done the same." I hug her again. "I'm sorry. I'm so sorry."

She pulls back and wipes her eyes. "We've got a lot to catch up on, huh?"

"You have no idea."

"Anything in particular?"

"Uh," I scrunch my nose. "I might be gay?"

She chuckles. "That's the least of my worries."

After a long catch-up with my mom, I make my way back to LA. I told her all about Jo, and she encouraged me that first loves are difficult, but that I'll make it through, I always do. I hadn't considered that at 36, Jo was my first love, but it's true: she is. Well, was.

Mom and I promised to see each other soon to make up for lost time. It feels right, even though nothing else does.

Back at the office, I sit at my desk, reviewing the freshly written letter on my laptop. Max knocks on my door, their forehead lined with worry.

"Can you proofread before we send it?" I ask.

"Are you sure this is what you want?" Their eyes glisten a little. "You've put so much heart into this company, Ava–"

"Tech isn't about heart," I cut them off. "I can't do it anymore."

"But you could create so much change."

I shake my head. "You don't have to tell me what I want to hear anymore, Max."

"You know I never did that."

I stand, leaving the laptop open for them, and gather my things.

"You can go enjoy Christmas trees and caroling and all the stuff you've missed out on working with me," I say. "I won't ruin it all anymore."

A tear runs down their cheek and I quickly run to hug them.

"I was kidding! Mostly!" They cry-laugh into my shoulder. "I'll make sure you still have your job, don't worry about that either."

"I'm more worried that I'll miss doing your dirty work."

I choke up. Our years of working together all day, every day, are coming to an end, and it's all because of me. I can't drag Max along, wherever I'm going. They deserve the best, and that's not me yet.

"Oh, I forgot." I head back to the computer and scroll to the bottom of the letter. In my signature I add one word:

Ava Garcia-Greene
Former CEO of Gramsta

EMMA and I are in an Uber, hurtling down the freeway in Los Angeles, a few hours till midnight on New Year's Eve.

"It's weird not to be in the backseat of George's Corolla," she remarks.

"Definitely not in Harmony Springs anymore."

The sun has barely set and already fireworks are exploding across the skyline.

Neither of us have been to LA before, and as I take in the sheer mass of people living their lives in this one place, I'm intimidated. This is a city where Ava belongs, where she rules her elite techie roost. Could she ever have been as enamored with Harmony Springs as I dreamt her to be?

I drop my head into my hands, starting to panic again. "Maybe we should turn around."

Emma nudges me with her knee. "Your mother did not buy us these tickets so that you could make a loop around LAX in a taxi and come back home."

I take a deep breath. "I'm good. I'll be good."

I'm dressed a little nicer than Ava is used to. Lena FaceTimed me while nursing and made me pick out what she calls a "wow-fit". Turns out it's just a nice sweater and khaki slacks with some jewelry borrowed from Carol, but I look good, and that's giving me, oh... 2% extra confidence.

We pull up to a gorgeous beachside office building with GRAMSTA spelled in chic minimalist neon lettering.

Emma walks up to a call box and taps in a number saved in her phone. It rings a couple times, then we're buzzed in.

The interior is as chic and minimalist as the outside of the building, with a few straggler employees wrapping up work before they hit the town to party until midnight.

Max bursts out of a stairwell, panting. They wave to both of us, doubled over, trying to catch their breath. Emma starts to say something but they hold up their finger. "Elevator. Getting repaired. Must. Hurry."

"Hurry?" Emma asks.

"No... time... to... explain..." they huff out, turning on their heel. Emma and I have to chase them to keep up as we begin sprinting up more flights of stairs than I've ever summited in my life.

"Why... are we... running...?" I manage to pant out.

We make it another couple flights before Max ekes out, "Ava's... resigning..."

I'm so shocked that what little words I could squeak out fail me.

We reach the top, and Max uses their key card to beep us onto Ava's floor. Photos of her line the walls, along with cases displaying every gold plaque imaginable. My eyes follow the hallway down to a pair of frosted glass doors. Max, after some forceful inhales, follows my gaze.

"We didn't pass her on the stairs, so she's still in there." Their face is solemn. "Jo, she's a mess. I've never seen her like this."

I don't wait a second longer. I fast-walk down the long hallway as Max and Emma trail me.

What awaits me behind those frosted glass doors?

I don't get to find out, because Ava bursts through, glued to her phone, before freezing as she notices us.

"Jo? What are you doing here?"

I close the final distance between us until I'm standing in front of her. "I'm here to apologize, but it sounds like I've done even more damage than I thought."

"You don't need to apologize, I deserved it. I thought I was doing something good for you, but it was selfish." She's distraught. "This job, my company, has reduced me to outcomes and appearances, and I let that drive the way I tried to fix your problem."

I shake my head. "No, I do need to apologize. You didn't deserve the brunt of my anger. Chrissy breaking down, you leaving–it was a perfect storm. When you rolled out the new truck, I latched onto it as a safe target for my anger and my residual grief about my dad, rather than dealing with the real issues."

"What were the… real issues?" she asks quietly.

I gulp. This is the harder part of my apology. "That you were leaving. Without so much as an acknowledgment of what this meant to both of us. I was afraid to bring any of my bigger feelings up–afraid of facing your rejection, of ending our time together on a sour note, or tarnishing your memories of it by asking for more than you were ready to give."

Ava toys with her lower lip. "I figured I was already asking too much of you. Being so new and unsure. We hadn't known each other for long." She glances up to me. "As you pointed out."

I wince. "Please don't resign. If my words made you question what you were doing with your life, they were said in anger, and I wanted you to feel my pain. That was not fair to you. I don't ever want to be the source of your pain."

Ava steps forward and takes one of my hands in hers. "I accept your apology. But even though you dealt me some zingers, you didn't push me to resign."

"I didn't?"

She shakes her head. "Spending time with you, in Harmony Springs, confronting the world outside of my bubble... All the good I witnessed the past couple weeks brought me to this decision. Your words might've been said in anger, but I *have* pushed people away because of the life I chose to lead. And I don't want that anymore. I want to be authentic." She takes my other hand in hers and gazes into my eyes. "Like you." A pause, then: "*With you.*"

At that moment, Max clears their throat, breaking our spell.

"Totally not listening in," Max proclaims, "but catch."

Max hurls something at me. I catch it and realize...

"Gay mistletoe." My face cracks a smile and so does Ava's. I hold the Harmony Springs memento over our heads. "Second time's the charm?"

We dive into a passionate kiss, back in our world once again.

I pull away. "But if you're resigning, what are you gonna do?"

Ava grins at me. "I have a few ideas."

That's all the reassurance I need.

I lean back in, and we lose ourselves in a sea of kisses, no longer two ships passing in the night, but rather a brand new, third vessel that we built together to better weather the waves.

EPILOGUE

AVA

358 Days Later.

"IT'S ALMOST TIME," I say, hurrying Jo along.

"Ava, if we're not on at exactly eight p.m., the world isn't gonna end." Jo stares at her phone screen as it dials. As I'm about to snatch it out of her hand, Emma answers her FaceTime.

"See?" Jo says, rubbing the phone in my face.

"You were right," I admit. Admitting I'm wrong has been coming easier these days, even if my patience isn't. "Now make it quick."

"I didn't pick up fast enough for Ava, did I?" Emma asks.

"Nope," Jo laughs. "How's my lead LA photographer doing?"

"The West Coast manager and I are doing well, thank you very much," she says, panning the phone to Max who stands beside her.

I flew back from Los Angeles this morning to officially promote Emma and Max as heads of our West Coast Photo Truck division, and Jo couldn't resist one of her chosen family calls, just in time for us to go on stage at the Chosen Family Festival.

She's sentimental as hell, and I love it.

"How is it over there? I can't believe we had to miss this year!" Max says.

"Oh, same ol', same ol'." Jo pans from backstage to George and Jeffrey dancing in the crowd, despite the lack of music.

"Ugh. That love will never get old," Emma coos.

"Actually, hold on," Jo says, handing the phone off to me.

"Jo!" I shout, but let her go once I see her pull out the Olympus. Instead of using up all her free time on truck maintenance, Jo has spent her idle hours shooting on film. Her favorite spot, besides in my arms, is in the darkroom of our new Harmony Springs home together.

She grabs her shot and runs back to me. I plant a big kiss on her cheek.

"Spare me," Emma grimaces. "But also never stop. Talk to you two tomorrow?"

"Of course," Jo waves and hangs up. I drag her toward the stage.

"Do you ever chill?" she asks.

"You know the answer to that," I tell her. Her lip twists up in that classic Jo grin.

"We've got all the time in the world," she says, always there to keep me calm.

"Please welcome to the stage... Jo Fisher!" the emcee announces.

Before I can even give her my look, I push her out behind the podium. I watch from the wings as she takes the mic in front of the applauding crowd. Matt and Lena watch on as Carol soothes baby Rog.

"Hello and welcome to Harmony Springs' annual Chosen Family Festival! We are so honored for The Photo Truck to be sponsoring this year's event."

The crowd whoops and hollers, rowdier than any Pride parade we've attended.

"As many of you know," she continues, "this time last year was the beginning of our expansion and we haven't stopped. The Photo Truck is now spreading love and belonging all across the country."

The crowd cheers again. She glances offstage at me. My heart still flutters from that gaze of hers.

"And it wouldn't have been possible without our brand-new CEO and my super-hot genius of a partner, Ava Garcia-Greene."

Before, I would put on my fake smile and wave to the crowd, a consummate professional. Now, I can't help but run out to Jo and give her a kiss in front of everyone.

The crowd 'awws' and whistles as I hold her face and say those three words I can't get enough of. "I love you."

"I love you," she says back, before patting my butt forward to take the mic.

"Thank you! Thank you all," I say as the applause dies down. "I have to admit I haven't always been the biggest fan of Christmas." *Understatement of the year.* "But with the help of the Harmony Springs community, especially Jo, my life was forever changed. With people like you, I wish everyday was a holiday."

Jo's corniness has rubbed off on me. So what?

"Without further ado, follow us up the hill for some fireworks… and our grand reveal!"

Jo looks at me, confused.

"Go!" I urge her.

"What could you possibly have up your sleeve now, Ms. Garcia-Greene?"

I take her hand, leading the crowd up the famously steep hill.

"I told you it'd be hard to walk up this thing in heels," she scolds me.

"One of us has got to wear something other than flannel," I tease. "I'll still race you."

"Oh, you're on," she says, already sprinting ahead.

I purposely hang back as I watch her crest the top of the hill. She stops, speechless.

Before her is the completely restored original Chrissy, albeit... a little different. While insurance wanted to scrap her completely, I made sure we had her saved and restored to become a permanent fixture in the community, trading her wheels for a cement foundation. After a year and some help with the permits (thanks, Wynnie), Harmony Springs now boasts its first public photography studio–Roger's Light–where residents can book time to hone and develop their film and digital skills for free.

This is all detailed on the plaque in front of Jo, who turns to me, misty-eyed.

"This is...?"

"This *is*," I say.

The crowd's murmurs of amazement echo behind us, yet their opinions hold no weight for me. I just want Jo to be happy.

She embraces me tighter than she ever has before, and I hug her back.

"You and your damn surprises," she says through tears.

"Maybe you could teach the studio's first cyanotypes class?" I suggest.

She sniffles. "I would love that."

"Come on, there's someone you need to meet." I usher her toward the open back of the truck where Mikey Stutz stands, beaming.

"Mikey!" Jo eyes me like I'm on my CEO bullshit again. "We *know* Mikey."

"I'd like to introduce you to the inaugural studio manager of Roger's Light," I announce proudly.

"Are you serious?" Jo asks. I laugh giddily as she wraps Mikey in a hug.

She pulls back from their embrace and eyes me. "You think of everything."

"I know," I say, pleased.

"All right, time for the first official photo taken at Roger's!" Mikey says.

"Wait, of us?!" Jo asks.

"Of course of us, silly," I smile at her.

We stand in front of the backdrop and pose, arms wrapped around each other.

"All right, say cheese!" Mikey says.

But Jo nuzzles up to my face and gives me dainty butterfly kisses with her lashes. It tickles, and I can't help throwing my head back in laughter.

Mikey snaps the photo and turns to the monitor. "Oop, we've got a blinker!" He goes to delete it.

"Wait!" I say. Mikey halts.

"Rule number one of The Photo Truck. Never delete a memory that precious."

ACKNOWLEDGMENTS

This book has been a wild ride, and it would not have been possible without the wonderful, beautiful, amazing, supportive people (and pets) in our lives.

We'd each like to thank our parents for supporting us through the silliest of careers, always knowing we were silly enough to make it happen for ourselves.

To Sari Sapon-White, thank you for being our earliest reader and fueling us with the encouragement and feedback to keep pushing forward.

We'd like to thank Michael, but we can't. He mostly distracted Ella.

Our gratitude to Shelbie Janocha, who specifically proofread the lesbian sex scenes and is also beautiful and definitely did not dictate her own acknowledgment.

Charlie Laud, thank you for being our real-life Christmas Card Generator and crafting our author photo, which features... many fingers.

Thank you to our friends who got us through writing this thing and life in general. We talk about how awesome you are, like, constantly.

Jim Kaufman: thank you for your invaluable business savvy and mentorship. We're just two gals, and you've helped us become business moguls (well... future ones, at least).

To our editor, Sophia Blackwell, thank you for helping us distinguish between all 600 em dashes and hyphens throughout the novel, and for your myriad other insights that allowed this story to truly flourish.

To our IndieGoGo contributors, we could not have done this without you. A very special thanks to: Amit Mehta, Ana-Julia Cavana Altaffer, Anjelika Washington, April Moreau, Astrid Carlen-Helmer, Brent Bailey, Brianna Chomer, Carie M., Charlie Laud, Cici Sparks, Cole Fowler, Colleen Donovan, Dan Matthews, Darci Price, David & Sadie Sacks, Danielle Fox, Emila Akrapovic, Emma Morgan, Eric Jaffe, Evan Alicia Skiera, Genevieve Mifflin, Guillermo Rojas Hernandez, Haley Manrique, Holly & Christian Chapman, Janis Brody, Jessica Saul, Jessie Rowlands, Jim Kaufman, John Buell, Jordan West, Joy Matthews, Kathryn Kilbey, Kat Barnette, Kerstie Sabo, Laurel Weill, Lauren Mahn, Laurie Buell, Leah Feiger, LeeAnn Egolf, Liam Doherty, Linda Schildkraut, Lingxi Chenyang, Luke Ausley, Mackenzie Horras, Madison Linnihan, Micah Swann & Erin Bump, Mikki Hernandez, Morgan Elizabeth, Oscar Lemus, Ramona Criss, R.E. Langley, Rhonda & Dick Schaefer, Robert McAvinue, Sari & Richard Sapon-White, Sandra Kate Burck, Santana Audet, Sheena Santamaria, Stacy Kwon, Stas Schmiedt & Leander Roth, Surya Marissa, Tandava Malone, Taylor Coffman, Tim Anderson, Troup & Alyssa Wood, and Yuni Kim. Thank you, thank you, thank you. We could never say it enough.

And lastly, we extend our undying gratitude to Wynnie and Murray, the furry little loves of our lives. We do everything for you.

Thanks for reading!

If you enjoyed this book, please rate and review on Amazon and GoodReads, and share with friends.

Join our mailing list at
www.smokeshow-entertainment.com

@smokeshow.press on Instagram and Threads
@sm0kesh0w.press on TikTok

9 798999 913003